THE *wicked* PAVILION

DAWN POWELL

THE *wicked* PAVILION

STEERFORTH PRESS
SOUTH ROYALTON, VERMONT

The Wicked Pavilion was published in 1954 by The Riverside Press
and reissued in 1990 by Vintage Books

Library of Congress Cataloging-in-Publication Data
Powell, Dawn
    The wicked pavilion / Dawn Powell.
      p. cm.
    ISBN 1-883642-39-6
    I. Title.
  PS3531.0936W53   1996
  813'.54--dc20   96-23041
                         CIP

Book design and typesetting by Stacia Schaefer

Manufactured in the United States of America

FIRST PRINTING

" . . . oh this wicked Pavilion! We were kept there till half-past one this morning waiting for the Prince, and it has kept me in bed with the head-ache till twelve to-day. . . ."

Mrs. Creevey to Mr. Creevey
from *The Creevey Papers*

PART ONE

Shortly after two a sandy-haired gentleman in the middle years hurried into the Café Julien, sat down at Alexander's table as he always did, ordered coffee and cognac as he always did, asked for stationery as he always did, shook out a fountain pen and proceeded to write. Considering that this was the very same man who spent each morning staring, motionless, before a typewriter in a midtown hotel, it was surprising how swiftly his pen moved over the pages at the café table. At five, just as the first cocktail customers were arriving, he paid his check, pocketed his papers and went to the desk in the lobby.

"Keep this for me," he said to the clerk, handing over the manuscript.

"Okay, Mr. Orphen," said the clerk, and opened the safe to put it with Mr. Orphen's other papers.

The sandy-haired man went out, buttoning up his overcoat in the flurry of snow over Washington Square, hailed a taxi and drove back to the hotel room where he sat for a while staring at the empty page in the typewriter until he decided it was time to get drunk.

That was the day he had written on the Julien stationery:

There was nothing unusual about that New York winter of 1948 for the unusual was now the usual. Elderly ladies died of starvation in shabby hotels leaving boxes full of rags and hundred-dollar bills; bands of children robbed and raped through the city streets, lovers could find no beds, hamburgers were forty cents at lunch counters, truck drivers demanded double wages to properly educate their young in the starving high-class professions; aged spinsters, brides and mothers were shot by demented youths, frightened girls screamed for help in the night while police, in pairs for safety's sake, pinned tickets on parked automobiles. Citizens harassed by Internal Revenue hounds jumped out of windows for want of forty dollars, families on relief bought bigger television sets to match the new time-bought furniture. The Friendly Loan agent, the Smiling Banker, the Laughing Financial Aid lurked in dark alleys to terrorize the innocent; baby sitters received a dollar an hour with torture concessions; universities dynamited acres of historic mansions and playgrounds to build halls for teaching history and child psychology. Men of education were allowed to make enough at their jobs to defray the cost of going to an office; parents were able, by patriotic investment in the world's largest munitions plant, to send their sons to the fine college next door to it, though time and labor would have been saved by whizzing the sons direct from home to factory to have their heads blown off at once.

It was an old man's decade.

Geriatricians, endowed by the richest octogenarians, experimented on ways of prolonging the reign of the Old and keeping the enemy, Youth, from coming into its own. Pediatricians were subsidized to strengthen, heighten and toughen the young for soldiering; the eighteenth-birthday banquets were already being planned, the festive maypoles of ticker tape set up, the drummers hired, the invitations with government seals sent out, the marching songs rehearsed. The venerable statesmen and bankers were generously taking time off from their golfing, yachting and money-changing for the bang-up affair that would clear the earth once again of these intruders on old-men pleasures and profits. Some who had triumphed too long were deviled by fear of a turn of fortune and besieged their psychoanalysts for the expensive reassurance that they were after all boss-men, superior to their victims and the ordinary rules. When the stifled conscience croaked of justice to come they scuttled feverishly to the Church and clutched their winnings behind the King's X of the sacred robes.

In the great libraries professors studied ways of doing away with books; politicians proclaimed reading and writing unnecessary and therefore illegal, for the action of written words on the human brain might induce thought, a subversive process certain to incite rebellion at robot leadership. All the knowledge required for the soldier generation could be pumped in by loudspeaker; eyes must be saved for target practice, hands preserved for bayonets. Why allow an enemy bomb to blast our accumulated culture when we can do it ourselves by government process?

In the city the elements themselves were money: air was money, fire was money, water was money, the need of, the quest for, the greed for. Love was money. There was money or death.

But there were many who were bewildered by the moral mechanics of the age just as there are those who can never learn a game no matter how long they've been obliged to play it or how many times they've read the rules and paid the forfeits. If this is the way the world is turning around, they say, then by all means let it stop turning, let us get off the cosmic Ferris wheel into space. Allow us the boon of standing still till the vertigo passes, give us a respite to gather together the scraps of what was once *us*—the old longings for what? for whom? that gave us our wings and the chart for our tomorrow's.

There must be some place along the route, a halfway house in time where the runners may pause and ask themselves why they run, what is the prize and is it the prize they really want? What became of Beauty, where went Love? There must be havens where they may be at least remembered.

The shadow that lay over the land was growing mightily and no one escaped it. As in countries ruled by the Gestapo or the guillotine one must only whisper truths, bribe or be bribed, ask no questions, give no answers, police or be policed, run in fear and silence ahead of the shadow.

. . . a young man against the city . . .

At half past nine that February evening the Café Julien around the corner from Washington Square was almost deserted. Solitary gentlemen on the prowl strolled in expectantly, ready to crowd into any corner if the place was jammed, but horrified into quick retreat at sight of the empty tables. Three young teachers, briefed by *Cue* Magazine on how to have a typically French evening in New York, had cast a stricken glance into the bleak expanse of marble tables and mirror walls, then backed out.

"This can't be the place," one cried out. "It looks like a mausoleum."

The remark brought complacent smiles to the grim-faced old waiters, guarding their tables with folded arms like shepherds of old. The Julien waiters were forthright self-respecting individuals who felt their first duty was to protect the café from customers, their second to keep customers and employers in their proper places. The fact that only two of the marble-topped tables were occupied was a state of business perversely satisfactory to these waiters, who had the more leisure for meditation and the exchange of private insults. A young Jersey-looking couple peered curiously in the doorway looking for some spectacular rout that would explain the place's cosmopolitan reputation, then drew back puzzled at seeing only two patrons. Karl, the Alsatian with the piratical mustaches, turned down a chair at each of his three empty tables, indicating mythical reservations, folded his arms again and stared contentedly at the chipped cupids on the ceiling. The more excitable Guillaume, given to muttering personal comments behind his patrons' backs, flapped his napkin busily as if shooing out flies, and shouted after the innocent little couple, "Kitchen closed now, nothing to eat, kitchen closed."

The two solitary diners who remained at their tables after the dinner crowd had departed smiled with the smug pleasure of insiders at such a typical demonstration of the café's quixotic hospitality. The plump monkish little waiter, Philippe (said by many old-timers to resemble Dubois, the celebrated waiter of Mouquin's where the artist Pennell, you may recall, hung a plaque in his honor, "*A boire—Dubois*") turned from his peaceful contemplation of the old fencing studio across the way to twinkle merrily down at his favorite patron, Monsieur Prescott. He liked Monsieur Prescott first because he loved youth and beauty, seldom found in this rendezvous dedicated to testy old gourmets, miserly world travelers, battered bon vivants and escapees from behind the frank-and-apple-pie curtain. Philippe liked Monsieur Prescott above all because he had the grace to appear only every two or three years, while other customers were exasperatingly regular. Philippe felt young and refreshed just looking at Ricky Prescott, a young man built for the gridiron, wide of shoulder, strong white teeth flashing above square pugnacious jaw, long legs sprawling under the table, hard black eyes ever looking for and receiving friendship and approbation. Other Julien visitors were always asking Philippe who was this breezy young man, so obviously from the wide-open spaces, and what did he do.

"It is Monsieur Prescott, a very good friend of mine," Philippe always replied with dignity, as if this covered everything. Hundreds of people all over the world would have given the same answer, for Rick had the knack of getting on with all classes and all ages, ruling out all barriers, loving good people wherever he found them. Stray dogs followed him, office boys called him by his first name; cops, taxi drivers, bootblacks never forgot him, nor he them. He had been back in New York for several weeks and had been popping into the Julien almost everyday. Tonight he and Philippe had gone through their usual little game of ordering the dinner.

"What do I want tonight, Philippe?" Rick had asked.

"Blue points in *sauce mignonne, pommes soufflées,* squab *sous cloche,*" Philippe had said, straight-faced.

"Fine, I'll have pork chops and Schaeffer's light," Rick had answered, and as always during this routine Philippe had demanded to know why a strapping fellow with the appetite of a bear and no taste for good food should ever leave those big steak-and-pie places on Broadway. Why did he choose to come to the Julien anyway?

"Why does anybody come here?" countered Ricky.

Philippe gave this question some judicious thought. "They come because they have always come here," he said.

"Why did they come here the first time, then?"

"Nobody ever comes to the Julien for the first time," Philippe said, and as this was a thought that appealed to him hugely, his plump little body shook with noiseless chuckles. Recovering his gravity he leaned toward Ricky's ear and asked, "You tell me why you come here."

Rick frowned.

"I guess because something happened to me once here and I keep thinking it might happen again, I don't know what, but— well I'm always expecting something I don't expect."

He grinned with a confidential wink that captivated Philippe, whose inner chuckles began all over, this time ending in a little toy squeak.

"Maybe you expect Miss Cars, hey?" he said slyly.

Miss "Cars" (and Philippe was tickled to see that the young man flushed at the name) was a young lady romantically identified with Monsieur Prescott, indeed the real reason for Prescott's devotion to the Julien as both of them well knew. It was on Prescott's first visit to the café that he had met Miss Cars, it was Miss Cars he sought in the café every time he returned to New York. It was here they quarreled and said good-bye for ever, it was here they made up after long separations, here they misunderstood each other again, and here Prescott once again was seeking the lost love.

"Oh, Miss Carsdale," Ricky said. "How is Miss Carsdale, Philippe? "

"I no see Miss Cars, like I told you," Philippe sighed. His feet were too tired after a lifetime of carrying trays to and from the distant kitchen to tramp out the final syllables of long words. He would have liked to be able to produce Monsieur Prescott's little lady or at least to give him advice on how to find her again. He had a vague recollection of some scene last time the two had been there and of Miss Cars running out of the café alone.

"Maybe Miss Cars think you not nice to her," he ventured vaguely.

The young man was righteously offended.

"Me not nice to her?" he repeated bitterly. "After all she got me into?"

He was about to recite his grievances to Philippe, decided they were too complicated, and allowed Philippe to waddle away for another beer while he sat brooding. It was undeniably Miss Cars who had made him reject the fine job in Calcutta after World War II for the simple reason that he was wild to get back to her. It was Miss Cars's fault he had got tangled up with three other women just because of her maddening virtue. Yes, there was no question but that Miss Cars, fragile and sweet as she was, had precipitated Rick Prescott from one mistake into another. It was her fault entirely, and this was how it had happened.

Seven years ago in the excitement of our-regiment-sails-at dawn, Monsieur Prescott had made a heavy-handed attack on Miss Carsdale's virtue on the spittle-and-sawdust-strewn staircase of an old loft building on East Eighth Street where she rented a work studio for her photography. Whenever he remembered that night Rick cursed the mischievous jinx that had twisted the most magical day of his life into a sordid memory. It was the first time he'd ever been in New York, the city of his dreams, the first time he'd worn his officer's uniform, the first time he'd been drunk on champagne. New York loved him as it loved no other young man, and he embraced the city, impulsively discarding everything he had hitherto cherished of his Michigan boyhood loyalties. In Radio City Gardens he looked up at the colossal Prometheus commanding the city's very heart and thought, Me! He wandered up and down in a kind of smiling daze, slipped away from the buddies and home-town friends supervising his departure, and strolled happily down Fifth Avenue, finding all faces beautiful and wondrously kind, the lacy fragility of the city trees incomparably superior to his huge native forests. Under the giant diesel hum of street and harbor traffic he caught the sweet music of danger, the voices of deathless love and magic adventure.

My city, he had exulted, mine for these few hours at least, no matter what comes after. He wanted to embrace the Library lions, follow each softly smiling girl to the ends of the earth, bellow his joy from the top of the Empire State building. Wandering on foot or bus in a joyous daze he suddenly came at evening upon the treasure itself, a softly lit quiet park into which the avenue itself disappeared. Bewildered, breathless, as if he had come upon Lhasa, he walked around the little park, seeing couples strolling, arms about each other, windows of vine-covered houses lighting up, hearing church chimes, as if the city outside this was only a dream. The sign on the canopy of a corner mansion, CAFE JULIEN, told him he was in Greenwich Village and this café was the very place he was to meet his friends for dinner. And here they were waiting for him, not believing that he had stumbled there by chance, not even believing his day's adventure had been with a city and not a girl.

He kissed all the girls enthusiastically, regardless of the men in the party who were all spending the war comfortably in Washington or at 90 Church Street. He was handsomer and younger than they, and grateful for his departure they sang his praises while the girls found patriotic excuse to stroke his black hair or urge soft thighs against his. Rick loved them all, loved the café, loved even war since it had brought him here. With each fresh champagne he looked for the wonderful surprise, the special adventure that the city had surely promised him.

All around the café he could see little groups chattering happily, new arrivals being joyously welcomed, tables joining other tables, and though eyes strayed to the good-looking young soldier, Rick had a pang of knowing they were complete without him, they would be complete long after he had left on his unknown journey. Tomorrow night these very friends of his would celebrate without him; even Maidie Rennels, who felt she had home-town rights to him, was already planning a theater party with someone else. The city he had fallen in love with would carry no mark from him, this café would not know he was gone. Impatient with these glimpses of future loneliness he suggested going to other spots, gayer and louder, where tomorrows could be drowned out in music.

"But we have to wait for Ellenora," Maidie Rennels kept explaining. "Don't you remember I wrote you all about Ellenora, the girl I met when I was studying at the League? She has a studio around the corner and we told her we'd be here."

"You mean Rick doesn't know Ellenora?" someone else asked, and shook her head pityingly.

You may have observed that whenever you enter a new group there is apt to be constant allusion to some fabulous character who is not present, someone whose opinions are quoted on all subjects, someone so witty or unique that you find yourself apologizing for not having met him or her. You may think you are having a perfectly good time, but how can you when this marvelous creature is not present? The name "Ellenora" was dangled before Rick until he began working up a foggy hostility to the absent one. Ellenora was everyone's darling, all painters wanted to capture her charm on canvas, and she herself, a child of artists, was wonderfully gifted, studying art on money she earned as a photographer. How exciting for her to be engaged to marry Bob Huron who had proper security to give an artist wife, and who adored her as she deserved. What a pity Ricky might never be privileged to meet her! Ricky began to feel that her absence was a subtle snub to him, and her being engaged to another man without even waiting to meet Richard Prescott was an insult. Then the sudden arrival of Ellenora in person changed everything.

"Darling—you did come after all— Look, here's Ellenora. See, Ricky, here's Ellenora, the girl we've been telling you about—"

"Just for a minute," Ellenora had said, as they pulled out a chair for her. "I'm on my way to the studio to pick up some proofs but I had to stop in to say hello."

Ricky's unreasoning prejudice wavered at first sight of her radiant little face. He had braced himself for a blasé beauty from a Hollywood picture of artists' life, a too clever poseur, full of arty talk and sophisticated repartee. This girl was nothing like that nor was she like any girl Rick had ever known. She had a delicate, quaint femininity that belonged to the past and seemed all the more striking in the New York setting. All in a moment the others seemed blowzy, their gaiety heavy-handed, their friendliness aggressive, their flattery obvious. He marveled that he had ever found hearty Maidie Rennels even mildly desirable. Ellenora had the teasing fascination of a light perfume, hovering in a room long after the unknown visitor has vanished.

She disarmed him by being no beauty, yet he couldn't keep his eyes away from the luminous pallor of her face, the delicate, humorously tilted nose, the tender, voluptuous coral mouth, the wide-apart eager hazel eyes with the soft babyish shadows beneath and the fine silky blond hair drawn sleekly up from the pretty ears, from which hung heavy topaz earrings. Whatever it was she wore—the tiny brown chiffon hat with its scarf falling over the shoulder of the cinnamon wool dress, the unexpected glimpses of bright emerald green silk somewhere in the lining of her brown cape—seemed special to Rick and made the other women appear drab. Whatever it was she said made the others seem stupid. They sounded shrill beside her soft breathless voice that seemed to quiver on the verge of either tears or laughter, just as the gentle comments she made seemed halfway dolorous and halfway comical but always miraculously right to him. At that time there was a special vocabulary college girls used as a precaution, it would seem, against communication. But Ellenora talked, as many articulate artists do, in terms of visual imagery and it was new to Rick. Even her long narrow hand fluttering to secure a stray lock of hair or to stamp out a cigarette in the ashtray bewitched him, hinting of the sweet helplessness of long-ago ladies.

He felt himself back again in his schooldays, a halfback when he wanted to be a bookworm, always too big for his age, clumsy and oafish, hands and feet all over the place. It angered him that she should have this effect on him, reducing him to the old boyish sense of inadequacy. He felt rebuffed when she took a seat on the other side of the table, and to show how little her presence affected him he found himself directing idiotic taunts at her, which she received with polite indifference. There was a lacy unreality about her that reminded him of the ailanthus branches or the Chrysler Tower he had admired. He suspected she must be amused by his too obvious subjugation, and he tried to restore his happy self-assurance by challenging every remark she made until the others cried out, "Rick, stop picking on Ellenora, she's such a darling!"

Any person experienced in love recognizes these outwardly hostile first encounters between a man and woman as the storm signal of immediate attraction, but fortunately for the two, the ordinary bystander reads only the exterior antagonism. Ellenora, only recently engaged to her nice young broker, was immediately conscious of the electric bond between her and this soldier and it frightened her that whatever this new feeling was—reckless, dizzy, ecstatic—she had never had it for Bob Huron, the man she was going to marry. Even when each of them spoke to someone else they were saying something wild and dangerous to each other. Ellenora tried to tell herself that it was the young man's situation, not the man himself, which was shaking her emotions as they had never been shaken before. He was going away to war, that was all. She hated the other men, her friends, for their safe jobs. She hated the tenderness with which the gods protect mediocrity while the rare irreplaceable specimens must be tossed into danger. She wished it was Bob Huron who was saying good-bye and as soon as she found herself thinking this she knew she could never marry Bob, never, never, not even if she never saw this soldier again. These strange sensations and thoughts filled her with terror. She did not know what she was saying, when she spoke, except it must be something he willed her to say. She kept her eyes from him lest they fill with frightened, revealing tears, and it relieved her that he construed this as a snub. Let him think she disapproved of him rather than guess that her lips must be guarded to keep the word "Love!" from flying out to him. The more he mocked at her sobriety in contrast to the merry party the more shaken and foolishly bewitched she felt. Nothing like this had ever happened to her in her twenty years and surely this kind of sudden sickness must betray itself to everyone else if not to him. Bob Huron, she thought, appalled, how could I ever have thought of marrying him when I know there is this man somewhere in the world? She would have to leave, before whatever in the air swelled into an explosion.

"I have an early appointment tomorrow and have to leave," she said, rising. "You know I told you I had to pick up some work at my studio and couldn't come along. But I couldn't resist saying hello—"

"See what you've done, Rick," the Barnard girl exclaimed. "You've teased her so much she's going."

"I told you I had to leave early," Ellenora said almost sharply. Rick's face looked suddenly desolate.

"I won't have it said I drove away a lady," he said and pushed back his own chair. "I'll walk her to her door to make up for it."

Going out the café door they had walked along in a tense silence that was like a fierce embrace. These things did happen, one did meet the one love, knew it at once, fought it, surrendered to it, stayed forever true.

"Where have you been all my life?" he finally asked and the question seemed brilliantly original to the bemused girl.

"Nowhere, I guess," she answered helplessly.

"What will you be doing until I get back?" he asked.

"Nothing," she murmured and they were hushed as if they had just exchanged solemn vows. They walked slowly along Eighth Street, hand in hand, and the silence seemed to fill in everything that Ellenora wanted said. She was beginning to wonder if she dared risk asking him up to the studio, for legally the students and artists were not allowed at night in these condemned old buildings except for emergencies. If they did manage to creep up there, if she could manage to build a fire in the fireplace—for really this was an emergency, once in a lifetime you might say—

"Here we are," she whispered at the entrance to the bleak loft building where she had her studio. At that instant, without warning, Rick made a wild predatory lunge toward her. When she pushed him away he backed into an ashcan that tipped over in the gutter with a tremendous clatter and suddenly the spell was broken and Rick was roaring with laughter.

"Please be quiet, Rick, or I'll lose my studio!" she cried.

The humiliation of his chasing her up the dirty staircase where any passer-by could see the clumsy struggle, her shame at her own sentimental expectations when all of their friends back at the café must have anticipated just such shenanigans made Ellenora give a heartbroken sob and a slap that sent him off balance tumbling down smack into the ashheap. She bolted the door behind her and stood there trembling, afraid to go on upstairs now and afraid to go out and back home to her apartment on Irving Place until he had gone. Everything that had seemed true between them now seemed a romantic schoolgirl distortion. He was just a soldier on leave, nothing more. She should have expected nothing more. He must have thought she was a complete fool. And she was, she was! She would never forgive him, but now she would never marry anyone else, never.

Prescott, for his part, was furiously disgusted with himself. The moment she had said "Here we are" he realized this was the end and he had swooped on her like some cave man, fully as astonished at himself as Ellenora had been. The ashcan episode restored him to his senses but then in his disappointment and embarrassment he had worked up a rage at the girl who had led him on to believe she had the understanding of angels. Didn't she realize that finding the city of his dreams and dream girl to match on the very night he plunged into nowhere was a miracle no man could handle? He was twenty six, decent, already an officer, and if he was good enough to be killed for his country he deserved some help in his emotional crises even if he had acted like a lumberjack. More unfair still was the fact that he, a prize marksman and athletic champion, should be sent hurtling down ten dirty steps into a garbage pile, forced to spend his precious hours before sailing in a doctor's office having three stitches taken in his head, all caused by a feeble little tap from a small white hand.

So this was Love at First Sight. So this was what happened when you met the dream girl. Brooding over this with mounting indignation on the flight to England, Ricky had celebrated his first night there by gallantly getting engaged to a Liverpool barmaid, also disappointed in love, who had listened sympathetically to him and who did him the inestimable favor of eloping with a corporal before he had his first leave. Three years later the armistice brought him back to New York and since New York was Ellenora he was in a fever to find her again, past error forgotten. He was so sure she had not married, so sure his own mark was on her, that it did not even seem chance to find her in the little art shop near the Julien. Of course he would find her. Of course she had not married. Of course she would meet him whenever he asked. And of course everything would be the same as before.

They met every day at five at Philippe's table in the Café Julien—same place, same waiter, same table as their first meeting, for they must start all over from scratch they tacitly agreed. They laughed a great deal, spoke very warily of personal matters, maintaining the gay exterior intimacy possible only in café relationships, where a man is as rich as his credit and a lady is as glamorous as her hat. Ricky, reduced again to being overgrown boy with tiny dainty woman of the world, knowing too well the sudden wild impulses that carried him away, tried to maintain his masculine poise by cagily indicating that this relationship was only a delightful oasis in his otherwise full life. Ellenora, being all loving and as dangerously bemused by the young man as before, guarded her susceptibilities by behaving archly worldly and mysterious. The very violence of their attraction for each other put them fiercely on guard, as often happens to people who use up their resistance on one great desire and have none left for the mildest of future temptations. They skipped gracefully around the edge of love, retreated when it compelled them to look into its blinding face. Avoiding major issues they found minor ones turned major wherever they turned. How strange that they had both read *The Life of the Bee,* odd that they both knew cummings' poetry by heart, rather uncanny that they preferred the bare charm of the Café Julien to uptown gayer spots. Prescott had a dim idea that Ellenora had come to New York to study art from somewhere in New England; Ellenora gathered that Prescott stemmed from Michigan, and that he had studied some kind of engineering.

They asked no questions of each other, barely mentioning other names or other places in their lives but finding each other out in a kind of breathless, intoxicating hide-and-seek. And the truth was that everything else faded away in the excitement of each other's presence. They would have forgotten to eat or drink if Philippe's affectionate supervision had not nudged them. Wary of allowing strong drink to betray his emotions as it had at their first meeting, Rick suggested vermouth cassis for the first week of their postwar cocktail meetings, and they parted discreetly at seven with great checking of wrist watches to imply other important claims. The second week, confident of their civilized control, they graduated to the pernod that was just coming back on the market, and though this heightened their pleasure in each other they still pretended that their daily meetings were accidental, a continuous lark maintained as a joke on the friends who thought they hated each other. A little more lax under pernod they did not look at the clock until the tables were filling with diners, tablecloths being whisked over marbletops. Then with little exclamations of alarm each must rush out to the hall to telephone explanations to importunate dinner companions waiting elsewhere. The third week they did not even try to part but stayed until the café closed and then Ellenora allowed him to take her to her door.

Ellenora's female pride made her take pains to indicate that though she enjoyed his company, her availability was purely accidental; she was by no means a girl to be forgotten for three years (war or no war) and then picked up at a moment's notice. She hoped he would never find out that the day after he had sailed she had broken her engagement to Bob Huron. She hoped he would not hear about the young doctor she had been on the verge of engaging herself to just at the moment Rick next came into her life, changing everything. She was afraid to risk seeing him alone in her studio, not for fear he would take advantage of her, but for fear this time she would surrender too easily. Rick was smart enough to make no demand, his own pride (as long as he could hold on to it) was in demonstrating that he never made the same mistake twice. The fourth week they discovered French Seventy-fives, a seasonal favorite concocted of brandy and champagne which made them laugh long and loud at their newfound wit, reach across the table for each other's hands over some delectable comment, find each other's eyes suddenly and stop laughing for a breathless moment. By this time Ellenora was recklessly putting all her eggs in one basket, refusing dates with nice fellows who adored her, and arranging for special permission from the landlord to live in her work studio since the apartment she shared with two other girls left no privacy for love. She intended to resist stalwartly of course, but she was desperately eager for the opportunity to show her strength.

One night they were in the café dawdling over French Seventy-fives, putting off the moment of parting, when some army pals of Rick joined them. Ellenora hoped they would go for she had decided this was to be the night, but Rick kept urging them to stay. Their drinks were two dollars apiece and the check was bound to be big enough to send an ordinary young couple on a week-end honeymoon (for Ellenora was ridiculously thinking on those lines), but what really stabbed her was hearing Rick, who had told her nothing of this, carelessly mention to his friends that he expected to take a job in Chicago next week. Stunned at the foolish dreams she had been building on this man for a second heartbreak, mortified at the thought of how close her surrender had been, Ellenora sipped her drink, smiling stiffly at the loud jokes about other girls in other places, Rick's record as a wolf, and how they might have known he would hide a creature as lovely as Ellenora in some out-of-the-way place like this where no one else could have a chance at her. It was then that Rick, a little disturbed perhaps by his friends' obvious interest in Ellenora, took it into his head to relate the story of their ashcan romance, embellishing it to his advantage, declaring that he had noticed this kid had had One Too Many and had gallantly offered to take her home from the restaurant.

"I was drinking Coca-cola that night," Ellenora had protested, but the men paid no attention and she realized that every one of the warriors would have told the same story in the same way so she couldn't really blame Ricky too much. But when it came to the payoff, the part where one little tap from her sent him sprawling, Ricky's version for the boys was that this poor sweet kid couldn't make it up the stairs and he had tried to carry her upstairs so her folks wouldn't be worried—

"My folks!" Ellenora had interrupted in indignation. "They weren't even living there!"

—then the girl, whose name, mind you, he had not even caught, took her purse trimmed in heavy gold and slugged him with it so he had to have eighteen stitches taken, all because these New York girls insisted on mistaking simple kindness as attacks on their honor. The loud laughter of the men, Rick's humorous admission of getting his only war wounds from a five-foot virgin infuriated Ellenora, fearful as she was that Rick might guess the thought of him was all that had kept her a virgin in his absence.

"At least he came out alive," she said, managing a sweet smile. "What Rick never knew was that I was trying to save him from getting killed by the man waiting for me upstairs." With these words, which she noted had the effect of turning the laughter on Rick, she picked up her coat and said, "That reminds me, somebody might kill me right now if I don't get home. Good night, everybody. And incidentally, Ricky, I'm five-feet-five."

It was such a mean trick to humiliate him in front of his pals, implying that he wasn't getting anywhere with her and had been so naïve as to think her a virgin, that Rick did not even rise for her departure, merely saluting her with smiling fury.

"A second round for you, my dear," he said. "I assure you there won't be a third."

Having successfully ruined her own good name and future happiness Ellenora marched out victorious, all ready to embark on months of weeping nightmares over her insane act. That was what happened when you held on to your normal impulses so rigidly, your whole being got deranged and trained for every other kind of self-destruction. They had ruined the reality with their foolish little game. Grimly flinging himself into a two-day binge Rick took one buddy's drunken challenge to fly to Texas next day. There he signed up with the fellow's oil company, and generously married his sister, a good-natured big girl who had tearfully confided men didn't like her because she had no mystery and didn't play little games. In another year she was no longer good-natured (having been praised for that alone too often) and he was a free man again, celebrating the annulment in New Orleans during Mardi gras, when the desire came over him for Ellenora. He was in his room at the St. Charles, drinking sloe gin with a lot of fine strangers in masquerade costumes, when his forgotten long-distance call came through, and when Ellenora heard all the babes giggling she hung up, thinking it was one more cruel joke. This time he didn't come to his senses till a month later in St. Croix with a girl he had taken along for a Mardi gras gag (after Ellenora's brush-off), and it took plenty of time and legal business, for this babe was no fool, to get rid of her and then, happily, a transfer to the New York office. He was still with the Glistro Oil Company, doing very well, though he knew and had in fact known for some time that the job bored him, and each unasked for promotion depressed him. His friends and family irritated him by their praise of his success with Glistro Oil as if this was a loftier career than they had ever dreamed of for him. In these moments of unreasonable dissatisfaction he longed for Ellenora, as if Ellenora and New York would resolve his future, Ellenora would somehow illuminate the wonderful road he was destined to follow. Until then he must mark time, venting his unrest in wild ruinous ways, and someday they could not be undone. Ellenora was his future, his dream, his harbor.

He still hated to admit her spell over him, and he put off surrendering to it, certain she would be around and available, and he could save his vanity by letting her make the first steps. Again he would make it a casual reunion, he thought, strolling into the old Julien café and running into her. Only this time it didn't happen.

At first in this 1948 winter he didn't even ask for her, just took to occasionally dropping into the café, then daily as his stubbornness got aroused. Finally he asked a question idly here and there, and at last he made a definite quest. From a walk down Eighth Street he saw that her old studio was torn down, from the janitor of her old apartment house on Irving Place he found that her two roommates had married without leaving their new names, from a telephone call to her old fiancé Bob Huron, he received the chilly news that neither Mr. Huron nor his new wife had kept in touch with Miss Carsdale. From the corner florist he learned that flowers had been sent to her at some uptown address a year ago but he could not discover by whom. Nor was their mutual friend, Maidie Rennels, to be found at her apartment. By this time Rick was leaving messages, in case anyone met her, to call him at his office or leave word in care of the Café Julien. He moved from his hotel to a furnished apartment near the Julien, not admitting to himself that he proposed to trap her in there before she could get away next time.

"You're sure you haven't heard anything about her?" Rick asked Philippe, the waiter.

Philippe shook his head.

"Maybe she got consump," he ventured politely.

"Funny she should stop coming here," Prescott said.

"I no see Miss Cars for maybe two year," Philippe told him as he had several times before. "Maybe she come on my day off. Maybe she got married. Hah. Monsieur Prescott married, no?"

"No," Prescott said impatiently. "I got enough wives already."

"Maybe Miss Cars got husband and big family, too," Phillippe suggested mischievously.

Prescott gave a short laugh. He was not worried about her being either dead or married because he simply would not have it so. He was not unfeeling in his conviction that she was in no trouble, he was merely showing his profound faith in Ellenora's powers over destiny. That little slap that had felled him had left an enduring respect for Ellenora's might. He could tease her with his anecdotes of other women, leave her, but she would always be the winner, and while this angered him it also continued to fascinate him. It bewildered him, too, that he could not settle down to the flirtations and pleasures of his New York life until he had got Ellenora pinned down. A fancier of beauty, wit and flamboyance in women, he could never understand why he had pegged Ellenora as his special property from the minute he laid eyes on her. He never could remember her features and sometimes thought perhaps she hadn't any—just a couple of smoky eyeholes in that sort of luminous Laurencin mask. She was taller than you thought and plumper than you thought; he had reason to know she was stronger than you thought. He had a couple of photographs of her but they didn't look anything like his inner picture of her. He knew he laughed most of the time he was with her but for the life of him he couldn't remember a single funny thing she ever said. He liked a sleek flawlessly tailored woman and it was strange he was so amused and delighted by Ellenora's penchant for feathers, ruffles, tinkling jewelry, softly swishing silks. They were so definitely and ridiculously ladylike in an age of crisp business girl ensembles. Like a peacock, he thought, silly and lovely; she walked like a bird, too, fluttering along the street helplessly and prettily as if her feet were made for perching on high branches and not for walking.

In distant places it disturbed him that he had so little to remember about Ellenora, for after all he knew little about her. She was homesickness, he knew that much, though God knows she represented nothing secure or known. It was New York he loved and he guessed Ellenora represented New York or his idea of New York the way the mind arbitrarily elects some unsuspecting cruise acquaintance to embody the hopes and glamorous expectations of a Caribbean trip. He would be in some deadly dull little southern town or on some desolate ranch and suddenly he would ache for Ellenora—not Ellenora as a body, mind you, but Ellenora complete with name band, Blue Angel, Eddie Condon's, El Morocco, Chinatown, Park Avenue cocktail party, hansom ride in the Park, theatrical lobby chatter between the acts, champagne buckets beside the table, keep-the-change, taxi-cab characters, and ha-ha-ha, ho-ho-ho, kiss-kiss, bang-bang, tomorrow same place. This was Ellenora, who, as a matter of actual fact, was not tied with any of these memories. He had never even danced with Ellenora and if he had been to any nightclub with her would certainly have been too polite to leave his drink sitting alone at the table while he whizzed Ellenora around the floor. Very likely the reason she represented this fictional and legendary Manhattan to him was that they had spent too many hours in one spot postponing going someplace else until what they had not seen together was more real than what they had.

The Ellenora who figured in his dreams knew everything about him, for he had long soul-satisfying conversations with her, telling her everything and being understood completely. She knew that he was meant to do something finer than just bury himself in business. He'd even told her—in these imaginary conferences—the dreadful way his mother had let him down, doting as she had been, too, on his twelfth birthday when she asked him what he intended to be when he grew up.

"A foreign correspondent," he had whispered almost choked up with the awe of putting it into words. It was the year he was reading Vincent Sheean and Walter Duranty, and besides he had been made sports editor of the school paper. His mother had burst into spontaneous, crushing laughter, and then explained to him fondly. "But Ricky, darling, nobody in our family is ever a journalist. We've never been the least bit clever that way. We're always lawyers."

"What about Grandpa Weaver?" he had shouted furiously, angry at her laughter after he had opened his heart so foolishly.

"He wasn't able to finish law so he went into business," his mother said. "And that's lucky for us, because now he can see you through law school."

"He doesn't need to," young Ricky had said, obstreperously, "I'll go in business myself since you think I couldn't do anything else."

But Ellenora knew he could have done anything, this Ellenora he always carried with him. Later whenever he found the real one it was a surprise to have her not know, for it was fixed in his mind that his thousand mental confessions had miraculously reached her and most of the time it really seemed as if they had. But what had gone wrong with the connection now? He had to find her. She *must* know that.

On this February eve Prescott had been drifting in and out of the Julien since five, sitting down for a while, then wandering up University Place to the stationer's, glancing over the magazines, exchanging track news with a messenger boy, getting his shoes shined across the street, anything to pass the time till he might enter the café again, all primed to see Ellenora seated at a table. He would act as if he didn't know her at first, he decided, one of the harmless jokes they used to have; pretending the other one had made a mistake, summoning Philippe, always in on the joke, to please remove this presumptuous stranger.

But Ellenora never came, and disturbed by this defection Rick drank fast. A person traveled, knocked around, liked to see new places and make new friends, certain that the harbor was always there safe and sure whenever the mood came to return. It was outrageous to find the shore line changing behind one, no lamps waiting in windows for the returned wayfarer. Let everyplace else in the world change but let Manhattan stay the way it was, his dream city, Rick insisted in his thoughts, the way it had been that first day, the day he met Ellenora, the way he pictured it in far places. He was not a man to admit things could be other than he wished, and now, he thought, let other lovers default as they would, if he sat tight and willed it the world would stop at the spot he insisted—*here, now,* with Ellenora smiling across the table.

He would give chance a little more time, he decided, and summoned Philippe.

"Save our—my table," he said. "I'll be back."

Outside once more for the restless stroll down the block, a peep into the Brevoort, a look into the Grosvenor, then back to the Julien stubbornly hopeful. She wasn't there, and he wavered between childish resentment that he couldn't *make* the wish come true (this was Ellenora's fault and if she walked in this minute he would not even look up, just to punish her) and the uneasy suspicion that he was making a fool of himself. He ought to shrug his shoulders and call up Maidie—there were dozens of girls, thousands! Still, now he was here, no reason why he shouldn't stay on and have dinner, and after that wait just a little longer. He knew this was only an excuse; he was chagrined to find himself still dawdling there hopefully at half past ten. For a full hour there had been nothing worth observing in the place except the patron at the opposite end of the room whose beard showed above his French newspaper. Earlier in the evening the relief telephone operator, a majestic blonde, had been emerging from her switchboard every half hour with the regularity of a cuckoo clock to stand at the café door and cluck "McGrew? McGrew? A call for Mr. McGrew." Each time Prescott was hopeful that one of his messages left in every possible place, from delicatessen shop to Art Students League, had reached Ellenora. But each time the lady's eyes rejected him, traveled thoroughly up and down the room again, not at all convinced by the bareness of the room. Each time she raised her hand to her eyes and peered at the red velvet curtains, the cuspidors, the cupid-strewn ceiling, as if clues were concealed there by mischievous colleagues. At ten-thirty she appeared again, but this time she stood in the doorway quietly scratching her blond chignon with a pencil and staring intently at Rick Prescott. Hopeful and happy he started to rise.

"A call for Prescott?" he asked.

"No," she said haughtily, "Mr. McGrew."

It was too much. Rick sent her a look of deep reproach followed by a burst of plain fury, as if the poor woman was personally responsible for telephones refusing to ring for him. Whoever McGrew was he hated him, too, for it seemed to him they all must have guessed the depth of his infatuation; they must have sensed that his desire was now so violent he would have begged Ellenora to marry and stay with him forever if only she would walk in the café door this instant. They thought he was making a fool of himself once again, and they all knew Ellenora was deliberately teasing him, trying to see to what lengths he would go to catch her again. How they would laugh when she came into the café with her fine New York boy friend and there would be the old Middle Western yokel waiting at the same old table with his silly heart on his sleeve!

All right, let them laugh! He would laugh, too. Fully as outraged as if Ellenora had publicly mocked at his honorable offer of love everlasting, Ricky leaped to his feet and followed the operator back to the switchboard.

"Is the same lady calling McGrew who called before?" he inquired.

The girl nodded, and he said briskly, "I'll take the call and tell her where she can find him."

A lady disappointed in not finding a McGrew might be in the same reckless mood as a man disappointed in an Ellenora. He was in Booth One speaking into the telephone before the operator could make up her mind whether this was permissible.

It was a matter of supreme indifference to the tall Catalan waiter at the opposite end of the café that his lone customer, Dalzell Sloane, was making the decision of a lifetime. For the Catalan every hour of his life had held a problem of terrific moment, whether to punch a fellow worker, throw a plate at a customer, resign his job, present all of his possessions to a daughter momentarily the favorite, enter a monastery, return to Spain, go west, east, north; all problems ending in the decision to have another cup of coffee in the kitchen.

But Sloane, so it seemed to him now, had never had to make a decision before in his life. There were always two paths, and if you stood long enough at the crossroads, one of them proved impassable. There were always two women, but one of them wouldn't have you or one of them kidnapped you. There were two careers but at the crucial moment one of them dropped out, something happened, somebody made an appointment, and there you were. For Dalzell, destiny had shaped itself only through his hesitation. But though he had hesitated over this one problem, waiting for chance to decide, it would not solve itself. Something must be done, once and for all, and tonight. This necessity had produced in his head nothing more constructive than a kind of perpetual buzz that was like a telephone ringing in some neighbor's apartment. He tried to draw counsel by detaching himself from his body, watching the bearded stranger in the mirrors across and beyond, assuring himself that such a calm, distinguished-looking citizen could have no real worry. He knew the beard made him look older than his fifty years, but at least it made him look successful, and after half a century one has the right to at least the appearance of success. If someone were to ask, "What have you done with your fifty years, Dalzell Sloane?" he could answer, "I have failed in love and in art, but I have raised a beard." The beard had given him credit and character references, for people assumed in a vague way that a man with a beard had traveled everywhere, knew all about art and science, had influential friends and doting ladies tucked away all over the world, and was securely solvent. Dalzell had only to look at himself in the mirror to be almost convinced this was all true. "Thank you, beard," he saluted it silently, marking that the gray was beginning to dominate the brown as it did in his thick hair, though his brows were still as dark as his eyes.

The beard, like everything else in his life, owed itself to no decision of his, but had grown of its own accord during a long illness, and all that had been demanded of him was to select a cut from the page of style offered by a Parisian barber. Later his fellow painters, Marius and Ben, took turns cutting it during their merry parties, shouting hilariously all the while. Old Marius and Ben, Dalzell thought, the three of them always together then, and now Marius dead, Ben lost for years.

A group of diners emerging from the large dining room beyond the café paused to stare in the door, pleased to discover a bearded bohemian philosophizing over his glass, even though it was not absinthe, and he wore no smock or beret. Dalzell looked steadily into his glass, trained to tourist curiosity. He had noticed them earlier in the evening when they came in, the pouting, red-mouthed, bare-shouldered young girl in blue taffeta with the white camellias in her blue-black hair, the tipsy, pink-faced fiancé, the two busty, gray matrons in their mighty silver fox capes, the large, purple-faced, responsible men of affairs. Thirty years ago he would have noted it as an effective idea for a canvas. Family Outing, Engagement Dinner. Now he had learned to reject such inspirations on the spot as he rejected any flare of desire, thus protecting himself against the certain failure. Family parties such as this were familiar to the big dining room, usually chosen by the host as a place where the appetite was king, undisturbed by music, glamour or youthful pleasures. The young were inevitably bewildered and disappointed as they discovered that the excited clamor of happy voices did not mean gaiety and dancing but sheer middle-aged joy over bouillabaisse, venison, or *cassoulet Toulousaine* with its own wedded wine. Dalzell was sympathetically amused at the youthful impatience with stomachic ecstasy, and it amused him, too, that the naughty word "café" made responsible men herd their families into the respectable safety of the dining room. Where did they get the money to feed Julien dinners so casually to five mouths? Thirty dollars at the least, more than he spent for food in six weeks, Dalzell thought.

There were people, and Dalzell was one of them, who were born café people, claustrophobes unable to endure a definite place or plan. The café was a sort of union station where they might loiter, missing trains and boats as they liked, postponing the final decision to go anyplace or do anything until there was no longer need for decision. One came here because one couldn't decide where to dine, whom to telephone, what to do. At least one had not yet committed oneself to one parlor or one group for the evening; the door of freedom was still open. One might be lonely, frustrated or heart-broken, but at least one wasn't sewed up. Someone barely known might come into the café bringing marvelous strangers from Rome, London, Hollywood, anyplace at all, and one joined forces, went places after the café closed that one had never heard of before and never would again, talked strange talk, perhaps kissed strange lips to be forgotten next day. Here was haven for those who craved privacy in the midst of sociability, for those whose hearts sank with fear as the door of a charming home (their own or anyone's) closed them in with a known intimate little group; here might be the chance companion for the lonely one who shuddered at the fixed engagement, ever dodging the little red book as a trap for the unwary. Here, in this café, were blessed doors strategically placed so that flight was always possible at first glimpse of an undesired friend or foe's approach. Here was procrastinator's paradise, the spot for homehaters to hang their hats, here was the stationary cruise ship into which the hunted family man might leap without passport or visa. Here in the Julien it was possible to maintain heavenly anonymity if one chose, here was the spot where nothing beyond good behavior was expected of one, here was safety from the final decision, but since the doors closed at midnight sharply, a bare two hours from now, Dalzell began wondering from where his solution would come. At this very moment in the dining room there might be someone he had known and forgotten years ago, now risen to great consequence in the world, and this person would pause at the café entrance to cry out, "Dalzell Sloane, as I live and breathe, the very person I'm looking for!" Or a theatre party, dropping in at the last minute for a nightcap, would carry him off to someone's apartment for midnight music, and one o'clock would pass, two o'clock, three o'clock—he would have missed the train, not the first time his future had been determined by negatives. But then what about tomorrow? Ah well, even if nothing else would be accomplished, at least he would have closed a door.

Dalzell had been sipping *mazagran,* for the strong coffee with the twist of lemon served in a goblet for twenty-five cents seemed less odiously economical than the same brew in a cup, but now he remembered that the last time he had been at the Julien with Ben and Marius they had drunk *amer picon citron,* and just as Marius had insisted, it had had a curiously magical effect on him, alcosomatic perhaps. It seemed to seep delicately through his bones, detaching his mind from his body, transforming him into a cool, wise observer of himself. Since he wished to observe instead of to be, he recklessly decided to spend eighty cents on a glass of the magic potion. He would step outside himself, perhaps change into Marius watching from the other world. Almost with the first sip his mood changed into a Marius-like desire for genial companionship. He was lonely. He'd been lonely for months, years. He regretted that he had been systematically avoiding people for so long, afraid they might guess his circumstances, or that he might be foolish enough to confide in someone. He had taken the back corner in the café to hide from possible discovery, but now that he was changing into the boisterous Marius he wanted to be found. He didn't want just anybody—the gray little half-people resigned to failure and poverty who had been creeping through his life all too long, demanding nothing, giving nothing. He wanted the bright beautiful wonderful ones, the stars in his dark sky whose fleeting presence raised him to their firmament. He thought of Andy Callingham, photographed only last week on arriving at the Ambassador. "Dalzell, you old son-of-a-gun, I'll join you in fifteen minutes," he pictured Andy as saying over the telephone, but that was nonsense. Andy would never go anyplace where there were no columnists, no gaping admirers, no publicity for his last novel. He wouldn't even pick up the phone except for Zanuck or a Rockefeller. Dennis Orphen, then, but this would be what Dennis called his "drunk time" and he'd bring all of his convivial cronies. Dalzell began berating himself for his folly in keeping up with his valuable friendships only when he was in the chips and didn't need such support, then scuttling down to Skid Row at the first drop in fortune, cowering under cover guiltily as if bad luck was a crime or contagion that must isolate one from all humanity. If the bad luck stayed on, as it usually did with him, you cut off all bridges back to civilized living and the chance of revival.

How long had it been, Dalzell pondered, was it months or years, that he had kept his door locked to his old friends as if Despair was a lady of the streets hiding in his room? A familiar voice on the telephone, a glimpse of an old friend on the street, was like a dun; the simple words "Let's get together" filled him with panic, as if "hello" committed him to horrifying expenditures—twenty cents worth of cigarettes, a beer, a cup of coffee— all these were obligations he could not face. After his emergence from his underground hiding—and how could he explain what had brought about his release?—the habit of friendship was hard to regain. The connection could not be won back with a simple phone call, the loving path was now overgrown with thistles and angry brush. Forget the solace of the old, then. Dalzell decided whatever was to save him must come from the new and unpredictable.

With a vague idea of tempting the unknown, Dalzell rose and strolled out into the little lobby that was now as deserted as the café. He observed the café's other customer emerging from the first phone booth. The other stood for a moment at the café door hitching his belt around his middle with the nonchalant pride of a big guy who knows how to keep in trim, knows what he wants, goes after it, gets it. There was something familiar-looking about him, and it struck Dalzell that he might be a film actor choosing this spot to get away from fans. Yes, he looked like that star Monty Douglass, and Dalzell was warmed by his grin, envisaging a quick friendship over a nightcap, an impulsive putting of cards on the table, a miraculous solution to everything. Childish dreaming, Dalzell scolded himself, and he went on his way down the stairs to the men's room.

He was slightly bewildered to find there a tall bushy-browed beagle-nosed man, coatless in a fancy mauve shirt and scarlet suspenders, his pinstriped gray jacket dangling from the door-knob, solemnly flexing his right arm with a regular rhythm before the mirror.

"Feel those muscles," commanded this gentleman, without taking his eye from the mirror, apparently not at all perturbed by an audience.

"Like iron," said Dalzell obediently.

"Of course they're like iron, because I keep them that way. Golf. Tennis. Sixty years old. I just put my arm through the door. Take a look at the other side. Right through. Wanted to see if I could still do it."

"You must be a professional athlete," Dalzell said, properly awed by the jagged hole in the door.

"Think so?" beamed the man. "Believe it or not, I'm in the advertising business."

"No!"

"I'm telling you. Here's my card, Hastings Hardy of Hardy, Long, and Love. I just don't let myself get soft, that's all."

It was the name of a leading advertising firm, one that had saved the lives of many a struggling artist by its sweet temptations. Dalzell himself in a low moment had offered to be corrupted there, but with no success. Maybe this was the time and this the opportunity, if only he knew how to make it work.

"Another thing, I eat right," said the tall man, patting his stomach. "The best food and not too much of it, three times a day, or don't you agree?"

"I do, indeed," said Dalzell.

"By best foods I do not mean health foods, understand," said Mr. Hardy, looking at him sternly. "Do you think I could have busted that door with my fist on a diet of health foods? I've always had the best food and liquor, and as a result how old would you say I am, sir?"

"Forty-four," Dalzell said, and was rewarded by a handclasp of deepest affection.

"Sixty next month," said Mr. Hardy, pleased to see Dalzell's expression of suitable astonishment. He took his coat from the door knob. With considerable care he managed to get the right arms into the right sleeves. After a complacent glance in the mirror again he looked at Dalzell.

"You look to me like a mighty intelligent fellow," he said. "I like a man who *looks* intelligent. What do you do?"

The beard again, Dalzell thought.

"My name's Dalzell Sloane. I paint."

This seemed to strike Mr. Hardy with tremendous force for he took a step back to stare at Dalzell.

"An artist? What do you know? As a matter of fact I'm talking to somebody right now about having my portrait done."

He seized Dalzell's hand and shook it vigorously, and then Dalzell saw that his eyes were brightly glazed like gray marbles staring straight past him.

"Look here, what do you say to joining my wife and me for a brandy when you come back up? We're with my daughter and her fiancé's family and we're arguing about the portrait right now. I'm going to tell them you're the man to do it. Sloane, eh? Frankly Sloane, I like you. I'd like to regard you as a friend. And what's the use of old friends if you can't do 'em a favor? We'd just about decided on some little chap I forget, oh yes, Whitfield. He did the president of Bailey Stodder, our biggest client. Did vice-president of General Flexmetals, too, hangs right there in the bastard's private office. Whitfield, that's this artist's name. Know him?"

The artists who make the most money from the bourgeoisie are usually never even heard of in the art world, and this name was unknown to Dalzell.

"I suppose he's good on tweed," Dalzell said, tentatively.

"The best in the field," declared Hardy. "On the Bailey Stodder job you can almost spot the tailor's name, it's that good. But why shouldn't I have a man of my own, why should I have to have Stodder's fellow? Come on back and join us and we'll talk it over. By George, I like to make my own decisions."

"That's mighty nice of you," Dalzell said, and again they shook hands. "I'll settle up first in the café and then join you in the dining room."

This was it, then, Dalzell thought with a deep breath, this was the crazy chance that was going to settle everything. After all these years Fate had decided to make him a portrait painter. Okay, Fate, this time he'd take whatever came. He washed his hands, turned back his frayed cuffs, flicked tentatively at his suit and decided he'd look better covered in topcoat, and then he followed his new friend back upstairs. The clerk was back at the desk in the lobby and the telephone girl was at the switchboard. Dalzell looked at the clock. Eleven. He tried not to let his hopes rise too insanely.

In the café he settled his bill, six eighty-five, as much as he had spent all last week. In his wallet there was still the eighty dollars he had reserved for his ticket from his—well, call it stolen profits—and it struck him that under the circumstances Alex deserved a larger tip so he drew out a dollar bill and left it in place of the seventy-five cents, but habit was so strong he could not leave the cigarette pack even if there was only one smoke left in it. Matches, too, went in pocket. He put on his loose brown topcoat, its shabbiness forgiven, he thought, by its English cut and the wide white scarf around his neck. He strolled through the center hall back into the dining room, surprised to find that in spite of all his experience hope was rising once again. The conviction that this-is-it was so strong that already he could visualize the rich portrait of Hastings Hardy, the belligerent marble blue eyes, the grasshopper jaws about to clench the biggest steak *Chateaubriand* or the biggest contract, the three-hundred-dollar suit, the twenty-dollar necktie (flight of ducks, black, *à la* Frank Benson in formation on a blue and white ground), the thirty-dollar fountain pen in hand signing the million-dollar contract nattily unscrolled to look like the Magna Carta—Oh no, not that way, Dalzell caught himself hastily, and altered the picture in an instant to a stern but wise executive, the mandibles parted in a paternal smile, the eyes and forehead Jovelike.

Hastings Hardy Hastings Hardy, he repeated to himself like a charm as he looked over the dining room, searching the small inside banquet room, then with mounting apprehension, the inner alcoves.

Every table was deserted.

He realized how firmly he had fastened on this last fantastic hope, because it took so long for his mind to admit that there were only waiters left in the darkened room.

"Mr. Hardy's party?" he asked incredulously of the waiter who was busily pushing a wagon of dishes toward the kitchen.

"But the dining room has closed," replied the waiter, as the last lights dimmed on the ceiling. "Everyone has left, as you can see."

Dalzell stood for a minute, a kind of panic coming over him. If Fate was sending him perfect strangers to play jokes on him at this late hour, then he would be compelled to make some move for his own preservation. He would go back to the café and summon enough assurance to invite the other lone customer for a final drink. In the café he looked all around but the other table was deserted.

"Has Monty Douglass left?" he asked Philippe who was going through the unmistakable signs of clearing up the table for the next customer.

"My gentleman?" countered Philippe. "That's not Mr. Douglass."

Now there was no one who might rescue him, and his fear returned. It might mean that at twelve o'clock, the very minute the last chair was piled on the last table, Dalzell Sloane must take a train to a lonely far western village perhaps for ever, perhaps to die and drop like a dried apple into the family graveyard, or—

and the dread of making a choice brought a dizzy seasickness over him—go back to the lie that would eventually devour him.

Quite pale, Dalzell sat down abruptly at Karl's table by the door. There was something ominous, he thought, in the mockery of last-minute hopes being raised only to be dashed. The furies indeed must be after him. He raised his hand to signal Karl for another drink but Karl, his arms folded majestically over his little chest, was staring fixedly at a poster advertising the skiing pleasures of the Bavarian Alps which hung above his table, and he made no move to ask the patron's pleasure. He was, in fact, asleep, in the manner he had perfected after forty years of avoiding the customer's eye. He was startled into attention by a sudden shout of laughter and blast of cold air from the outer hall as a clutch of ladies and men in dinner clothes plunged in, the valiant survivors of some party who must make a merry night of it now that they were in Greenwich Village.

"Dalzell Sloane, as I live!" boomed a male voice that could belong, as Dalzell knew, to no one but Okie, the indefatigable, omnipresent, indestructible publisher, refugee from half a dozen bankruptcies, perennial Extra Man at the best dinners, relentless raconteur, and known far and wide as The Bore That Walks Like a Man. "I've been trying to get hold of you for months."

Wonderful Okie, Dalzell thought joyously, dear, deadly, boring Okie, the friend in need! Fantastic that the day should ever have come when the sight of old Okie would make his heart swell with fond affection. And the beaming lady with him was none other than Cynthia Earle, Cynthia with new short ash-blond curls clustering around her narrow once brunette head, which swiveled, snakewise, in a nest of glittering jewelry. As her arms reached out eagerly to embrace him the thought leapt between them that he still owed her six hundred dollars.

"Darling!" she cried, flinging her arms about him. "We've come to this place dozens of times hoping we'd find you. Where on earth have you been all these years?"

"I've telephoned," said Dalzell evasively.

Her friends were busily drawing up chairs, tossing their wraps on neighboring tables, pushing Dalzell back into his seat against the wall until he felt himself plunged straight through the mirror, saved only by Cynthia's purposeful grasp on his arm.

"We've just escaped from a funny little dinner and I brought everybody here for a nightcap, only I haven't any money," Cynthia burbled on. "Do tell the waiter I want to cash a check. Waiter!"

But Karl was rudely obstinate about cashing Cynthia's check. He insisted that the Julien would cash checks only when sponsored by a trustworthy customer such as Monsieur Sloane. Cynthia's face reddened at this insult to her credit, and she looked on incredulously as Dalzell, equally appalled and embarrassed, wrote his utterly worthless name on the back of her check. It was such a typically Julien incident, so endearingly French-foxy, that he would have burst out laughing if he had dared. Cynthia, worth millions, whose mere name gave her credit any other place, must have her check certified by a man who owed not only her but the Julien itself for years past, and who could not even afford a bank account! He saw Cynthia looking at him half mockingly, her lips curled tightly to keep back some taunting query. She must be thinking he had had a great windfall and had been neglecting her, as other favorites had, because of brighter opportunities. He was on the verge of setting her right but if he said he was no better off than ever, then she would be on guard against impositions. People like Cynthia enjoyed observing the ups and downs of artists' lives but they became bored and irritated when it was all *downs*. One could not blame them. Dalzell himself was bored by the monotony and shame of always needing fifty dollars, forever needing fifty dollars, fifty dollars to go, fifty dollars to stay, fifty dollars to pay back some other fifty dollars. Cynthia's eyes were covering him sharply after Karl's rebuff to her and he fancied she recognized the topcoat as the one he'd worn in London fifteen years ago. The sudden withdrawal of her radiant emanations told him—how well he knew the signals!—that she regretted mentioning "checkbook," cautiously anticipated a request from him, and a minimum sum had already lit up in the cash register of her mind. You didn't have to be a mind reader to know the reasoning of the rich.

No, he couldn't endure it, Dalzell thought angrily. Better be considered ungrateful, forgetting true old friends in his heartless climbing, rather than be found beaten, tired and afraid. Let them think he dined regularly on Julien squab and Moselle with only the richest and noblest. To confirm their suspicions he smiled vaguely across the room at new groups of visitors crowding into the café.

"How are things going, old man?" Okie asked, throwing an arm around Cynthia's slim shoulder as if to protect her from contagious poverty.

"Very well indeed, judging by his credit here at Julien's," Cynthia said dryly.

"When you never hear from a fellow, you can figure he's in the chips, ha ha," Okie told her.

"I did have rather a run of luck in Brazil," Dalzell said.

He had always found it saved pride, on emerging from retreat forced by poverty, to claim in London great success in Hollywood, in New York to boast of Continental favor, and in Paris or Rome to ascribe his disappearance to ethnological pioneering in unknown isles. Better to have people jealous and skeptical than pitying or scornful.

"I thought you looked disgustingly cocky," Cynthia answered. "No wonder your real friends never hear from you."

There, he congratulated himself bitterly, he had delivered himself into their hands. They could blame him now for chronic ingratitude but not for chronic poverty.

"Wouldn't you know it?" Cynthia exclaimed petulantly. "I never see them when they're having their success. Okie, you are so right. About them."

Them, of course, meant the artists she had "subsidized" in the past, the subsidy consisting, as Dalzell well knew, of never more than a hundred dollars a month for a year or two, which gave her a fine philanthropic reputation, dictator rights and the privileges of the artist's bed and time. He himself had been a bargain, having been young and naïve enough to think he was really in love with her and that she really admired his talent. Later, of course, he and Ben had laughed over the printed interviews in which Cynthia had modestly excused her largesse to artists: "I don't want to spoil them, really. I just think a little security doesn't hurt real genius."

Security! As if Cynthia herself had ever had it! She kept her iron fingers on his arm possessively, and he recalled an old trick of hers of fondling one man publicly while planning to sleep with someone else. He wondered which one of these others was her present lover and was surprised to discover he was still capable of a twinge of jealousy.

"You might at least have answered my letters!" she reproachfully hissed in his ear.

What would he have said in answer to that last letter of hers six years ago? *I am not pretending that I need the money, Dalzell, but if you are in the chips now, as someone who saw you in Paris was telling me, why not return at least part of the loan so I can pass it on to some young artist who really needs it?*

"Order up, everybody," Okie roared genially. "Cynthia Earle's money is no good here, but Dalzell Sloane's is, ho ho."

"Allow me," Dalzell said calmly and motioned to the waiter.

Now he was in for it. He was into his ticket money already just because he couldn't stand Okie's needling. It was going to be

Okie, then, who decided his future and he resented this intrusion even though it was all his own fault. He could see that Okie was showing off his intimacy with Cynthia, reveling in his new eminence as right-hand man to rich lady, a role that allowed him to regard the rest of mankind as beggars, borrowers, swindlers, pennypinchers and imposters.

Okie had become important through the passage of years merely by never changing, loyally preserving every trait, however disagreeable, of his youth, adjusting them to his spreading figure and whitening hair until he exuded the mellow dignity of an ivy-covered outhouse. For years he had been a last minute telephone call, an emergency escort, for Cynthia in bleak periods between her lovers and marriages, until finally these caesurae in Cynthia's life totted up to more than the big moments and here was Okie at long last Cynthia's Man—not lover, scarcely friend, but reliable old Stand-In, glorified by garlands of snubs from the best people and bearing his scars from Cynthia's whip as saber cuts from royal duels.

His bulging frog eyes were beamed at Dalzell and then at Cynthia with the permanent anxiety for her approval. Do we insult him or is he going to insult me? Do we like this person or should we put him in his place? Do Cynthia and he gang up against me? Dare I count on Cynthia to gang up with me against him or may I have the delicious relief of ganging up with him just for a moment against dear Cynthia? Who moves first? Do I jump on his lap or at his throat? The throat is always the most fun, but what if the mistress's whim was the opposite?

Dalzell was sensing Okie's problem when Cynthia's lips tickled his ear once more.

"Talk to Severgny," she whispered urgently. "He's been trying to find you for weeks."

A dealer looking for him? Dalzell's heart beat faster.

"We talked about you all evening," Cynthia said mysteriously. "Wait, I'll tell you about him, while they're yakking about the drinks."

The sudden influx of last minute customers created a din outside the din at his own table and Cynthia was obliged to shout introductions. No one heard or paid any heed to the names and all Dalzell could hear was the loud buzz of Cynthia's voice in his ear sometimes punctuated and sometimes obscured by a wild squeal from one of the ladies or a bellow from Okie. It was easier to study them in the looking glass in tableaux whose titles were zealously furnished by Cynthia.

It was the looking-glass world, at that, he thought dazedly, and it must be that he was the rabbit.

"Severgny is the new proprietor of the Menton Studio, getting a terrific reputation in moderns and everyone thinks he's French but of course he's just Swiss," Cynthia buzzed in Dalzell's ear, "and he would never have been anything but an interior decorator except for the war, and he spent that in Hollywood painting monster murals over those monster beds, but it's all paid off as you know. The woman beside him talking about this café's Old World charm—" she nodded toward a gaunt spinster in bony but dauntless décolletage—"is Iona Hollis, steel mills and Picassos, you know, and that egghead is Larry Whitfield, the portrait painter—Laidlaw Whitfield, that is—"

"Indeed," murmured Dalzell. The tweed specialist himself, no less.

"—and the little cotton-haired dried-up doll is Mrs. Whitfield. He had to marry her in order to meet the right people, of course, but the joke was the Social Register dropped her right afterward." A sudden lull in which Mrs. Whitfield bent toward her made Cynthia continue shamelessly, "As I was saying, there we were at this strange little dinner tonight."

"I've barely met Jerry Dulaine and I can't imagine why she asked me to dinner," Iona Hollis' deep voice sounded, "or why I went."

"Come now, we went because we wanted to meet Collier McGrew," Okie said benignly. "It was a damn fine dinner even if he didn't show up, but Elsie Hookley drove us out, that's all."

"I was positive that any party a girl like Jerry Dulaine would give would be really wild, in a chic way of course," Cynthia complained. "But it was as stuffy and correct as one of Mother's own dinners. I wouldn't want her to know I said so but she must be disgustingly respectable at heart."

"Do you suppose she or Elsie had something up their sleeve?" Miss Hollis pondered. "Why should anybody throw a party like that for nothing?"

"I'm sure there was some reason we were asked and some reason McGrew backed out," Cynthia said. "He's no fool. I'm sure we were about to be tapped to back a play or a little magazine or adopt some refugees. I noticed Elsie's brother wasn't there, whatever that meant. Anyway it was worth coming down for just to run into Dalzell here at the old Julien.

"I've been most anxious to see you." Severgny leaned across the table toward Dalzell and Dalzell's heart missed a beat. A Fifth Avenue dealer anxious to meet him? More people arrived with more introductions and Cynthia's documentary going on and on in his ear, but Dalzell was thinking only about Severgny, waiting for the moment to resume conversation with him, wondering if this was the chance he had known was coming to him. Feverishly he tried to think of plausible excuses for being without a dealer at present. He could do himself no good by confessing he'd broken with the Kreuber Gallery because Kreuber insisted on charging him storage rates for holding his canvases, so dim was his faith in them. In his mind he began sorting out pictures suitable for his first one-man show in fifteen years. There would be the terrible cost of framing, at the outset . . . Cynthia's elbow dug into his ribs.

"Severgny is asking you a question," she said.

Dalzell made the effort of jumping back through the looking glass and directing himself toward the trim little mustached gentleman leaning across the table towards him.

"Could I count on having some of your time very soon, Mr. Sloane?" Severgny repeated, and before Dalzell could answer he went on, "I understand you and Ben Forrester knew more about Marius than anyone else."

Marius? Dalzell came down to earth.

"Severgny's working on a big memorial show for Marius," Cynthia explained. "It's to be the same month Okie's definitive biography of Marius comes out."

"We need your help in tracking down certain canvases we know existed," Severgny pursued while Dalzell arranged a smile to conceal his stricken hopes. "Did he leave a large body of work in Rome, for instance, or where would you say he left most of his paintings?"

"Ask Household Finance," Dalzell replied grimly. "Ask the Morris Plan. Ask the warehouses and landladies all over the world who sold it as junk to pay storage rent, or else took it along with his furniture and clothes to auction off when he couldn't pay."

"Not literally!" Okie laughed. "He's joking, of course, Severgny. Dalzell, surely you have an idea of where his stuff is. You have some yourself, I know. If Marius had only been like Whitfield here, who keeps a record of every scrap of work he ever did!" Okie exclaimed.

"Can you imagine anybody ever caring?" Cynthia whispered in Dalzell's ear maliciously, though she might have shouted without giving offense, for two new young men were crowding around the table exchanging shrill introductions, more chairs were being drawn up until Dalzell, squeezed against the mirror, was dizzy with claustrophobia. Severgny was trying to tell him something and Okie was obliged to relay the words.

"Severgny got hold of Ben Forrester," Okie said. "He reached him through a San Francisco dealer, and he's promised to help us with the Marius show."

Dalzell's first thought was of the burst of new hopes that must have flared in Ben's breast at the urgent summons from any dealer, and the double disappointment on finding the call was not for Forrester, the artist, but for Forrester, bosom friend of Marius! How well he knew that hurt flash of jealousy on learning that Marius had been the one to win the Grand Immortal Prize of death which opened the gates closed in life to all of them! Marius is my dear friend, Ben must have said just as Dalzell had, and he is a fine painter, but what has he got that I haven't got except a coffin? The feeling had lasted with Dalzell for days after the first funeral fanfare in the papers, a perfectly ridiculous resentment at Marius for "selling out," quite as if he had started toadying to patrons and critics, dropping his old friends merely for the publicity and success of death. Then reason had set in, and as the definitive articles and kiting of Marius prices grew, the affair became a wonderful joke, something Marius himself would have loved. Ben must have gone through all these stages, too, thought Dalzell, for in the old days Ben had more intermittent bouts with success than any of them. If they could only meet, check the comedy step by step, wipe out all the bitterness with wild laughter! If Ben were really in New York—

"Remember when Marius would have been glad to take a thousand dollars for everything he had in the studio?" Okie was shouting. "Yet that little oil we saw tonight in Miss Dulaine's—just a boy's head looking up at clouds—would bring five thousand. Remember? The brown eyes, torn blue shirt, the clothesline—"

Did he remember? Dalzell gulped down his drink.

"Marius had his different periods, too," Okie was pontificating, waving a cigar at Severgny, "but as I point out in my book, they were not right-about changes, they were logical transitions and all consistent with his marvelous gusto and what I refer to as his greed for beauty, that is to say beauty complete—to be *completely* drunk, *completely* mad, and that reminds me I want you to give me a few of those wonderful anecdotes about him, those bawdy—ha ha ha—Rabelaisian, ha ha, sayings of his we all used to love."

In his ears Dalzell could hear again Marius mockingly mimicking Okie, *My sense of humor is as good as the next one but I find nothing funny in bawdiness for the sake of bawdiness, after all, Marius, one is a gentleman first and a clown last and I must ask you to leave my room if you will not be a gentleman.*

"My theory on Marius' final use of white—" said Okie, and suddenly Dalzell felt that he must get out of here, he must find Ben and laugh before the joke became too ugly for laughter. What did these people know of old Marius? The mere circumstance of Okie knowing a woman rich enough to back a magazine for him made him a mighty critic of all the arts with trespasser rights to all of them. The fact that Severgny knew how to bargain (it might have been real estate or canned beans for all he cared except that he liked the social advantages of more elevated wares) gave him the right to encourage or discourage Titian himself. Cynthia Earle's ability to buy a porkchop for an artist or writer when they were hungry endowed her with the most exquisite perceptivity and the right to judge their work. Marius was dead and these were the people who had killed him, these were the demons who had destroyed him as they were destroying himself, too, Dalzell thought. These were the embalmers, the coffin salesmen, the cemetery landlords who carved up the artist. There was some consolation, though, that had Marius's success come during his lifetime he would have had to play the idiot success game with these buzzards. He would have been obliged to listen to Okie's asinine pronouncements on technique, he would have had to defer to Severgny and to Cynthia; the stench of success would have risen higher than that of his moldering carcass. Still, let's face it, he would have had the satisfaction of knowing he was good, his talent would not have been corroded and crippled with doubt.

Or would success have corroded and crippled, too, as some said it did? It was a risk he himself was willing to take, Dalzell reflected. If his integrity, morals and whole spirit were to be corrupted, why then let it be by Success for a change.

"Think about it and make memoranda of canvases you remember and where he did them," Severgny said. "Ben Forrester is doing the same thing."

"Funny Ben hasn't looked you up yet, now he's here," Okie remarked. "Such old pals." Ben here? A quick apprehension struck Dalzell.

"I'm not surprised he didn't look me up," Cynthia said plaintively. "I know artists better than you do, Okie, and they never look anybody up unless they need them. And when you need *them* you can never find them, because they're always hiding out someplace from creditors or wives or something. And lies! Once I gave a marvelous party for Dalzell and Marius when they were going to Spain, and then they told me the wrong ship so I couldn't find them to see them off!"

Dalzell suppressed a faint grin, remembering that the name of the ship had been that of a Staten Island ferry and their Pyrenees had been the hills around Tottenville. It was one of their jokes that whenever the going was too tough they could discover havens within subway or ferry fare from Manhattan. Rooming houses in the Bronx, abandoned beach cottages, river barges, the wastelands of Queens—how often they had announced some proud foreign destination and then merely disappeared in a subway kiosk until luck turned!

"Ben didn't give us his address," Okie said. "I sort of gathered there was a lady friend. All I know is he took the Queens subway at Fifty-Ninth."

"I'll bet Dalzell knows perfectly well where Ben is," Cynthia said. "They always covered for each other. You do know, don't you, Dalzell?"

Why then, perhaps I do, Dalzell thought with a sudden glimmer of light. Perhaps . . . Before Cynthia could tease him further a new couple entered the café and there were screams of recognition, more introductions, more chairs pulled up at Cynthia's insistent invitation. Guillaume crossly insisted the place would close in ten minutes, but even with this repeated warning, the same three young teachers were in again, pushing past him purposefully, convinced that the mounting uproar indicated something exciting was surely about to happen.

"We'll all go up to Cynthia's," Okie shouted. "Dalzell, you'll come."

"Later," Dalzell said.

In fifteen minutes his train would leave, but for him it had already left. Through his mind raced a series of pictures, the closing gate to the Sunflower Special in the Station, the certain desolation in his heart as the train sped westward to that old attic bedroom looking out over the peaceful prairie, the burned church with the ruined cemetery (the painting that had won him the prize money to leave home) and his sister's face smiling a tired welcome to the prodigal, home at last in final defeat. Dalzell shivered. In the confusion of last minute noise he rose and slipped out to the hall. The porter was talking excitedly to the clerk at the desk.

"I tell you, someone has broken the door downstairs! Ah, Monsieur Sloane, you were downstairs, yes, did you see what had happened?"

"No," said Dalzell, and went out the door. He had to move fast before his courage failed him, but whether it was the *amer picons,* the idea of having escaped Cynthia and Okie, the thought that soon the train would be moving westward without him, liberating him, as it were, for whatever might happen, or whether it was the thought of having at last made a decision, feverish elation possessed him. It carried him along East Eighth to the B.M.T. station where he had to compose himself for a moment, trying to bring back that long ago—had it been ten or twenty years?—address. Uptown, under the river in the subway, or over the Queensboro bridge on the bus, the last stop, then the local bus—no by George, he'd take a taxicab to—where? Keane, wasn't it, but what number?

"Something about the Battle of Hastings," he remembered, and then laughed aloud triumphantly. "Ten Sixty-Six Keane Place."

Unexpectedly for this hour and this neighborhood a taxi's lights came toward him from downtown, and taking it as a sign Dalzell hailed it. At least a three-dollar tariff but magic was brewing—that is, if the driver happened to be in the mood to transport anyone to another borough.

He was. He happened to live in Queens and was on his way home.

It was his lucky night, just as Dalzell had known it would be. He would have thought so even if he had known that Mr. Hastings Hardy at that moment was back in the Julien looking for him.

. . . ladies of the town . . .

In the living room of a charming made-over brownstone house
four blocks north of the Café Julien and one block west of Fifth
Avenue there sat this very evening two ladies in the most festive
of evening dresses in the most profound of melancholies. The
scattering of half-filled coffee cups and liqueur glasses about
the little tables, the atmosphere of mingled perfumes and cigar
smoke, the grouping of the chairs hinted of recently departed
dinner guests; the gloomy faces of the ladies, the earliness of the
hour—it was not yet eleven—and the visible signs of elaborate
expectations indicated all too clearly that the party had not
"come off." The dresses and even the living room had the look of
stage properties about to be packed off to the warehouse now
that the play had failed.

Whatever had gone wrong, the fault had certainly not been
with the *mise en scéne,* though the eyes of the hostess had traveled
anxiously over every inch of the room, looking for some guilty
flaw. The wallpaper was the correct silvery-patterned green; the
crystal-beaded lamps glittered with suitable discretion; the shining striped satin of the sofa and chairs, the unworn blond rugs,
the cautious blend of antique and modern furniture all murmured of "taste" or that decorator's strait-jacketing of personal
revelations that is accepted as taste. Through an arched door
could be seen a dining room, china cabinet, chandeliers and all, a
daring gesture toward formal tradition for such a small apartment, and a soft coral light on the opposite side of the entry hall

led not to the wings but really and truly to a white and gold little gem of a bedroom.

"When you think of how long it took us to cook up this party," mused Elsie Hookley bitterly, "then to have us right back where we started in just three hours! Look at the place! You wouldn't know anybody'd been here, even!"

"Did you expect them to wreck the place?" inquired the other tartly.

Of the two ladies you might have surmised that the older, ferocious-looking one was chaperon, singing teacher or stage mother for the other, but then Miss Dulaine looked far too glossily self-sufficient to need such protection, and Elsie Hookley (she had dropped the "Baroness" along with the Baron Humfert himself) was the merest babe in the wood, as she admiringly confessed, before the younger woman's knowledge of the world. Consider them as bosom friends by necessity in spite of the twenty years difference in their ages, bound together by a common foe and at the moment by defeat. They had known each other hardly two years, they had nothing in common but a profound distaste for women friends and a passion for private life, but friendship had spread under them like an invisible net waiting for the certain catch. Both had moved from more fashionable sections of New York into the Washington Square quarter at the same time, with identical motives for marshaling their resources while unobtrusively retrenching. Being the only solitary ladies in the Twelfth Street house they spent months fending off possible neighborly advances from the other. Finding themselves on the same bus they carefully hid behind their newspapers, bumping their carts into each other in the A. & P. Supermarket with identical cocktail crackers, club soda and red caviar, they looked carefully past each other; hands touching at the Sixth Avenue newsstand as they reached for the same columnist's newspaper they did not exchange a single smile.

Months of this wary circling finally persuaded them that they had nothing to fear from each other, and extravagantly relieved, they backed into a minuet of neighborliness, courting the casual encounters and excuses for the very conversational exchange they had formerly spent so much time in avoiding. Elsie looked for her neighbor's name or picture in gossip columns; Jerry was impressed by society page references to Elsie's family. Without being aware of it they fell into a companionship that on the surface made no demands or encroachments but consisted of confidences over nightcaps when they arrived home at the same hour, intimate revelations one makes to someone safely in another world or in another country. They felt completely safe with each other; neither could conceive of the possible intrusion of the other in her own sphere. They could tell about their own sins or those of their dearest friends with all the pleasure of spilling the beans and without the attendant fear of just reprisals. Never going to the same places they exchanged little worlds like party favors whenever they met, cheered and amazed that their offerings were so highly prized, their discarded and discounted currency so valuable. Each was fascinated by the vice the other wished most to hide; in Elsie it was her respectability; in Jerry it was her lawlessness. They had never known anyone like each other, but in their blind progress towards opposite goals they had reached a simultaneous stalemate, and the temporary collision seemed a rare union of minds. Whatever it was they wanted in life, they were confident it was not the same thing; they would never be rivals, but between them they might play a winning hand.

Like shipboard acquaintances they confided freely everything about themselves except what they did last night or were going to do tomorrow. Elsie talked about Boston, to Jerry's great delight, for Elsie was an escaped Bostonian, in perpetual and futile flight from everything that city represented, as obsessed with it as any excommunicated Catholic with the Vatican. She derided her brother Wharton for being a proper Bostonian, horrified by the democratic waywardness of his sister, and she chose to fancy herself voluntary renegade instead of involuntary exile.

"Boston is supposed to be the center of culture, but there's no place on earth where money is so much worshiped. Talk about Chicago or the oil cities! Good God!" Elsie was wont to rant. "In Boston a family is supposed to be distinguished if some scalawag ancestor socked away enough loot to keep the next five generations in feeble-minded homes and keep their lawyers in yachts. Nobody's ever read a book in Boston, they just have libraries. Nobody likes paintings, they just buy them. They go for concerts in a big way because all real Bostonians are deaf as posts so music doesn't give them any pain. I tell you in Boston the word "ignorance" just means no money in the family. That's the way my brother Wharton thinks. Boston! Ugh! I'm ashamed to admit the twenty-five years I spent there trying to conform. But give me credit for pulling out finally, even if I had to marry a European crook to do it."

Elsie could not understand that the more elegantly eccentric she made her family out to be the more delighted Jerry became. The running stock of tidbits about family quarrels, scandals, lawsuits, feuds and hidden passions opened a curious world to Jerry and she followed it, fitting pieces together as she might have a jigsaw puzzle. It seemed that after Elsie's marital debacle brother Wharton felt it was her duty to stay with Mother in the great house on Marlborough Street, but Elsie absolutely refused, so Wharton and his family had to live there and of course simply ROBBED dotty old Mama. Finally Mama, with her last shred of intelligence, had put the house up for sale and went to live in happy senility at the Hotel Vendome with an ancient dependent. Brother and sister continued to accuse each other of filial neglect but Elsie didn't feel a bit guilty because Mama had never forgiven her for the scandal about the Baron. And Mama and Wharton had been so gaga about him at first, so dumbfounded that it should be Elsie the barbarian who had brought the Almanach de Gotha into the family and vice versa. And even after the Baron von Humfert had gotten into that swindling jam and had to be bought out, brother Wharton still enjoyed baronessing his sister in public until Elsie, just for pure spite, had dropped the title.

"Of course the man was a crook," she quoted Wharton as fuming, "but the title left us a little dignity. But oh no, Elsie won't leave us even that little shred of pride!"

Elsie swore that wild horses would not drag her into her brother's stuffy clutches now that he had taken up residence in New York on Gracie Square. But after a few months when it became apparent that the Wharton Hookleys were in no way importuning her to be one of them, Elsie began to worry. Perhaps she had been too blunt. She heard everywhere of their social activities, so evidently they did not need her introductions. A furtive familiar that she usually took to be her conscience reminded her that blood was thicker than water, a brother was a brother and then there were the children, her nieces. God forbid that she should ever be the snob her brother was, but the fact was those girls soon to enter society needed the experience and guidance of an aunt who was a woman of the world. Nita, their mother, was nothing but a child herself.

So Elsie had nobly decided to make the overtures and sacrifice herself. She called and magnanimously offered herself as chaperon for the older girl who had just come out.

"I would be perfectly willing to take Isabella shopping or driving," she reported to Jerry she had told Wharton. "I have lived in New York for years and therefore know everyone and would see that Isabella got to know them too. I could arrange little parties for her—take her to the right galleries, the right plays, the proper restaurants, in a word prepare her for a successful marriage."

And what do you think Wharton, the stinker, had said?

"My dear Elsie," he had said, and in repeating her brother's incredible words Elsie gave him a quavering sort of village idiot voice just as in quoting herself she used an ineffably dulcet, benevolent whinny, "what in the world would it do to my daughter's future to be seen about with your sort of friends? I'm sure they're the most interesting people in the world to you but what would it do to little Isabella's reputation?"

Those were her brother's very words.

This absolutely killed Jerry, though Elsie thought the story merited indignation rather than laughter. On second thoughts she decided it made her feel better to be amused by Wharton rather than insulted so she joined heartily in the laughter.

"But believe me, my dear," Elsie sighed, "these are the moments I just wish I'd kept the Baron."

She said this as if the Baron was a wool hat she'd given away not knowing a blizzard was coming.

From Elsie Jerry got the general impression that the best Bostonians rattled their family skeletons at each other as proudly as Texans flashed their jumbo diamonds. She concluded that Elsie's whimsicalities were a proof that the Hookleys were gloriously rich.

But if Jerry was spellbound by Elsie's Boston legends, Elsie was even more entranced by her peep into Jerry's world—a world without trust funds, no windfalls from forgotten relatives, no estates to be settled, no wills to fight, no salary, no family, yet a world illuminated with vague opulence. How on earth did a girl without a boat, so to speak, sail triumphantly through life, knowing the best people and the best places? It couldn't be that Jerry was merely a shrewd manager for she was always tipping grocery boys in dollar bills for bringing up a quart of milk, or handing out five dollars to a taxi driver and saying to keep the change. When Elsie rebuked her for this folly Jerry shrugged.

"I just remember what a thrill it was when some uncle gave me a buck when I was a kid," she explained. "And then I figure that anybody in a three-thousand-dollar mink coat hasn't got any right to be waiting around for eighty-five cents change from a cabby."

No, Jerry was certainly not the shrewd type. Of course a good-looking girl with a figure for clothes and a model's opportunities (for that's how Jerry had started) could always assemble a fine wardrobe on credit or gravy, and have unlimited dates, but how had Jerry managed to collect so many important men as close friends? Gossip columnists never seemed able to link her name in shady romances, her escorts varied from Cabinet members to industrialists, bankers, yachtsmen, and for bohemian relief older editors of *Fortune, Life* or play angels. How could a girl without family or social sponsors acquire such a circle? Elsie could not rest until Jerry would consent to clear up this mystery. It took Jerry a little time to figure it out herself.

"I guess I learned a lot watching the other girls make mistakes," she finally confessed, rather enjoying the luxury of being candid about herself. "I'd see how some of the girls scared men, big men, I mean. I knew big shots want to have fun the same as anybody but they're awfully skittish. They're afraid of their jobs and publicity and their wives and their children, and of being used. If a new girl flatters a man too much he's afraid she's going to move in. If she finagles a couple of drinks out of him he's scared she's going to stick him for a sable coat. You've got to calm him down right away like you would a nervous virgin. He feels easier if he finds out right away that you know bigger shots than he is and could introduce him to them, or tell him about them. You ask his advice about business. You show him you're not on the make, you're just trying to make friends with him because you admire him. Maybe you surprise him by buying him a tie or a book. Look, he says, here's somebody doing something for me at last, instead of me having to do something for her. After that he relaxes with you—and he can't do that with many people, see."

From a sharp little lawyer Elsie sometimes consulted and whose work gave him the opportunity to observe Jerry Dulaine's rise, Elsie heard another angle.

"Jerry's antecedents and background are so hopelessly low grade she's never had anything to lose," he explained. "Nothing surprises her, nothing awes her, and never having made any particular class in society she's at home in all of them. Like genuine royalty, you might say—or the oldest peasantry."

Elsie congratulated herself on providing herself with such juicy nourishment for she had devoured most of her old friends, her enthusiasms were thinning out, and she had reached a time of life when the zest for adventure properly takes itself out in belaboring a daughter-in-law, ruining a grandchild or defending a worthless son. Having been denied these natural channels for her robust energy she had satisfied herself in years past by feeding on younger people who had talent, or a capacity for unique mischief. She liked to be in the midst of uproar without leaving her rocking chair, and for her chosen ones she was always ready with a shoulder to cry upon even though it was often she who had to make them cry. Certain disappointments in the last few years had made her more cautious but had not lessened her appetite, and after her preliminary reserve she plunged into Jerry's private career with the single-minded gusto of a folio collector. It delighted Elsie that there should be individuals like Jerry, wild cards, you might say, being anything the dealer named, anything that was needed for winning.

It was the first time she had encountered one of these girls so inexplicably in the city spotlight, girls everybody seems to know or ought to know, whose names invariably euphonious or amusing, ring a very faint bell, and rather than admit ignorance the businessman assumes she is a débutante, the débutante guesses she is an actress, the actor deduces she must be rich, all credit her with

distinction in some field of which they are ignorant. With no letters of introduction she builds a kind of social security for herself
simply on the importance and dignity of her escorts. Here was
democracy, Elsie thought, a joke on the bourgeoisie, particularly a
joke on her brother, who for all his position and influence, could
not know half the great names in Jerry's date book. She chuckled
to think of the elaborate hocus-pocus he would have to go
through to get suitable matches for his daughters when little Jerry
Dulaine, runaway girl from a Kansas small town, could know
anyone she wanted. It was a pleasure, at those times when Wharton used the outrageous excuse of having some very important
visitor, too important to risk meeting his sister, for Elsie to mention that she had just met that very gentleman on her doorstep
escorting her dearest friend home from the races. Wharton could
not disguise his helpless irritation that a sister he liked to reproach
as surrounding herself with cheap wastrels and Bowery bums
should have contacts he himself had made with difficulty.

"He's always knocked his brains out for something you take
right in your stride," Elsie chortled privately to Jerry.

It was just as well that Elsie was completely in the dark as to how
her young friend had gotten her start "taking everything in her
stride," miraculously keeping her name above water at the same
time. Jerry herself could not disentangle that first introduction
from the chain of subsequent introductions that had been her
staircase. The fact was, her success, such as it was, stemmed from
an error made fifteen years ago.

This was what had happened, only a few months after Jerry
had landed in New York.

A young couple of some social distinction, pondering their financial woes in the bar of a midtown hotel, remembered that an
elderly uncle, high in government affairs and rich in oil, usually
kept a suite at this hotel. Brave with double Manhattans and last
hopes of fortunes, they rushed up to his suite to surprise him,

which they did indeed, for they found him entertaining a personable young woman, two gay goblets on the coffee table, a serious-looking bucket of champagne on the floor. In the ensuing embarrassment the young couple hastily stated that their visit was for the purpose of inviting Uncle George to Oyster Bay for the week end with some marvelous people, and of course they would be delighted if Miss Dulaine would come too. Miss Dulaine went, and since her appearance and deportment were perfectly acceptable, the girl wearing the proper clothes, saying the proper things, playing tennis and swimming well, she interested influential men who issued invitations to places where she met higher figures who moved her further along, and no one ever discovered that Uncle had picked her up in the lobby of his hotel a bare thirty minutes before his nephew's call. Even if they had discovered this, it would have been too late to matter, for Jerry was already being mentioned in gossip columns on the fringes of both glamour and fashion.

A likable, good-looking young woman without affectations, on speaking terms with the leading names, can always get along in New York, and Jerry got along. She was blessed with that easy confidence that all men are men and everybody's only human that often induces the world to behave as if this was true. She had quit high school in her Kansas home to come to New York on her father's railroad pass (he was a fireman on the Southern Pacific Railroad), met another girl in the Grand Central Station ladies' room who got her a job in a wholesale garment house where she modeled. Tessie also took her to her rooming house on West Fifty-Fifth, invited her on a couple of double dates with a press agent boy friend and a photographer, and Jerry was started. She made enough money, had a good time, and was happy enough for a few months.

But the social popularity she began enjoying after her successful début in the Biltmore lobby made the demands of her job seem increasingly oppressive. Staying up all night in the best nightclubs with the easiest spenders, who themselves need not get up next day till dark, made Jerry's own alarm clock seem a cruel dictator. She had quickly picked up the standards and patter of the garment trade, could appraise within a dollar every rag on every back, see through fur and leather to the designer's label, nose out makeshifts and imitations until her tastes and needs were elevated hopelessly beyond her ability to satisfy them. Her modeling job, well paid as it first had seemed, became merely a means of meeting spenders, and the truth was that as a model Jerry was not as pretty as others at that time (that radiant sheen of youth came to her much later) and she was much too grateful. Older men liked to take her out, because a more conspicuous beauty would have caused gossip. Jerry looked like just a nice girl. She had the clean healthy look of a Western niece or the suburban bride of some junior associate. Her friend Tessie and other play girls in her shop and hotel called on her when the party required another girl who could be trusted not to encroach on their special game. Wives did not bristle jeaously at her presence, or if they did they were reassured when some respectable older citizen spoke to her. Older men were flattered that she seemed to prefer them to younger, hotter blood, and Jerry really did. Younger men demanded too much, drank too much, cost too much, and got you nowhere, as Jerry had seen by watching her friend Tessie's occasional lapses into love. A floater herself, and from a family of floaters, Jerry reacted to a man of fifty or more, of established reputation in business or public life, securely solvent, the way most women react to a fine masculine physique. She cut out pictures of such men of affairs from *Time* and *Newsweek,* pinned them on her mirror, and if opportunity came to acquire a personally autographed photograph she framed it in silver for her dresser.

But the camera lens was cruel to sleepy eyes and her modeling jobs dwindled as more and more men depended on her ready assent to last minute calls, "Come on over to the Stork and help me get rid of a branch manager, Jerry, atta girl." What had first seemed her chief asset turned out to be her misfortune: looking like a nice girl who would never accept diamonds or foreign cars, these were seldom offered. Even the ordinary negotiable loot of a popular girl got less and less. Open-handed men of substance, half tempted to settle a good sum on her, looked into her clear, honest blue eyes and switched to vague offers of marriage (with a big home and ready-made family out in Nebraska) or else proposed a regular job with fine opportunities for a girl with personality. Her girl friend, Tessie, who had launched her so kindly, was no longer her friend for Tessie had counted on some gratifying male skepticism at her loyal claims for Jerry's beauty, brains and wit. It was a betrayal of confidence, Tessie indignantly felt, that her men friends were taken in by her praise and soon went so far as to prefer Jerry to her prettier self. Jerry had naïvely thought her sponsor would be proud to see her accepted, but to her surprise she soon saw Tessie's eyes fixed on her with unmistakable hostility, lip curled in accusing scorn; and presently Jerry realized that Tessie's fondness had been based on her unflattering faith that Jerry was merely a good foil, and could never make out without Tessie. There were bitter words. No, Jerry discovered, you could not depend on girl friends in this little world, not after you moved up into their class. Just remember not to grieve over them, but save your tears for that ominous twilight when their flattering jealousy turns to kindness.

The girls separated, Tessie to marry a natty-looking promoter named Walton simply to stop him making passes at Jerry, who honestly detested him and had not wanted to offend Tessie by rebuffing him. They knew too much about each other to dare be enemies outright but each felt, when they divided their joint possessions, that she had been robbed. They spoke to each other only when they chanced to meet head on, once or twice a year.

Catching a glimpse of each other in a crowd they made a swift estimate of the other's appearance, saw that muskrat had replaced mink or vice versa, wondered a little, and ducked out of sight.

Jerry who had moved to the Pierre slid back to Lexington Avenue hotels. She took to leaving the receiver off the hook mornings to block early assignments for work. The simple truth was that with her increasingly extravagant tastes she really could not afford to work. A miserable hundred or so a week (taxes and social security deducted), did not pay the upkeep of a job like hers. As for settling for the safety of marriage, that seemed the final defeat, synonymous in Jerry's mind with asking for the last rites. Then suddenly—all in a day, it seemed—men friends were looking at the girl next to her instead of at her, and were saying, "Who was that attractive girl in your party at the Café Julien the other night?" or "What a little beauty over there at the corner table!" Not daring to analyze these warning signals Jerry was only conscious of a growing desperation, hidden and solitary, a desperation never to be faced openly but nevertheless lurking for her in mirrors and in men's eyes. She found herself hiding iodine and sleeping pills from herself, avoiding edges of penthouse roofs, afraid.

It was Uncle Sam, the one with the red, white and blue pants, who eventually cornered Jerry. One of the pleasanter tasks he had assigned his internal revenue men was a secret investigation of the patrons of expensive restaurants, shops and entertainments. The larger spenders were, of course, able to come to a gentleman's agreement, or else were lavishly protected by distinguished lawyers or politicians, so the industrious officers must make up their records with names of minor lone unfortunates whose clothes, companions, residences and checks were out of all proportion to their avowed incomes. Jerry Dulaine was one of these, and like a sporting fish showed such guilt, terror and impudence as to guarantee her constant persecution with fines, threats, warrants, superfines for not paying fines. In particular there was a cadaverous Mr. Prince in the Empire State head offices who had made Miss Dulaine's tax deficiencies a gruesome case for the government far more evil than the million-dollar lapses of mighty corporations. Nothing less than a small fortune was needed to appease these bloodhounds, and Jerry had observed that nobody reaps a fortune nowadays from working union hours or even double-paid overtime. As for saving for these quarterly raids, if such a thing were possible any more, the slogan of the new economy was "Save the pennies and the bank will charge you double to take care of them." Luckless citizens with no genius for major crime were obliged to apply themselves to figuring out quick-profit schemes unique and complicated enough to elude tax classification. There must be a Gimmick, they told themselves, and toiled night and day to find how to make the quick dollar without toil. They were constantly goaded onward by news of a lady relaxing in her bubble bath who thought up a perfumed chewing gum and made a fortune; a retired but restless black marketeer bronzing his pot on Miami Beach thought of a dolls' roller derby and was back in big business; a radio bit-player, between shots, thought of a sound-skip device that would eliminate all voices but the one desired; a bartender on Rubberleg Square thought up the idea of a juke-box psychoanalyst, two backward students at Penn State thought of a Baby-Naming Personal Service. All through the night and all through the land the geniuses, the bums, the experts and the birdbrains were pecking away for the golden gimmick that would fell the great enemy, Taxes.

Jerry Dulaine, who knew everyone, learned by listening, introduced Ideas to Capital, shuffled contacts personal with contacts professional, joined the quest for the Gimmick. She got a bank ten good clearing-house days away from her New York bank, took a $500 option on a $100,000 business block, "sold it," "bought" a suburban movie theatre, borrowed on it, "bought" a textile works, traded it for a piece of a musical show, wangled advances to pay past losses, her distant checks passing her local checks on slow trains, one deal juggling the other, all maneuvered so swiftly that the eyes never quite caught up with the prestidigitator's hands.

For the past five years—Jerry was not thirty-four—she had lived perilously on the brink of disaster, but she had lived well and still clung to the brink. It was still a good show, Elsie Hookley declared, mystified and admiring. But Jerry was beginning to wonder. How much longer could she keep it up and where was it leading? Instead of the game being easier it was getting tougher. She was calling up more men than called her up and, worse yet, some of these gentlemen belonged to the older and lower part of her ladder. And there were the lunches every day with other girls whose luck was running out except for restaurant credit.

Elsie, once Jerry's apprehensions had penetrated her consciousness, was far more disturbed than Jerry. Taxis, instead of private cars, were bringing Jerry home, and earlier besides. Jerry's doings had filled Elsie's life and made her forget her uneasiness about her own. She had countered Wharton's victories with Jerry's and if the show was not to go on forever then she must see that the curtain came down on a triumphant finale that would pay off both star and audience. Elsie made wild plans in her worried sleep to rent a bigger, finer house than her brother's where she would bombard his finest guest list with royal dinners at which Jerry would shine. She would pick up the old exclusive club memberships gaily discarded decades ago and install Jerry in the inner circle. She would rent a palace in Capri or Rome where Jerry would preside over international royalty.

"It wouldn't do," she always had to sigh before resigning herself to sleep. "I'm too old and too tired."

The great inspiration came at last on the morning she had carried Jerry's mail up to her from the hall table and found the young lady sitting cross-legged in bed absorbed in scissoring a photograph out of *City Life*. The sight of the worldling's tousled head bent over her paper-doll cuttings, shining black locks loose, brow knit, pajama coat carelessly unbuttoned down to the twinkling childish navel, charmed Elsie. An innocent little devil-child, she thought, her innate generalissimo instincts deeply touched. Oh yes, she vowed, she would fight to protect this happy picture. Who would dream that this dear child, so simple and guileless-looking without make-up, pretty mouth puckered in concentration, small pink bare foot peeping out of blankets, had been probably night-clubbing all over town most of the night?

Elsie looked fondly about the room. There always seemed such order in its disorder, the dresser drawers always half open, the satin puff always sliding to floor, coffee cup with cigarette butts always on night table, a book always face-open on the floor where it had slid, mottoes and cartoons that had appealed to Jerry pasted on the mirror. ("It's just our club motto," Jerry explained, seeing Elsie puzzling over one card: The Lady Flounderers Club. *They said* I *couldn't do it so* I *didn't even try;* Fishback, Elsie read, and saw pasted below this inspirational thought, *Better half-done today than not at all tomorrow.*) These touches, with the jet slippers toppled wearily in a corner where dance-tired feet had kicked them, gave the place a jolly, inviting air, as cozy as a kitchen fireplace.

At the moment Jerry was carefully inserting the clipped photograph into the silver frame that always contained her Man of the Week. Elsie dropped the letters on the bed, noting from the corner of her eye that the envelopes had ominous cellophane windows, and then looked at the latest idol, relieved that this ones' face didn't look like a trail map through the Badlands as the *Time* cover men always did.

"Collier McGrew?" she exclaimed and took a second look.

"Isn't he a dream?" Jerry demanded happily. "The most marvelous man I ever met in my life."

Elsie sat down, shaking her head in speechless amazement.

"I knew you got around," she finally sighed, "but Collier McGrew! Where on earth did you meet him—the White House?"

"Why shouldn't I meet him?" Jerry asked, squirming off the bed and sliding her feet into rabbit-furred mules. "He's in public domain. Let's have some coffee."

"But he doesn't go to nightclubs or any gay spots. How did you meet him?" Elsie eagerly followed Jerry into the kitchen and took two cups out of the cupboard as Jerry adjusted the Chemex.

"I had lunch at the Julien the other day with Judge Brockner and he was there with some Congressman Brockie knew," Jerry explained. "Brockie and the Congressman had to go to some meeting and McGrew and I had a brandy and he walked me home. Then there was that benefit fashion show. I was with the fashion people and he was bored with his benefit people so he took me out for dinner. Just a quiet little steak house. He hates crowds he said. Then last night a drip I knew took me to a newspaper party and there was McGrew with some Washington bigshot and bored stiff. I was the only person there he knew, he said, so he and I slipped out and had a quiet snack, then he drove me home."

"Well!" Elsie exclaimed. "When I think of everybody in the Pentagon and U.N. after him, my brother Wharton quoting him on everything and bragging about how close they are, and then you walk away with him just because everybody else bores him!"

"The most attractive man I ever met," Jerry declared with such an unwonted dewy look that Elsie gave her an approving thump on the back. They carried their cups to the living room and Jerry dropped on the sofa.

"I could marry a man like that," Jerry said, dreamily stirring her coffee. "I swear I could."

Much to her surprise Elsie did not take this as a joke.

"Now this is something I'll buy! " Elsie shouted, and clapped her hands as the idea began burgeoning in her brain. "Don't you see it? You've been wasting your time on small stakes, but this is the time for the big kill. You're thirty-four and still gorgeous. You've got a chance at the biggest man you've ever met and you ought to play it big. How would you like to be an ambassador's wife?"

Jerry's answer was to burst out laughing. How would Elsie herself like to be Pope, she countered. Who wanted to get married, for heaven's sake? All anybody asked was some ready cash and a good time, and besides McGrew wasn't any ambassador.

"Everybody says he will be," Elsie insisted, her eyes beginning to glitter and her nostrils dilate at the whiff of the marvelous mischief she was about to launch. In her excitement she began to stride about the room, holding her cigarette aloft like a torch and waving it about as she swooped back and forth until it seemed to Jerry the room could not possibly contain this mobile statue of Liberty. "And let me tell you something about marriage, my dear girl."

"Now Elsie!" Jerry cried in alarm. "Not the facts of life!"

"You don't realize what a future there is in marriage," Elsie said, ignoring the interruption. "Why, I've seen women without looks and no talent for anything else be perfect geniuses at marriage. They really clean up. You marry your man, pop a baby right off the reel, enter it in Groton or Spence on its christening day, have the father set up a trust fund for it right off with you as guardian, get your divorce, marry the next guy, pop another baby with trust fund, repeat divorce and same deal all over. Finally you're living high on the income from four or five trust funds, without lifting a finger."

"Like a prize stud," Jerry observed. "Frankly I don't see myself as a breeder, old girl."

Elsie was obliged to admit that it might be a little late for Jerry to get into that field, but there were other ways of making a business out of marriage.

"You work it out like a big merger," she said with a large gesture. "After all a girl like you has a lot to offer and you expect top price. A man like McGrew needs a woman like you and you need a man like him."

"He's done all right for himself all these years without a wife," Jerry objected. "Why should he need one now?"

Elsie could answer that one. First, everybody said he should marry and mothers all over the world were throwing their daughters at him. He had been so busy dodging daughters ever since the New Deal had flushed him out of an aristocratic private life into public service that he'd been afraid to marry. But now that he was rising in importance, honored from the Pentagon to United Nations and Wall Street, he needed a hostess to help share his tremendous social obligations. Brother Wharton said so and Elsie was positive he was grooming his eldest daughter for the job, a little goon like that, mind you! When obviously the one woman in the world equipped to handle such a man of affairs was Jerry. And the great part of it was that evidently McGrew himself had recognized this.

"Tell me again just what he said," she urged.

Jerry looked dreamily at the photograph.

"He said I was the first woman he'd met in years he could talk to without feeling she was either a competitor or a responsibility," she said in a faraway voice, and then remembered something fresh. "He said I was plastic, that's it."

"Plastic?" Elsie queried doubtfully.

"Not like Dupont products, silly," Jerry said, impatiently. "He said he was frightfully tired and bored and I had a plastic charm that gave to any mood. He thanked me for refreshing him, he said."

"That does it!" Elsie cried. "He admits you've got the quality he needs. If we follow this up right you'll be Mrs. McGrew and all your future will be solved."

"What do you want me to do—blackmail him into it?" giggled Jerry. "Elsie, darling, don't be an idiot."

"There you are!" Elsie exclaimed. "You just don't know your own value. Believe me, I've been around enough to know how high you could go if the right person handled you. Why, I could put this across myself if you'd let me handle you and do just as I said."

Jerry's continued amusement made Elsie the more resolute. She swore she was going to study this problem and map out a campaign that Jerry would have to follow. The idea of Elsie as marriage broker and talent manager kept Jerry in hysterics for several days, but she stopped laughing when she had to buy her own dinner two nights in a row and another envelope frank-stamped from the Collector of Internal Revenue arrived. This letter turned out to be a warrant form with penciled-in threats and rebukes by the clerk. Hopelessly Jerry tore up the letter and turned to Elsie. The hour had come for her to put her destiny in someone else's hands.

Elsie, seeing that she had made her impression, set to work. She devoted herself to planning her strategy with the thoroughness of a long pent-up housewife going after a belated college degree. She pried all the information about McGrew she could get out of her brother by the ancient technique of disparaging the man so that Wharton would angrily blurt out everything he knew. By poking around she ascertained that little Isabella was studying cooking at a fashionable cooking school (McGrew was a Chevalier du Tastvins); little Isabella was also boning up furiously with tutors in French, Spanish, and Persian (there was a rumor that McGrew might be sent to Iran on a government mission); little Isabella was having a second début in Washington, D.C., on the excuse that Hookley cousins there demanded it. Obviously Wharton was doing his best to land McGrew and Elsie's nostrils quivered happily at this familiar challenge.

McGrew was to leave that week for Florida, Elsie learned, for conferences with certain politicos there and best of all he was to spend some time, at Wharton's insistence, with some Palm Beach Hookleys. They were her cousins, too, Elsie joyously cried, and they could just as well sponsor *her* friend as they could Wharton's. Jerry would meet McGrew under finer auspices than she ever had in New York and a different background often acted as a forcing spot for romance. A long-distance call arranged for ten days at the cousins' estate and after that Jerry could bide her time at a hotel—McGrew's hotel, if possible.

"My cousin's set is the last word in stuffiness," Elsie said. "I want McGrew to see that you can handle a stuffy set as well as you can a party crowd. A diplomat's wife has to know all kinds. But above everything else she has to know food and wines. I'll teach you."

"Nobody has ever complained that I didn't know how to order a fine dinner," Jerry laughed.

"I mean to serve it in your own home," Elsie said. "Why else do you think Wharton and Nita are forcing their poor daughter to study gourmet cooking when all she knows is chocolate malties? But leave this to me. I'll arrange everything."

While Jerry was away Elsie was to have decorators do over her helter-skelter apartment into a tasteful background for a lady of discrimination. Good books, a fine modern painting or two, and the ultimate in equipment for serving such dinners as would melt away all barriers of class and race in any capital where a diplomat might be sent.

"I'll loan you my Iola to cook for you," Elsie said. "We will stage a marvelous demonstration dinner for McGrew the minute you get back just to sew him up if Florida hasn't already done it."

Jerry was ready to do anything or go anywhere that was financed. Cheered by Elsie's generosity, she set out with a fine southern wardrobe privately sure she could get McGrew one way or another. Hadn't he refrained from making any passes at her? Wasn't that how you knew a man had seriously fallen for you? At her door he had kissed her good night, a sweet, warm, sexless sort of kiss that had left Jerry absolutely dewy-eyed, knocked for a loop as she admitted dizzily to herself afterward. This must be It. No groping, no clutches, just a boy-girl kiss. Jerry was thankful she hadn't been in the least tight or she might have been fool enough to make a pass or two herself. But McGrew or no McGrew she had a few private ideas for making the most of a Florida trip, though Elsie, suspecting that in her present state Jerry might give up the game at the drop of a hat, gave her last minute warnings.

"Don't you dare forget this deal isn't just a flop in the hay," Elsie said severely. "It's a roll in the orange blossoms. So don't get mixed up with any fly-by-nights down there, don't get plastered except with the best people, don't forget you're not there to have yourself a good time but to build a respectable marrying background for yourself. You've still got a good reputation, God knows why. You've had sense enough to know you can have more fun with better people that way, but that Irish in you is beginning to come out more and more so watch out for it. You be working on being top drawer down there while I get the nest all ready. When you get back you're going to start making your name as hostess in your own home instead of party girl."

"But I hate staying home," Jerry complained. "I hate ending up in the same place I started out and with the same people."

"There you are!" Elsie exclaimed, quite shocked. "Don't you know that no matter how many men you get by being seen around all the spots with all the big shots you only get a husband by having him see you in your own home? You've got to give dinners—fine dinners. Once you've got people at your own table you've got the edge on them. They've as good as admitted they're your friends and are committed to stand by you. Wait till you get back and see all the things I've planned for you. It's a new life, my chick."

So off Jerry went, glad to be away from creditors, returning weeks later radiantly bronzed, confessing to many happy hours with McGrew and allowing Elsie to deduce she had practically won her game when the truth was she had, to her own bewilderment, merely been playing McGrew's. He was too experienced a bachelor to permit any pressure, and she sensed soon enough that her appeal for him was in her demanding nothing but being *there* when he chose to see her. No use hoping to rouse his interest by her popularity with other men of his rank, for he would not compete. If he was so delighted to find her alone with no plans, then she would be that, like a back-street mistress, she thought, without the romance. He was a new kind of fish to her, and for the life of her she couldn't understand why she would feel so flattered and elated after a perfectly harmless swim or ride with him. She knew most men would class her as desirable but McGrew gave her the dizzy delusion that she must be intellectual, and that was a new sensation indeed.

Just as she persuaded herself she was getting someplace she found that the gentleman had left for New York without so much as a good-bye. A curious man, she reflected, slightly chilled by his efficient use of her for exactly what and when he liked, with no loose ends or wasted time, just as he dropped being charming to order the dinner, then resumed charm the minute the headwaiter left. She did not betray her doubts to Elsie when Elsie suggested she give a dinner for McGrew as soon as she got back to town. It gave her an excuse to telephone him, and he was in the mood to find it amusing to be invited to "test her new cook." Happily relieved, Jerry made out a guest list but Elsie immediately crossed off all Hollywood or Broadway names and substituted more worthy ones.

"I hardly know these people," Jerry protested at Elsie's list. "Why should they accept any dinner invitation from me?"

"On account of the guest of honor, silly," Elsie said. "You'll see."

Indeed it had been funny, Jerry admitted, the way people hemmed and made excuses till the McGrew name was mentioned and how fast they accepted then. But now the masterly plan had been tested, the dinner was over, and at eleven o'clock the two ladies, deserted, knew they had failed. Jerry had known it was a flop for hours but Elsie refused to admit it till the last guest had fled. Then she decided to be philosophical about it, for she feasted on catastrophe, and there had been so many subtle angles to the evening's failure that she anticipated a whole season of warming over tidbits, souping and hashing. She enjoyed her power as secret entrepreneur of a grand comedy. She was not vain enough to expect gratitude from Jerry or personal applause if the game had succeeded; all she had dreamed was a slow trickle of fury through her brother's future thoughts. She did not think yet about the financial loss to herself, not because she was generous but because she was vague about money, blind in arithmetic and only spasmodically foxy. For her it was chiefly a dazzling, amusing scheme that had missed fire. It had occupied her energies for a while very nicely, and she did not realize how serious it was for Jerry. Her young friend's gloom gave her the opportunity for a few cheerful words on errors in strategy. She felt there might be consolation in analyzing the whole situation, now that the show was over. Which Elsie proceeded to do.

"At least my husband was a gentleman," Elsie Hookley suddenly announced, helping herself from a decanter of Jamieson's Irish which she had drawn within cuddling distance. "What if he did ruin my life, the bastard? He had a great many women, true enough, but he was a gentleman and he treated them like ladies. He paid them and he paid them well. All right, what if it was my money? The way he put it was that a real gentleman expected to pay and a real lady expected to be taken care of. That's your European aristocrat for you."

"So McGrew isn't a European aristocrat," Jerry Dulaine replied crossly. "So I don't get paid. It still doesn't explain why he didn't show up."

"And not one word out of him," Elsie said happily, for she was beginning to enjoy the enormity of the catastrophe. "Not a telegram. You're sure he understood he was to be guest of honor?"

"He's known it for two weeks," Jerry said wearily, for they'd been all over this a dozen times. "You know perfectly well he told me his favorite dishes and you had Iola make them especially for him."

Elsie nodded sadly.

"Guinea hen, broccoli in creamed chestnuts, wild rice—my God, my brother would do murder for a dinner like that! And Iola all gussied up in turquoise corduroy uniform from Clyde's! I had counted on McGrew telling Wharton all about it just so

he'd burn up." She thought of something new. "You're sure he
never came to your apartment before we fixed it up? He's such
a wine and food man he might have been afraid your dinner
would be a weenie roast."

"He brought me home but he never came up," Jerry said.

"You're sure you remembered not to sleep with him?" Elsie
asked with a meditative glance at her friend.

Jerry had a flash of righteous indignation at this insult

"I told you this was *serious,* Elsie," she exclaimed. "I told you
it was his never making any pass, just saying little things to me—
never anything personal, too—that made me know he meant
something serious."

"You mean nothing really happened when you were with him
so much in Florida?" Elsie asked as reproachfully as any designing mother. "For goodness sake, what did you do when you were
alone?"

"Talked, like I told you," Jerry muttered.

"What about, for God's sake?" Elsie demanded.

Jerry shrugged and lit a cigarette.

"Art," she admitted defensively. "He buys paintings, doesn't
he? And I asked his advice a lot about investments and—oh,
things. He liked my ideas, he said."

She lit a cigarette and looked at herself in the mirrored wall,
thinking back ruefully of how important it had seemed to get exactly the right white taffeta to show off her tanned shoulders and
enhance her cloudy hair. Every square inch of that sleek bronze
skin cost a good fifty dollars if you measured it in Florida hotel
rates, and when you considered that this gilding encompassed
her whole body you realized that here was indeed complete folly.
Staying on down there week after week just because McGrew
was there, borrowing and charging right and left to anybody she
could think of (particularly Elsie), writing post-dated checks on
bank accounts she'd long outspent, counting on one big throw of

the dice to recoup. Even so, she wouldn't have got in so deep if she hadn't been carried out of her depth by Elsie's enthusiastic urging. Elsie had really shoved her into this mess, and God knows Elsie had certainly made the whole evening a hundred times worse, but you couldn't say that.

"I know you wish I'd go home," Elsie said, kicking off her slippers and stretching out her long bony legs in their stockinged feet to the fender, her skirt pulled up above her knobby knees in the careless sexless way that always obliged people to look studiously away. "You wish I'd gotten out sooner, so you could have gone out with the others. They wouldn't invite me of course, because they couldn't stand me. I don't care. Right now, I feel like a little cozy post-mortem. A party that's a flop is more fun to talk over than a good party. Now get yourself a drink and sit down."

She wants me to drink with her so I'll blubber out more troubles and it'll cheer her up, Jerry thought. She knew Elsie loved her best when she played her cards badly and any other time she would have humored her by reporting a whole book of errors, the way pretty women mollify their enemies by stories of childhood freckles and miseries. But tonight she could not bear consolation or advice. She wanted Elsie to go home, for the sight of the gaunt, brassy-haired confidante of her misadventures, like the half-filled glasses left about, the inordinately festive profusion of fresh flowers (forty dollars' worth) smote her with the grim evidence of the evening's disaster. She didn't even dare put her fears into words; she could say it, but if she ever *heard* it she would surely gobble her bottle of Nembutal on the spot. It wasn't that she had counted too much on this dinner party to which the guest of honor had failed to come. It was the hint that her luck had run out and would never come back, that this was the beginning of worse disasters to come, of situations her blind knack could not manage. Already she could see the sunken black eyes of the dreadful Mr. Prince of Internal Revenue, wagging his bony finger at her and thundering, "If I can't afford to buy my wife or girl friend dresses like yours, then you ought to be in jail!"

In another minute she might burst into tears, Jerry thought with horror, and then where would she be? You didn't start sniveling until you'd given up hope of getting anything out of life but pity. Hastily she poured herself a stiff highball and sat down on the rug, doing her best to suppress her ungrateful exasperation with her friend. It was turning out to be exactly as she had always feared intimacy with a neighbor would turn out—and she should be kicking herself instead of blaming Elsie.

The trouble with accepting Elsie's devotion in an off-guard moment of need was that she moved in on you, so to speak. You should have been prepared for that. It was only reasonable. You thought it was fine that you knew how to spend beautifully without knowing where your money was coming from, but unfortunately Elsie, who had it and was willing to back your imagination, had to have an orchestra seat at the show. Elsie saw no unfair irony in herself wearing a ten ninety-five rayon crepe from Klein's-on-the-Square while Jerry wore a two-hundred-dollar dress she'd charged to her account at Bergdorf's. That was perfectly natural, Elsie thought. Pantry and cellar were her only indulgences, her sole requirement of clothes being that they should either be or at least look like basement bargains, but she placed no limit on what Jerry demanded for her proper setting.

"I should be grateful," Jerry reproached herself.

Of course it had to be a boomerang. Elsie financed you to a party designed to settle your whole future, then she queered everything by attending it. It was the first time they had attempted to fit together the odd sections of their social jigsaw, and in spite of all the knowledge they had of each other through after-hours confidences, they appeared to each other before an audience in a completely new light, like summer lovers suddenly popping up in winter clothes. Elsie, for her part, was more than satisfied with Jerry's easy manner in handling a large dinner party, and her loud compliments with hearty pats on the back made guests and Jerry wonder just what vulgar hi-jinks she had anticipated.

"Would you have dreamed that Jerry Dulaine could have managed a thing like this?" Elsie crowed again and again. "Isn't she marvelous? Just see what Colly McGrew is missing! "

Even if he had come, Elsie would have bollixed everything, Jerry knew. The more Jerry tried to pass off the slight from her missing guest the more Elsie insisted everyone should be mortally insulted. McGrew had decided they were none of them worth his while, Elsie reminded them again and again, and she just wondered what lies her own dear brother Wharton had said about Jerry Dulaine to keep McGrew from coming.

Jerry was accustomed to making a party go under the most trying handicaps, and after the hour's delaying of dinner, beautifully prepared and served by Elsie's precious Iola, she expected to salvage a pleasant enough evening for the others, with no further reference to the truant guest, loss though it was to herself. But she had never bucked against Elsie Hookley, and seeing her on show, so to speak, for the first time, Jerry thanked her stars that Prince Charming had not come, for if he had, Elsie would have driven him off forever. In those friendly hours when they had let down their hair, Jerry had taken for granted that Elsie, like herself, put the locks up in public. The picture Elsie had given of herself was of a worldly-wise gentlewoman, obliged by her station to put up with certain silly conventionalities, carrying on properly with straight face, but all the time saving up her real democratic feelings for the private orgy of honesty. Now Jerry saw that Elsie not only let her hair down in public but pulled out everybody else's hairpins as well. The spectacle of a few people dressed up to go through the motions of a genteel social routine inflamed Elsie, as she saw in it a masquerading dragon sent by her enemy, Boston, which she must attack with fiendish vigor. No simple exchange of amenities could pass without suspicion, the merest mouse of a polite compliment to the hostess must be harpooned and held up as deadly rodent. *Don't believe him when he says this is the finest Montrachet he's ever tasted, Jerry, he's got too good a cellar himself to kid anybody, though fat chance anybody ever gets of sampling it these days. . . .* An escape of talk into general fields while Elsie enjoyed a bite of fowl had her stopped only momentarily and then she was loudly declaring that were she the hostess, God forbid, she would never speak to anybody present for their neglecting to appreciate the marvel of the cooking, the equal of which she defied them to find short of Julien's, the *old* Julien's of course, not the new one her dear, dear brother Wharton continued to be so devoted to.

The fact was that Elsie was being herself, never less than overwhelming. Youthful years of excessive shyness, awkwardness and suppressed desires had fitted her out with a perfect treasure chest of home-truths conceived too late for their original cues but all waiting for some victorious day when they could be uttered. There was something pernicious, she felt, in the efforts of the others to pretend the party was a success; she felt she must prove her contempt for society's emptiness by emptying it before Jerry's very eyes. By the time they had arrived at dessert general conversation had been pretty well blocked, Elsie tackling, singlehanded, every sentence that ventured down the field. The withdrawal to the living room for coffee offered a dim hope of loosening Elsie's grip.

"By George, that's an early Marius," Okie, the publisher of *Hemisphere,* had exclaimed, studying the painting above the fireplace. He had been invited as the last of a vanishing race, the Extra Men, and moreover Cynthia Earle, whose family background paralleled McGrew's, was using him these days as escort. Jerry nodded modestly to him, hoping Elsie had not overhead his remark for she would certainly declare that the picture was hers and that she knew more about it than Okie.

"An early Marius, at that," Okie went on. "You are lucky, Miss Dulaine."

"You must come in the gallery sometime and talk to me about it," murmured Severgny, the art dealer who sometimes employed Jerry as decoy to bring into his place certain rich collectors. "I am extremely interested in Marius right now."

"Let me tell you what Marius said the time I bumped into him at the Whitney—" Cynthia Earle began.

"But Marius is dead!" Elsie Hookley had boomed.

"This," Cynthia had patiently conceded, "was before he was dead. I mentioned his Paris show and you know how terribly, terribly funny Marius always was—"

"But Marius hasn't had a show in Paris for years!" shouted Elsie.

"This was 1939," Cynthia continued graciously. "The year before I met him at the Whitney as I was saying—"

"I can't understand why the Whitney didn't buy more of Marius," Elsie said. "They overdid on Ben Forrester, if you ask my opinion, and then only one little Dalzell Sloane. And speaking of Dalzell—"

"So you met Marius." Jerry raised her voice pointedly to Cynthia, not only to get the ball away from Elsie but because a certain idea for a profitable deal with Severgny had just occurred to her.

"Oh I wish I could remember the exact words. It was so—so *Marius.*" Cynthia's little-girl Tinker Bell laugh at this moment was a tactical error for she had barely got on to her story again before Elsie charged.

"Oh I admit Marius was funny, oh screamingly funny. But Dalzell Sloane was a genius and a gentleman." Elsie placed one hand on the tense knee of Park Avenue's pet portrait painter and fixed the others with a beady blue eye. "I know geniuses aren't supposed to have any decency, they're supposed to be just sexy and funny like Marius, but let me tell you, Dalzell could paint rings around all of them. Just because he was too much of a gentleman to *use* people, the way you have to do, Mr. Whitfield—"

"Cynthia is telling a story about Marius," Jerry chided without conviction, and then since everything was already lost she gave up to a mild speculating on whether Cynthia could ever get the ball any nearer goal against Elsie's overpowering tactics. Cynthia had resolutely started her anecdote all over again when suddenly Elsie snatched the Whitney Museum from her lips and whooped down the field scoring a touchdown with a big inside story about a Hookley ancestral connection with the museum in Boston, a city where Collier McGrew's great-great-grandfather's South Boston wife had been unable to write her own name, and how do you like that, you people who think he's so perfect. Cynthia gave up, as indeed did everyone else, for Elsie was trimmed to take on every verbal offering, shaking an argument out of the merest name, questioning the pronunciation of a word before the speaker had gotten out the last syllable, finding political affronts in the first sentence of some attempted joke, pouncing on some orphan cause barely mentioned as needing noble defense, cutting through whispered asides like a school monitor, finally managing to keep the conversational ball on her big nose and batting it up and down like a trained seal. No use, Jerry thought, almost admiringly. No use, concluded the guests, and surrendered to glazed apathy as Elsie triumphantly regaled them with detailed grudges she had had for years against characters they had never known and never wished to know, delicately prefacing her remarks with a "Jerry's heard me say this before but since I'm on the subject—" convinced she was making the talk general by keeping one hand on Whitfield's knee, the other on Cynthia's back and addressing herself across the room to Jerry as if she was in a distant cornfield.

Yes, Elsie had been in great form and the guests had fled as from a tornado at half past ten, and not one of them had invited Jerry to come along with them for a store nightcap for fear Elsie would come too. Let them go and the hell with everything, Jerry thought, she was a gone goose now, anyway.

Being sorry for herself Jerry spared some morose speculations on poor Elsie, who, it was evident, was a comforting flannel nightgown for lonely winter nights but not to be worn in public. There were people like that whose shoulder-chips, spiritual ulcers or painful vanities were fluoroscoped by a party, though the weaknesses never came out in everyday life. A kind of disease, really, and you simply ought to make allowances. It couldn't be any fun being fifty-four years old with no men left in your life, being sore at the world for the mistakes you had made in it, feuding forever with your ancestors while you boasted of them, sitting up there in your family tree dropping coconuts on yourself.

Poor, angry, honest, openhearted old Elsie, lavishing love and gifts on chronically unworthy, ungrateful wastrels! ("I'm as bad as the rest of them," Jerry guiltily admitted, "but how can I help myself and anyway if it wasn't me it would be somebody else"), then shrieking for vengeance when they behaved as she had so wonderfully predicted. Poor old Elsie, Jerry thought, she's so proud of having kicked over that fine old family and being so democratic, yet every time she meets a title or a millionaire she wishes she could mow them down with superior lineage. Instead all she can do is to bellow at them. And it was funny to see her heckle everybody like an old eagle, sort of brave, really, poor mad creature. They said she had once been rather striking, in that old Boston war-horse way, six feet tall with flame-red hair and legs right up to her shoulder blades as some contemporary had remarked. Her hair was now on the pink side, frizzed in front and looped into a limp bun on top. Her eyes were brilliantly blue and if she would use creams instead of a careless washrag her skin might have been more human-looking. As it was, her striding walk, her great height, her icy glare and booming voice quite terrified people and it was always necessary to reassure those who were backing away—"You know she comes from a very old family, the Boston Hookleys, you know, her brother's Wharton Hookley—he got the mother to do poor Elsie out of her proper place in the old Marlborough Street home just because Elsie refused to live in Boston—some legal twist, and of course she could call herself Baroness but she's so democratic—"

Good old Elsie, indeed, but that didn't give her the right to ruin everybody's evening and a great deal more than that. Now that it was all over there was no point in regrets or reproaches. Besides Elsie seemed blissfully unaware that she herself was responsible for anything going wrong. She sat there wiggling her toes before the fireplace and sipping her drink with the pleased expression of a day's wrecking well done.

"Did you hear me take down that little museum monster when he said, 'I had no idea Miss Dulaine did herself so well!'?" Elsie asked. "I simply looked him in the eye and said, 'Just what kind of an evening *did* you expect from Miss Dulaine, may I inquire?' and of course he was on a spot. And as for Okie—"

"You made him mad, too," Jerry acknowledged. "You told him he knew nothing about art."

Elsie's blue eyes widened in honest astonishment.

"Why should that make him mad? God knows Okie has always been the dumbest man on earth but at least I gave him credit for *knowing* it. Now *really!* Look, do you think I should telephone around some more for McGrew? Just in case—"

"No, no," Jerry hastily protested, for one of Elsie's tricks had been to keep telephoning various clubs and restaurants during the evening to track down the missing guest so that all present should realize all was lost without him. It might be funny someday but right now and tomorrow it was serious, so that Elsie's sudden chuckle as she comfortably poured herself a dividend made Jerry's kindlier thoughts switch to resentment that a girl of her own looks and capacities should have to sit around in a handsome new evening dress with a noisy old girl just because she owed her a fortune. The favors weren't all on Elsie's side. She had been bored and lonely for years until her frustrated appetite for holocausts had been gratified by Jerry's magnanimous sharing of her ups and downs. It was just as she was thinking this that Jerry's downstairs bell rang.

"I knew he'd come!" cried Elsie clapping her hands. "Just let me give him a piece of my mind."

But suddenly Jerry's cheeks flushed and her eyes began to glow.

"Pull your dress down, Elsie," she commanded briskly, giving herself a quick glance in the mirror. "This may be somebody else."

"But who—?" Elsie began, bewildered, and then she stared at her friend with dawning suspicion. "You telephoned somebody a few minutes ago, didn't you?"

"I told you," Jerry said evasively. "I called the Julien Café again just as you suggested and talked to a man who said he was looking for McGrew, too. He asked where I was—"

Elsie threw up her hands.

"And you invited him up," she accused incredulously.

"Good Heavens, Jerry, what's the matter with you? He might be a ripper or a lunatic. I can't understand you."

For no matter how thoroughly she approved and felt she understood her young friend there was always more to be found out. It was her turn to look with bewilderment at the change coming over the other, for if an audience brought out Elsie's disease the prospect of a strange man brought out Jerry's.

In any great crisis, financial or emotional, that would send most persons to the bottle or out the window, it had long been Jerry's habit to turn to a new man as restorative, someone unknown, hazardous, unique. She took care to maintain most circumspect relations with any man whose valuable friendship she knew was an important asset, not to be traded for a transient affair with awkward aftermaths. But a moment of pique, a broken date, a lost earring, an unpleasant interview brought out a wild lust for compensating abandon, the more fantastic the better. Elsie had her own outlets which she kept to herself, and she had gathered from cryptic references to "characters" and low barroom types that Jerry, too favored piquant contrast in her conquests. All very well and a woman's only human, but tonight was more than a mere broken date, it was a whole future, and weren't they in it together? But Jerry seemed slipping from her grasp, needing neither her sympathy nor her company. She tried to make Jerry meet her reproachful eyes but the young lady was busily spraying *L'Amour L'Amour* on her hair and wrists and humming happily.

"I always can tell you're up to something when you start singing 'Where or When,'" Elsie accused her. "I just wish you'd learn the rest of the words."

"There aren't any other words but where or when," Jerry said, and then exclaimed impatiently, "Listen, Elsie, this night has sunk me. But I'm going to have one good time before I give up and maybe this is it."

"With a total stranger!" Elsie gasped. "Don't you know this sort of caper will finish you with McGrew? You can't play high and low."

"That's how I play, old dear," Jerry said.

"I will not be called old dear, not by anybody," Elsie said as she stalked proudly out the door, a little miffed not to be called back.

The hall light was out and it was too bad she could not get a good look at the stranger as she passed him on the stairs. She stood outside her own apartment door listening for a moment as Jerry opened the door to him. Prescott was his name, Elsie overheard him announce.

"At least he sounds human this time," she reflected. "No *deses* and *doses*."

That the late guest must look as satisfactory as his accent Elsie could deduce from the sudden dovelike flutiness in Jerry's voice, a change she had observed before when her companion would be interrupted mid-sentence by a husky delivery boy or dreamy solicitor. The change in voice was accompanied, in these moments of fleeting lust, by a telltale glitter in the gray-green eyes that made the pupils tiny pinpoints of desire and the color go hard and unrevealing.

"The little devil," Elsie marveled with a chuckle. "I wonder how much longer she can get away with it."

The old great Dane, whose fur had a pinkish tinge similar to his mistress's hair, was waiting inside Elsie's door, and he rose with arthritic chivalry when she entered. Her living room looked small and untidy after Jerry's brand-new grandeur. Still, it was a cozy dump, Elsie thought, with the garden outside and the jolly little dining corner where Iola daily displayed her priceless culinary treasures. Elsie strode into the kitchen, which was larger than the living room, indeed had to be to house the extraordinary collection of copper and clay utensils, graduated pots and weapons and lordly equipment of herbs, groceries and general fodder sufficient to pacify the fussiest chef and feed a tribe of gourmets. Elsie opened the huge icebox with a fond pat on its

belly as if it was the favorite stud in a fine stable, and reached in
for her inevitable nightcap of beer—this time a good Danish
brand—and a prize hoard of chicken livers for Brucie.

"What'll you bet!" Elsie mused aloud with a reflective glance
upward, another shake of the head. But it wasn't funny, come to
think of it, it was downright asinine for a girl of Jerry's poten-
tialities and opportunities to throw her body and brains around
as if there were plenty more where those came from. Elsie had
always muffed her own chances and took for granted that she always would, but it angered her now that Jerry was bent on doing
the same thing, no matter how a person tried to help her.

Now what satisfaction is that going to be for her to wind up
this mess in bed with a strange man? Elsie thought, exasperated.
How is that going to fix up everything? If she'd only have let me
stay and thrash out things we might have figured out something.

She picked the *Evening Post* out of the wastebasket to read
Leonard Lyons' column in bed and her eye caught the pile of un-
opened bills she had thrown there earlier. It was an outrage to
have to think about money. It crossed her mind that her quixotic
vanity would ruin her some day, that idiotic pride she took in
being regarded as a woman of unlimited means. Whatever they
might criticize in her looks or brains she would not have it that
anyone dared be superior to her financially. Even with her
brother Wharton, who was supposed to be guardian of the family fortunes, Elsie had all sorts of little dodges to make him think
she had mysterious other sources of revenue of which he could
not guess. She switched off the kitchen lights and carried beer
and paper into the bedroom. The fine glow she had experienced
in carrying off the evening in such bold style, delivering so many
good punches at possible detractors of her protégée, faded and
she felt rebuffed for a moment. Brucie followed her to the
dresser where he stood beside her like a watchful valet while she

skinned off the blue rayon satin dress, the pinned-up magenta slip—imagine anybody paying more than two ninety-eight for a slip, though come to think of it a Hattie Carnegie slip for Jerry had cost thirty-odd dollars—the elastic girdle, the incredibly long nylons. It occurred to Elsie to study her naked length in the dresser mirror thoughtfully as if she was viewing it for the first time. The truth was she thought of herself seldom in physical terms, and even soaping herself absently in the shower she was as likely to wash Brucie's curious snout thrust through the shower curtains as her own bottom. She shook her head now in quizzical dismay over the roll of fat over her stomach and the lack of padding in proper places. No one can remain dissatisfied completely with one's body even if all one can honestly boast is a rare birthmark. So it presently struck Elsie that her upper thighs were evenly matched, her knees if knobby were knobbed in the right direction, and even if dressmakers did complain that her behind seemed to slope down all the way to her knees, still her shoulders were quite remarkable for her age, not too bony and certainly not flabby.

"Not so bad, eh Brucie," she asked her dog complacently.

Maybe she had given up too soon, she reflected. Maybe instead of fixing up Jerry Dulaine's lovelife she should have another go at her own. Maybe she could have hung on to that Portuguese lad on the Cape a little longer, maybe she should have given him the car he kept pestering her for. She'd gotten him away from her mulatto maid by promising him a secondhand motor bike with a fire horn but of course that was when the little bounder was in oilskins and before she'd put him into a Tuxedo and taught him to carry fancy canes. Yes, she could have kept him from that Gloucester widow if she'd given in about the car. Not a Buick, of course, but say a used Chevy.

"I'm just too damned Yankee, that's my trouble," Elsie sighed giving her hair a couple of licks with the brush. "I could have strung along that little monkey another summer or two just buy-ing him a couple of flashy shirts and a Tattersall vest. I always get stingy at the wrong time. Darned if I wouldn't like to have the little rat around right this minute."

Musing on love, Elsie gave another deep sigh and hopped into bed, thrusting her long bony feet over the edge to make room be-side her for Brucie.

Rick hurried purposefully up Fifth Avenue, savagely proud of having conquered his weakness for Ellenora. It was no good telling himself that she had no way of knowing he had been waiting for her; he felt as righteously injured as if she had deliberately stood him up to make a fool out of him. At the corner he hesitated just a fraction of a minute, half turned to catch a dim glimpse of some people getting out of a cab in front of Longchamps, firmly dismissed the wild idea that the girl might be Ellenora (which indeed it was) and pushed onward. He knew perfectly well he was about to get into trouble, the way he always did, as if spiting himself would make everybody else sorry. Chasing up some unknown dame from a phone call like a dumb freshman, he mocked himself, but nothing could ever stop him in these stubborn moods. You had to see these blind adventures through to the bitter end, though they were never worth the trouble and could ruin your life. Still anything was better than sitting on in the Julien waiting for someone who would never come.

When he saw the handsome girl who opened the door of her apartment he knew he was having the luck he didn't deserve. Jerry was congratulating herself along the same lines.

"Looks like a party," he said. "How nice."

"How do you do," Jerry said with a shrug. "It's all over and it was not at all nice."

"Then I'm sorry I missed it," Rick said. "I see McGrew isn't here yet. I was expecting him at the Julien, myself. That was why I suggested we might as well wait for him together."

"Of course," Jerry agreed.

Eying her new guest with increasing appreciation she felt cheered and elated. If she could produce a beauty like this out of thin air in her very darkest hour, then she was certainly not done for. The hell with McGrew, she thought.

"I gather you had important business to discuss with him," she said politely. "Will I be in the way?"

Rick hesitated and then grinned at her.

"Not as much as he will be," he said, and then they both laughed shamelessly, understanding each other.

"You never even heard of him," Jerry accused.

"I've heard of nothing but McGrew all evening," Rick defended himself. "Everytime the phone rang at the Julien it wasn't for me, always for McGrew. I answered it to put a stop to it, that's all. A man like that can get dangerous. I only wanted to warn you in case he is really a friend of yours. By the way, is he?"

"Of course he is," Jerry said. "Friend enough to stand me up."

"So that was it," Rick said. "I thought you were making it too easy for me, telling me to come on over. But I was getting tired of being stood up myself."

"Not you too!"

"Every night for two months," Rick said. "I'm damn sick of it."

"I'm sick of everything myself," Jerry said. "I was trying to get rid of the last guest so I could put my head in the oven."

"Could I help?" Rick asked. "Just show me the oven."

"It would have to be the pressure cooker," Jerry said. "Mostly I was considering pills, being a lazy girl. Then I rather hoped you'd turn out to be the killer type and save me the trouble."

"No, I'm just as lazy as you are," Rick confessed. His experienced eyes had taken in the carefully decorated look of the place, the kind of impeccable taste often used to mask the dweller's secret life. Kept, he thought.

"I wouldn't want to mess up such a pretty room," he said.

"Oh it's not paid for," Jerry said, and then to her surprise tears came to her eyes, and suddenly she was gulping and choking away like any Southern belle with the vapors. She snatched at the handkerchief her guest quietly handed her and would have started to bawl in earnest except for the curious fact that the young man showed no disposition to stop her. Indeed he was looking over a book casually as if the lady had asked him to look away while she fixed a garter.

"Thanks for not saying anything," Jerry said, surprised. "How nice of you not to say it will make me feel better to cry because it never does."

"I could have said things can't be as bad as all that," Rick admitted, putting the book aside to look at her. "But probably they're worse. I warn you, though, if you tell me anything I'm likely as not to blab it."

"If I did tell you anything I'd make out I'm just crying over a broken heart," Jerry admitted, "but it's much more important than that. To tell the truth—"

Rick put up a protesting hand.

"Can't we be strangers?" he asked.

"Then let's get out of here," Jerry said.

"Back to the Julien?" Rick asked.

"Too chummy," Jerry said. "I feel like loud company. Dingy bars with fine low types who could never do me any good. I know a few spots."

"I know a few myself," Rick said. "Better change your costume."

Jerry started for the bedroom door but turned to look at him.

"Do you always know the right way to handle people's troubles?" she asked curiously.

"That's what they tell me," he said. "Trouble is just what I'm good at. I have a feeling I see it coming at me right now."

"Let's not look, then," Jerry suggested. "Let's get even with everybody and have one good time before we die."

"Hurry up, then," Rick said. "We've only got all night."

This was the way it always ended up, he thought, resigned. Every time he tried to blot out Ellenora he wound up blotting out himself. He wanted to have a light gay adventure to make up for his romantic wounds but it always bogged down into his feeling sorry for somebody and getting himself in a mess trying to help them out. As if he was God's gamekeeper, his mother used to scold him.

Gourd's grimekipper, Geep's Godkimer, Gam's keep—he was muttering it angrily to himself hours later.

The electric light in the middle of the ceiling sent a steady unrelenting warning and it was this, more than the rhythmic moaning sound, that finally opened Jerry's eyes. What she saw was a dream, she knew, and closed her eyes again, reaching out an arm to the light she knew was by her bed but which somehow now was not there so she slowly opened her eyes once more. Her room would be a mess, she knew that from the fierce throbbing in her head which meant that she had drunk too much of something terrible, and of course her clothes would be thrown all over the place and probably the lamp turned over. But this bulb in the ceiling? The pale woman with long red braids lying in the other bed? The funny-looking windows with no curtains—dungeon-like windows—yes, with bars.

Suddenly it struck her that she must have done it—taken poison or dope pills just as she had been afraid she might. This was no dream, this was a hospital.

How had it happened, how long ago, and where? Frightened, she sat up in bed abruptly and the sudden motion made her sick. She leaped up to go to the bathroom but the door was shut.

"There's not even a doorknob," she gasped, and then saw the little pane of glass on a level with her own eye in the top of the door. It was a hospital corridor outside but she saw no one pass until a young mulatto nurse hurried by, paying no heed to Jerry's pounding on the door and outcries. Frantically Jerry looked around for a basin or sink but there was nothing in the room but the two beds and only one sheet. She was stark naked and there was no sign of her clothes. Her hands were bruised and she realized that her rings had been torn off.

"What kind of hospital is this?" she cried out.

The girl in the other bed, with the sheet pulled up to her chin and her braids lying on it, turned quiet empty eyes on her.

What had happened? Where had it happened and with whom? Another stab of pain in her head made her snatch the sheet and vomit into it. She rolled it up and sat on the bedticking, shivering. Think, she commanded herself, think hard. There had been the dinner party and Elsie's voice booming in the dining room, Elsie's voice booming in the living room, people sitting around, but clearer than anything else she remembered the sick desperation in her heart, a feeling that this was a wake for her because this was the end. She remembered being alone with Elsie, slipping to her medicine cabinet to count her sleeping pills, praying that Elsie would get out. Well, had she gone and was this waking up in hell? No, there was something else. Then she remembered the doorbell, the arrival of the angel, it seemed at the time, named Ricky, a crazy good-looking stranger who made her forget the medicine cabinet. They had compared notes—each was in a mood to kick over the traces, each was ready to trust the first passing stranger or, if requested, take a rocket to the moon. Oh, they had met at the precisely right moment for anything to happen. They had decided to go out on the town—not to the uptown places but to all the dives—Monty's on Houston Street, the Grotto down by the bridge, the Sink, the Bowery Lido—

The Bowery Lido. Suddenly Jerry saw it again.

The band was booming out "Rose of Washington Square," the grizzled chorus boys in straw hats were shuffling-off to Buffalo, arms around each other's shoulders, the Lido Ladies, old variety hoofers and stompers and ripe young strippers, were prancing off the stage, the mission derelicts were peering in the windows at the uptown slummers whooping it up inside, the cops were getting their handouts at the bar—this was the real New York, the real people, the good people, the bitter salt of the earth. None of the phoniness of Fifty-Second Street, or the fancy spots. "Isn't it wonderful? Isn't it fun?" That was what she and Rick kept saying to each other and whatever strangers they invited to join them, the Chinaman, the old streetwalker they prevailed upon the waiter not to throw out, the old hunchback. And then she remembered Tessie. That must have been when it started, she thought, pressing her hands to her head. Imagine seeing Tessie in a G-string and transparent fan marching along in the Lido chorus line, Tessie, her old roommate who had married a respectable customer's man and moved to Mount Kisco! Tessie, who had advised her ten years ago to give up the gay life and settle down before it was too late. Tessie, obviously fifteen pounds over model size sixteen and with the silveriest blond dye job on her too long flowing locks, strutting past the customers and so flabbergasted at sight of Jerry she had forgotten their past differences and shouted, "My God, Jerry!"

"Tessie!"

Next Tessie was sitting at their table and they were hugging and kissing each other like long-lost sisters, so Rick could never have dreamed that they hadn't been speaking to each other for a good ten years, and the waiter was bringing round after round of whiskey and fizz with Tessie sending drinks to all her buddies in the floor show and inviting them all to join them. What happened then? Was Tessie here, too? What had become of Ricky?

Jerry ran to the barred window and shouted their names into the stone-gray daybreak. A great animal roar answered her, lunatic laughter and a sustained inhuman moan that seemed to come from the stone walls shuddering into the new day. Jerry ran back to the door and peered out the aperture, pounding on it

furiously. This time she saw two eyes in a dark face in the peephole of the door opposite. Whoever it was shook her head as if
in warning and then lifted dark wrinkled hands to the peephole,
spelling out in sign language "W A I T." The eyes appeared
again and the head nodded. At least someone was a friend, Jerry
thought. The mulatto nurse hurried down the hall and this time
she came in the room.

"Shame on you, dirtying your bed, I'll teach you," she cried
out, and smacked Jerry smartly. "Shouting and carrying on, you
dirty thing, running around naked, disturbing everybody."

"I want a nightgown, I want to go to the bathroom," Jerry said
carefully.

"Oh yes, a private bathroom and a lace nightie, oh sure," the
nurse smacked her again. "When it's time to go to the bathroom
I'll let you know, you filthy little tramp, you."

This is a dream, Jerry said out loud over and over, this is a
dream but why don't I wake up?

"Shut up," said the girl. "If you behaved right you wouldn't be
here, you tramp."

"Can't we please have the light out?" Jerry begged.

The girl gave a jeering laugh.

"That light stays on, so if one of you gets killed I can look in
and see which one did it."

The door closed behind her.

A dream, a dream, Jerry chanted, pulling a corner of the wet
sheet across her nakedness, a dream, only all she could think of
now was of how to choke the nurse to death. She went to the
peephole again and her friend across the hall winked this time
and again spelled out "wait" with her hands.

The stone walls were still moaning; it was a hollow, beyond-
pain baying noise like beasts at the water hole, but now the sky
was a lighter gray and there was the croaking of river tugs, the

clatter of delivery trucks, and garbage cans. Out the window she could see the stone court surrounded by bigger gray stone buildings with barred windows, and there was a smell now of dead river rats, sour coffee grounds, boiling hay or mush, and Jerry vomited again into the sheet. No, this was not a dream, but what was it? She felt a little better now, except for the pain in her head and the sudden piercing desire to kill the nurse.

Back to Tessie and the Bowery Lido she pushed her thoughts. They had talked about what wonderful times they used to have, the limousines sent to take them to house parties in Bucks County, Saratoga, Montauk Point, New Haven—anywhere, private planes toting them to masked balls in Palm Beach, Hollywood, New Orleans, Texas, the big spending gentleman buying a name band to amuse them on his Miami-bound yacht, champagne raining all the time, oh the happy, carefree, days of old, the dear wonderful good good friends whose names were either forgotten or never known, ah those pure, unclouded happy times! And those two loyal, devoted, true-unto-death friends Tessie Baxter and Jerry Dulaine, such friends as neither had ever had before or since, all of which made this chance meeting here in the Bowery an occasion for unlimited celebration and hosannas.

"I'm just working here for laughs," Tessie said. "I wanted to get in off the road, no matter what I had to do. I've got the most marvelous midget, a real clown. You'll die."

Jerry tried to concentrate on what happened after Tessie's midget brought up the two punks who wanted to dance with her. Then Tessie took her backstage and they sat there gabbing, not listening to each other, until she remembered to go back in and look for Rick. But the place was suddenly in an uproar, full of cops and shouting. Someone snatched her arm and somebody else grabbed her when she struggled—that was as far as she could remember.

The door of her room opened and the nurse stood there.

"Well, get out to the washroom and on the double. Throw that sheet over you, you can't be running around here naked, you dirty tramp!"

Jerry's fists clenched but the open door was there and she ran out, the soiled sheet bunched in front of her, joining the sudden horde of half-naked women running down the hall, her red-haired roommate being shoved and yanked by the mulatto nurse. They were nearly all youngish women except for the tiny dark Porto Rican called Maria who Jerry realized must be her friend from across the hall. It was so wonderful to be in the washroom, able to wash and have a turn at the comb with the others that Jerry's murderous rage changed to the humblest gratitude for this privilege.

"That nurse wouldn't give me a sheet or open the door last night," she murmured, waiting behind her friend who was combing her short shaggy gray hair.

The little woman smiled.

"If she open door maybe you try to run out of place naked," she explained. "Maybe you get to next floor then they lock you up for crazy and maybe long time before you get out, like happen to me here once."

Jerry shivered, knowing it would have happened just like that because now she knew anything could happen. Everybody else seemed to be old hands here, calling each other by name—Babe, Chick, Bonny, Bobby, Flossie, Sally—taunting each other with having boasted that last time was to have been the last time and now look. It was amazing how quickly the human mind adjusted, she thought, for she felt more bound to these women than to any other group she'd ever known. When the day attendant, a hard-faced white woman, came in with a clean sheet for her to wear she surprised her with her burst of gratitude. And when the woman put down a cardboard box of used lipsticks, Jerry's joy equaled that of the others.

"Doctor says you tramps can put on lipstick this morning," the nurse shouted out. "But don't forget where you are and start making passes at him or it's the lockup for the lot of you."

"Where are we?" Jerry asked Maria.

"What's the matter, you forget?" said Maria. "City hospital."

"I never was here—" Jerry started to say but from the mocking smiles around her knew no one would believe her. What frightened her most was the curious way she felt in the wrong, as if the mulatto girl's cruelty must not be questioned, nor did she have any right to a gown, or any right to be anyplace else but here. She saw that there was a bump on her temple and remembered something.

"The policeman hit me, he hit me with his club," she exclaimed, and there was a titter from the others.

"They always do," said Maria. "The bump will go away before you get out."

"What do you mean?" Jerry asked. "I'm going home as soon as they give me my clothes."

"That'll be when," said the tall sixteen-year-old named Bobby with the translucent white skin. "Where'd they pick you up?"

"The Bowery Lido," Jerry said. "I don't know what happened, if I got sick and doctors brought me here or—"

"What are you talking about? The cops brought you, girl," Bobby laughed scornfully. "Same as they brought all of us. For cripes sake, what made you try anything in the Bowery anyway?"

"I wasn't trying anything."

"Break it up, you tramps, and come and get it!" the nurse yelled through the door, and again they ran down the hall, some in hospital shirts, bare-bottomed and barefooted, some, like Jerry, with sheets held in front of them or dragging behind. They slid onto benches at a bare table at the end of the hall, a bowl of watery farina and a cup of cold tea in front of each. The nurse and a new attendant went from one to the next, popping pills in each mouth. Bobby resisted hers and was slapped. Jerry held hers in her mouth, and slid it out on her cereal spoon.

"They have no right to hit us," she said. Maria shook her head at her.

"They got all the right they want," she whispered. "There's nothing anybody can do."

"When do the newspapers come?" Jerry asked, thinking that there might be some explanation in the news, but all heads turned to her again with a mocking smile.

"No reading's allowed here," Bobby said. "That's why they take away everybody's glasses. No radio either. They always take away Sally's hearing aid, too, and then when she doesn't hear what they say they let her have a good wallop."

"I like to read," stated the quiet, waxen-faced woman about Jerry's age with the chrysanthemum bob of black hair and the carefully manicured white hands. "I went to school when I was a kid and I was always reading."

"I know the school you went to, Bonny," jeered the nurse.

"Shut up, you creeps," said Bonny quietly, as everyone hooted with laughter.

"Some school," taunted the one named Chick. "Sunday school."

"I taught Sunday school class once, damn you," shouted Bonny, rising.

"Break it up, girls," the day nurse ordered. "The doctor's here. Good heavens, Bobby, this is the third time you've been in since Christmas."

"I had a fit in a subway station," Bobby said.

"She had a fit in the Hotel St. George, don't let her kid you," said Chick, winking at Jerry. "It scared this sailor she was shacking up with and he got the cops."

"Men are all jerks," said Bobby. "A girl has a simple everyday fit and they start screaming for the cops. A fellow I knew had a fit once, we were sitting on a bench in Prospect Park, and I was only a kid fourteen years old and did I call the cops? No, I stuck my handbag in his jaw so he wouldn't bite off his tongue, and the dumb cluck bit through the bag and got pieces of my mirror in his windpipe and darn near killed himself. But it was the right thing to do."

"How do I telephone?" Jerry asked.

"Are you kidding?"

"But people will be looking for me," Jerry said, and then stopped. Who would be looking for her? Creditors, maybe. Rick Prescott must have thought she had skipped out of the Lido when she stayed out so long with Tessie. What had happened to Tessie?

She could tell that some of the guests or patients or prisoners were locked in their rooms for the attendant was carrying trays in and out.

"Can you find out if my friend, Tessie Baxter, came in with me last night?" Jerry asked the nurse. "Is she here now?"

"That's none of your business, miss," said the nurse coolly, and everyone laughed. Obviously this nurse was regarded as a wag. "If your friend is the same kind as you she'll be here sooner or later, I can tell you that much."

"Are we allowed to telephone?" Jerry asked meekly.

"Sure, we all have private wires," said the one called Chick. She sat on the bench beside Jerry and suddenly patted her on the cheek. "I like you, kid. When we get out let's see what we can do together. Where'd you get your hair done?"

"Elizabeth Arden's," said Jerry and realized it was the wrong thing to say for there was a silence till Bobby said, "She had Elizabeth Arden fix her up so she could go down to the Bowery and get herself a man."

"I was kidding," said Jerry.

"There's a phone booth in the hall but your pocketbook's in the office safe so you won't have a dime to call, anyway," volunteered Maria. "Maybe somebody will call and leave a message for you.

Whatever name you told them when you were brought in."

Jerry knew it was no use trying to remember how she had come in or what she had said.

"Anybody want me to do any phoning for them when I leave this morning?" she asked.

"Who told you you were getting out?" asked Chick. "Tell me the truth, where'd you get your hair done like that? I like your fingernails. What shade is that?"

"Opalescent," said Jerry.

"You certainly did a job on yourself just to work the Bowery," said Bobby, admiringly. "Look, girls, the toenails yet!"

"Opalescent," repeated Chick, giggling. "Opalescent toenails!"

"It's nice." Maria nodded to her kindly, and Jerry felt a wave of love for her, as if here was the dearest friend she had ever had, one she would cherish forever.

"Would you like me to tell your family where you are?" Jerry asked her, wanting to do something wonderful for her.

Maria looked alarmed.

"No no, please," she said. "My husband will come wait for me outside and beat me up."

"Maria's old man gets drunk on Porto Rican rum and starts whamming the kids around and Maria clobbers him with everything she can lay her hands on," explained Bobby, while Maria smiled apologetically. "The neighbors call the police and they cart off Maria yelling her head off so they bring her here. Then her old man lays for her to get out so she doesn't care how long she stays here."

"I don't know maybe this time I killed him," Maria said thoughtfully. "Better for me maybe to stay crazy."

The girl with the red braids who had shared Jerry's room was standing in the hall facing the open door of the bathroom. The day nurse had stood her there like a window dummy and she had not moved.

"She's making up her mind to take a bath," explained Bobby.

"She'll stand there maybe all day and all night unless somebody lifts her in."

"The doctor's ready, girls," shouted the nurse, and the mere thought of a man around excited everyone to fever pitch. "Come on, you, he wants to see you first, miss."

Jerry got up, trying to cover herself with the sheet, and made for the office. The doctor was a young man, disguising his youth behind a short black Van Dyke. He had a card in front of him and looked at her over this briefly.

"Well?" he asked crisply.

"I want to know how I got here," Jerry asked quietly. It was funny how fast you learned. Any protest of injustice brought on more injustice, so you must be quiet, accept outwardly whatever punishment the powers give, and wait, as Maria had told her, just wait.

"You don't remember?" the doctor said skeptically, then nodded. "That's right, you were in such a state the cops said they had to give you a shot to quiet you. The report says you and some other prostitutes were picked up in a Bowery joint with a hunchback who peddles reefers which you were smoking—"

The blood swam in Jerry's head.

"He passed us cigarettes, I didn't know they were reefers," she said faintly.

"You gave him a five-dollar bill, they said," said the doctor. "You wouldn't give that for a pack of Camels."

"I thought he was poor, that's all," Jerry said.

The doctor looked at her still skeptically.

"Are you so rich? Anyway there was a clean-up all over town last night. Some of the girls went to jail and the ones that were hysterical were taken to alcoholic or psycho wards in the city hospitals."

"What made them think I was a prostitute?" Jerry asked evenly.

The doctor looked at her again and then shrugged.

"The place you were, the people you were with, the reefers," he answered. "The hunchback is a procurer in that section and you gave him money."

"I told you I was sorry for him being a hunchback," Jerry repeated. "Was he arrested?"

The doctor gave a short laugh.

"I doubt it. Those places always pay protection for their regulars. When there's word of a clean-up the cops go after the strangers."

"Is that how those other girls out there were brought here—just to cover for the really guilty ones?" Jerry asked, trying to keep her voice steady, concealing the anger with which she was filled.

"That's not my business," said the doctor. "I'm the doctor, not the law. I can tell you that most of the girls out there today are brought in regularly—usually drunk or hopped up, either a little weak in the head like Bobby, or so long in prostitution that they don't even know it's a bad word and knowing no other life and not learning it's considered a sin they go right back in it."

"Those aren't bad women," Jerry said. "I'll bet you always get the wrong ones and they are too scared to say so."

The doctor was annoyed, and tapped his pencil on the card.

"It's not my business to prove their innocence or guilt," he said.

"Oh we're all guilty, I know that," Jerry said bitterly. "I know now that you become guilty and you feel guilty as soon as someone treats you as guilty. The only innocent ones are the accusers so all of you try to accuse the other person before you're found out yourself. You know it will *make* him guilty."

"I can't give you more time, Miss—" he referred to the card, "Dulaine. I agree with some things you are saying, but I advise you to take care where you say them. You made the office downstairs very angry last night screaming accusations at them and at the police, and threatening to report them all to your fiancé, Collier McGrew, who would order a big investigation. He's on our board, of course."

Jerry drew a long breath.

"I said that?" she murmured. "I can't remember."

"Reefer smokers think it's funny sometimes to pass their cigarettes to greenhorns. They get a kick watching their reactions," the doctor said. "I'm surprised you didn't suspect that. It usually creates delusions of grandeur. Maybe that's what made you boast of all the important people you thought you knew."

"Yes," said Jerry. There were evidently a lot of things she had said and done that it would be better not to know. But bringing in McGrew's name! Her fiancé! She felt weak with shame.

"I'll see if we can get you out of here as soon as possible," said the doctor. "That's all for now."

His phone rang and he picked up the receiver. He motioned Jerry to wait as he answered and when he hung up he smiled at her.

"Well, that's one on me," he said. "It seems you did know Collier McGrew. You insisted on his being notified last night, and he has sent his car for you and arranged for your release. The nurse will bring you your clothes, and your valuables are down in the office. I can only advise you to stay in your own class after this, Miss Dulaine. Stick with the people you know."

"Thank you," gasped Jerry, plunging out the door, tears in her eyes thinking of how good everyone was, how incredibly kind people were. The other women were standing in line outside the door waiting their turn with the doctor and the nurse stood by with her clothes over her arm.

"I'm going, I'm getting out!" Jerry cried out to the others. "Tell me what I can get for you outside, whoever you want me to see. I'll telephone your office and say you're sick or maybe there's somebody you want to come get you."

"Listen, those tramps got no offices," muttered the nurse.

"You're all right, Jerry," Chick called to her.

"Send me a newspaper or something," said the quiet-looking one named Bonny. "I'd like to do a little reading instead of sitting around yakking with these creeps."

The pale girl was still standing looking into the bathing room, her red braids over her shoulder, the slender legs bare from the thigh down posed in an arrested step like the statues of Diana. Jerry hesitated beside her, wanting to do something.

"Your hair is lovely," she said but the blue eyes looked calmly, patiently off as if waiting for a magic word to waken her.

"She's all right, she feels no pain," the nurse said impatiently. "Here's your clothes, now get into them, you're so anxious to get out."

She tossed the clothes on the bed, frowning, not wanting to show her curiosity and respect for someone able to escape so quickly into a world outside her authority. Jerry hurried into her clothes, overwhelmed with the privilege of wearing stockings and shoes, powder, her own comb. It was a dream that she was really getting out—she must make the most of it before she wakened and found herself back in this room with no doorknob on the door. She was glad she had changed from party clothes to street wear before she went out for that good time last night with Rick Prescott.

The girls were lined up outside the doctor's office as she passed and Bobby ran up to her, her sheet dragging behind her thin bare childish body.

"Got any rouge?" she whispered.

Jerry took out her compact and gave it to her, and handed the others her comb, lipstick, perfume vial, handkerchief.

"She'll take them all away tonight but we can hold them till then," said Maria, nodding toward the nurse down the hall.

Jerry followed the attendant down the corridors and out, thinking of the doctor's advice to stick to her own class and with the people she knew, and she thought these were the people she knew, this was her class.

A chauffeur in livery was standing in the office waiting for her.

"Mr. McGrew's car is outside," he said. "I'm to drive you to your home. He asked me to give you this note."

She opened the note, sitting in the back of the car.

> I could not reach you last night as my plane from Texas grounded in the desert and the relief didn't get me in till this morning. My secretary took the hospital's message and tried to straighten out what seems to be some fantastic error, or was it a joke? It will be amusing to hear all about it from you. Can I make amends for failing you at dinner last night by having Swanson pick you up at seven tonight?
>
> As ever,
> McGrew

Jerry smiled faintly as she crumpled the note. Elsie would certainly get a bang out of that, she thought, though it seemed a long time ago and of no matter to herself. She caught a glimpse of a man standing in front of her apartment. A process server, she thought, and decided to ask McGrew's chauffeur to drive on but it was too late. He had already stopped and opened the car door for her.

"Any message for Mr. McGrew, Miss Dulaine?" he asked, as she got out. "He thought you might want me to call for you later."

Jerry hesitated. It was too late, she thought. Everything happened too late. There wasn't anything she wanted of McGrew now.

"Thank him and tell him I'm not free tonight," she said and walked bravely up the steps. But it wasn't a process server at all, she realized, just her good friend of last night.

"I was just about to dredge the river," Rick said to her, taking her keys from her hand. "I've been chasing all over trying to find out what happened to you. I went backstage hunting for you and Tessie. Then there was that raid on the place and they shooed everybody out of the joint. All of a sudden I sobered up and re-membered you said you were going to jump in the river."

"Me?" Jerry asked with a tired grimace. "I thought I said I was too lazy."

"You look pretty rocky," he said, surveying her doubtfully.

"Someday I'll tell you about it," Jerry said.

"Don't," he said. "I could guess when I saw the limousine."

"It wasn't that way at all," Jerry said. "That was just the happy ending that happens a day too late, at least that's the way I always fix it."

"That's the way I fix it, too," Rick said. "Born that way. Has something to do with the middle ear. Can't change it."

"Don't look so scared," Jerry laughed. "I won't faint."

"Sure you're all right?" He hesitated, about to go.

"Now I am," she said. She saw her mail on the hall table, topped by the long envelope from the collector of internal revenue, and sat down on the bottom stair suddenly, her head in her hands.

"Ever play crack the whip?" she asked, quite dizzy. "I feel like the one on the end that gets whirled off the faster they go.

Ricky turned and helped her to her feet.

"We'd better go make some coffee," he suggested. "We need a bracer. Let's face it, we had one hell of a good time even if it kills both of us."

He had intended to go back to his apartment, shower and shave, and get to the office around noon. But she was a nice kid and he couldn't leave her like this, half in a daze. It was just another one of those things he had started and had to see through.

Waking up in Jerry's bed later on, much refreshed, he asked Jerry why she was smiling.

"I can't get over that doctor taking me for a prostitute," she said.

PART TWO

Wharton Hookley had the most profound admiration for his sister Elsie's incorruptible character, and he often dreamed of the monuments and even scholarships he would institute in her name when she died, the Elsie Hookley Club for Art Students, the Elsie Hookley Orphanage, the Elsie Hookley Woman Travelers' Aid (all inspired by his sister's latest vagary and worked out in systematic detail by his insomnia), but the trouble was that Elsie never would die. This put her brother into a most exasperating position, for almost every time he saw her or heard about her he got into such a sweat that he was bound to betray the very opposite of those emotions he wished to have. How could he eulogize his sister's classic candor until it was conveniently silenced once and for all? How could he state that no matter how unconventionally Elsie had lived and through whatever gaudy gutters she had trailed the Hookley traditions, she herself was the soul of honor when he was forever hearing that Elsie bore him no ill will for doing her out of her rightful inheritance? "Wharton really *cares* about possessions and I don't," she had generously said—no sense in doubting this report for she often made the same statement in his presence—"Grandmother's diamonds and the Maryland and Boston homesteads really mean something to Wharton, and I don't deserve them since I don't appreciate them, so let him keep my share, I have all I need in my little income."

The fact was that Elsie's outspokenness was Wharton's hair shirt, or rather one of his hair shirts as he had rather a full

wardrobe of them, mostly the gifts of women as such unnecessary sartorial luxuries are apt to be. For most of his lifetime he
had been able to maintain a Christian forbearance in the face of
such vague aspersions from his sister's bohemian adherents, the
kind of gentlemanly poise possible when one is sure the world
is wise enough to wink at these fabrications. Wharton had been
so confident that everyone agreed with his own exaggerated admiration for himself that he felt he could afford to excuse, even
publicly defend his sister's eccentric doubts about his honesty.
Elsie had never been well as a child, Elsie had been taken in by
an early marriage to a titled foreigner, Elsie had been a child
beauty and then, at the age of twelve, shot up to a grotesque six
feet and been obliged to compensate.

But too late it was borne in on Wharton that the world secretly
believed Elsie. Who put on the big social show in Boston and
New York, after all, and how was it Wharton, with four expensive daughters, could live and travel in grandeur, fling around
pews, stained glass windows and cemetery lots in endless memo-
riams to related Hookleys, unless he was nibbling away at Elsie's
proper funds? Wharton, who had always been fiendishly metic-
ulous and efficient in money matters, rued the day he had
inherited the management of the family estate (though he would
have cut his throat if anyone else had been given the nerve-
racking privilege). Elsie, caring little as she did about diamonds,
forgot she had casually changed them into bonds on which she
now drew interest, and all that her loyal supporters saw was that
Wharton's girls wore the diamonds. So many people felt guilty
for finding Elsie Hookley's excessive heartiness and belligerent
bohemianism almost intolerable that they pounced gratefully on
any chance to prove they were not snobs, and after being chased
into the most queasily genteel position by her excessive earthi-
ness they were happy to proclaim their essential democracy by

denouncing her brother for lack of it. Often Wharton found himself waking in the middle of the night accusing himself of dishonesty, remembering that he had forgotten to notify Elsie of the sale of five acres of timberland in northern Maine, and he would get up and paddle to his desk in his bare feet to jot it down right then and there at his desk. These careful notes referring to the sum of $304.64 being deposited to her account only made Elsie, who hadn't even known of any timberland, speculate sarcastically on how much Wharton was holding back from her on the deal. The more Wharton heard of Elsie's reflections on him the more slips he made, like a child who's been told it's clumsy, until he sometimes wondered if he was not being slowly tortured into unconscious chicanery, and at these moments he fiercely cursed his sister for puncturing his good conscience. A fine head for figures and careful bookkeeping being his particular vanity, slurs on these were all that worried him; like someone so absorbed in boasting of his abstinence he doesn't know he's sipped away a pint of bourbon, Wharton was so engrossed in his careful bookkeeping accounts and business management that he never seemed to notice that all the family furniture, silver, china and other accouterments of solid living unobtrusively found their way into his possession. In all her life Elsie had never noticed whether she was eating off a gold plate or a picnic pasteboard and besides, with the hit-or-miss life she led, what would she do with things?

That was why her request for the cane was so astounding.

It was one of the days when Wharton Hookley felt he owed it to his peace of mind to sojourn down to the Café Julien to lunch alone in state, for Elsie's note about the cane had been the last straw. The only thing that soothed him in moments of stress was to buy himself and nobody else a lavish lunch in an expensive restaurant, and look about him at all the people buying expensive lunches with money they were obliged to earn themselves, whereas he did not have to work for his lunch money and therefore must represent a superior order of mankind. It always surprised him that acquaintances, seeing him exhibiting his superiority in this fashion, did not envy him but often attempted to join him under the fantastic impression that he was lonesome. He ordered with the loving care he always bestowed on his stomach, starting off with a solitary Gibson, and a green turtle soup with Madeira. Sipping his wine with a complacent survey of an adjoining table where three businessmen were feasting on what must have taken them a good half day's work to earn, he felt sufficiently composed to take out his sister's note.

"I hate to have to keep after you about Uncle Carpenter's ram's-head cane," the large flowing handwriting said—now why must she dot her r's and h's, he wondered pettishly—"but honestly, Wharton, this must be the tenth time I've asked you for it during the last few years, and why on earth you hang on to it when you know what it means to me on account of Uncle Carpenter being my favorite relative—etcetera, etcetera."

The fact was that every time Elsie remembered Uncle Carpenter's ram's-head cane, Wharton knew something nasty was in the wind. He and his older sister were poles apart, had never understood one thing about each other's nature, lived completely different lives that crossed only occasionally, on the surface of things meant nothing to each other, but somehow had never been able to make a single move unless they were convinced it was the exact opposite of what the other would do. Even when they were not in the same country they had some kind of radar that told them what the other was up to, always something extraordinarily wrong and inducive to a countermove carefully planned to cause equal irritation on the other side.

Take the matter of Uncle Carpenter. For several summers, Wharton had sent his younger daughters up to Uncle Carpenter's big place at Narragansett, and once in a while Wharton would have a faint twinge thinking that Uncle Carpenter was half his sister's property, too, but still if she didn't have sense enough to feather her nest he wasn't going to do it for her. On the old man's death the place, technically, was half Elsie's, but since she showed no interest—of course if it was ever sold, Wharton always said, she would get her half—he continued using it for family purposes, carefully deducting repairs and general upkeep from Elsie's as well as his own estates, fifty-fifty fair and square. Then—just as he was vaguely expecting some much more justifiable alarming demand—he received Elsie's request for Uncle Carpenter's cane. In his relief he was about to send it to her post-haste when a shrewd second thought came to him. Just what was there about that cane, one, incidentally, which he had never even remembered? He went through a hundred ancestral canes in the Narragansett attic until he found the one with the little ugly jade ram's-head. The eyes and horns were studded with emerald and diamond chips and it was made of some perhaps remarkable Malaysian wood, the head unscrewed for a dagger, but it was an ugly thing at best and certainly of no great value. Wharton did not remember ever having seen his uncle use it, and at first he just sat there looking at the damn cane shaking his head and thinking what a fool Elsie was. Why on earth did Elsie want it? Was it a museum piece, was there something about it that made it worth a king's ransom, and what mysterious enemies were behind Elsie in this strange request? Wharton hung on to the cane, reading up about cane collections, asking questions here and there, with Elsie making repeated demands. Something more important always came up and the cane would be forgotten, but maybe after two years of silence up popped the matter of the cane again. The worst thing was that he couldn't think of any reason for not giving it to her so he always promised to hunt it up. He went to Uncle Sam's Cane Shop on Forty-Sixth Street with it and they said it might be worth something as a curio, the ram's horns were remarkably carved and the end capped with a miniature hoof was a quaint conceit, but even though it might be worth five hundred dollars to some collector the cane shop would not offer more than two hundred at most.

"Why should Elsie have Uncle's cane?" fretted Wharton, and looking around at the bustling lunchers who surely could not enjoy their armagnac when they knew it was the sweat off their own brows, it seemed to him they were all his enemies, all of them knew what there was about the cane that made Elsie want it and they were all laughing at him. Well, she wouldn't get it this time, either, he vowed, and see how they liked *that!* He saw that everyone was laughing today and he wondered if maybe it wasn't the cane, but something else, something somebody might have said about him in Boston, for instance, or something about Nita, his wife—

The thought of Nita popped up like a jack-in-the-box from the bottom of his conscious mind, the way it had been doing lately, and it would not go away no matter how he tried to remind himself that it was not Nita but Uncle Carpenter's cane that was bothering him.

At the age of thirty-five (having lived dutifully with his mother in the Boston house during all of her strokes, pursuing his private eccentricities with the utmost discretion) Wharton had found exactly the right bride and had married her. She was the sixteen-year-old daughter of a Peruvian dignitary, so the step had none of the hazards of a union with some overeducated, wilful American woman but was like taking on a sweet, dutiful daughter with none of the inconvenience of creating her. Wharton was a frustrated mother, and far from having a mother complex, had only enjoyed his own mother when she was too feeble to resist his maternal care and dictatorship. Mother now retired, Wharton found Nita gloriously childlike, a blank page as so many carefully reared and protected South American young girls are. She had been an obedient daughter and except for occasional wayward weeping fits of nostalgia for tropic skies and convent playmates, tried hard to be an obedient bride. Wharton had never been nor wished to be a ladies' favorite, for the young ones were like his sister, arrogant and superior, and moreover he had constantly before him that particularly terrifying breed of Boston women, unsexed by age and ugliness, hairy with old family fortunes, the spayed witches of subterranean bank vaults, perpetual demonstrations of the Horror of Femaleness.

Wharton himself had been no beauty, licked at the start by a nose that did seem an outrage, a mongrel affair beginning as the Hookley Roman then spreading into Egyptian, and possessing a perverse talent for collecting lumps, iridescent scales, ridges and spots so that it seemed to reflect half a dozen colors simultaneously, ranging through bruise-purple, cabbage green, mulberry red, baby-bottom pink and chalk white. Wharton had such a terrific reputation for efficiency that many friends swore that the reason his nose changed colors before your very eyes was because of an elaborate Rimbaud color code, indicating varied reactions to his surroundings. But middle age had been kind to him, for nose, mottled skin, prim mouth, grim chin and irritable grape-green eyes were blessedly dominated and softened by luxuriant, wavy iron-gray hair and eyebrows. "Distinguished" was the word for Wharton at fifty-five at exactly the time in his life when the overpowering egotism built up by his marriage was being dangerously punctured. Ah, what a stroke of genius it had been for him to have found Nita! How happy he had been on his honeymoon and for years afterward basking in the safety of Nita's childish innocence where his intellectual shortcomings, sexual coldness and caprices—indeed his basic ignorance—would not be discovered. He corrected her language, manners, dress, aired his opinions on all subjects as simple gospel, but particularly he enjoyed her gasps of bewilderment when he lectured her on some new angle of art, literature, psychoanalysis, or perversion that had secretly shocked him. He was well aware that many men of his quixotic moods preferred young boys, but he dreaded to expose his inexperience to one of his own sex, and after certain cautious experiments realized that his anemic lusts were canceled by his overpowering fear of gossip.

Marrying Nita was the perfect answer, just at the moment when Boston had formed its own opinion of him. Against the flattering background of Nita's delectable purity he blossomed forth as the all-round-He-man, the Husband who knows everything, the reformed rake (as Nita's tradition informed her all husbands were) who was generously patient with her backwardness. He soon taught her that snuggling, hand-holding and similar affectionate demonstrations were kittenish and vulgar. He had read somewhere, however, that breathing into a woman's ear or scratching her at the nape of the neck drove her into complete ecstasy, and this was something he did not mind doing, lecturing her at the same time on the purpose of this diablerie so that the dear gullible child did a great deal of dutiful squealing. This success led him into reading many frank handbooks on the subject of sharing one's sex with women, his own instinctive revulsion neutralized by Nita's disapproval. In due course Nita bore him four daughters, a sort of door prize for each time he had attended. This was again fortunate since any male infant would surely have terrified him with the hint of future knowledge surpassing his. Nita allowed him to assume the position of hen mother, clucking and clacking rules for their every moment, herself in the role of conscientious older sister. But when the youngest turned six and Nita herself was thirty-two, looking, to tell the truth, a bare nineteen, she suddenly blossomed out before Wharton's horrified eyes as the complete American girl.

Wharton had grown so complacent in his role of tutor that it never occurred to him that his pupil might graduate. Nor had it ever struck him that the ideas he pronounced purely for dramatic effect would really take root in virgin soil. Suddenly he found his wife utterly changed, as if seduced by his worst enemy. The charming little doll wife was his Frankenstein monster confronting him with all the sawdust with which he himself had stuffed her. He groaned now at the idiotic satisfaction he used to take in nagging her for her convent shyness (he being a very shy man himself), telling her that now she was an American and must learn American confidence. He dared not remind himself of the daring new books, plays, pictures, philosophies which secretly appalled him that he maintained (against her shocked protestations) were necessary for the modern thinker. "You must learn the ways of the world, my dear child," he had patronizingly instructed her, smiling kindly at her naïve outcries, "this is the world, this is life. You're no longer a child and you're no longer in Mother Clarissa's convent in Peru. You're a woman of the world, a wife and mother, and an American!"

The first time Elsie had demanded Uncle Carpenter's ram's-head cane was the very year Nita had burgeoned forth with the bombshell that as an American woman of the world she could naturally waste no more time in the wilderness of Uncle Carpenter's Rhode Island estate or the Hookley morguish manor in Boston. A New York establishment was indicated as the suitable headquarters for the midwinter season of an American matron whose four ugly daughters were safely tucked away in boarding school, and in his consternation Wharton found himself doing exactly as Nita directed him, unable to answer her query as to whether he wasn't pleased with his little pupil, now that she had become the kind of wife he wanted.

Nita had learned more than he intended, and in that maddening way women have, had not been content to leave the knowledge in print the way it was supposed to be but must put it into practical use. She was enthusiastically modern now, frighteningly knowledgeable on all the matters he himself had pretended to be, as worldly and bold in her conversation as any American woman he had ever feared. Wasn't he proud, she demanded, that she was no longer the little provincial prude he had so patiently brought up? Now she could carry on the most fashionably free conversation with any man; wasn't he flattered when he saw how his years of patient criticisms had finally taken effect? It must make him laugh to think of the way she used to embarrass him by slipping her hand in his in public as if he was her papa, as he often said in scolding, and the way she had been afraid to talk to men, turning really pale when the conversation turned openly on sex! How sweet and patient he had been, reading to her, explaining and scolding until she was now—as you see—a genuine woman of the world. She no longer drew back in consternation when some male guest kissed her or casually caressed her, for she knew her husband would mock at her foreign backwardness, and if necessity arose she could breathe in their ears and scratch the napes of their necks like any other proper American woman.

Baffled as he was, Wharton was certain she had not gone to any lengths with any other man because if she had—and it tortured him to face it—he had a terrible conviction that she would never have returned to him. With a herculean effort he adjusted himself superficially to the new order, saw with newly opened eyes that his wife was not regarded as an appropriate detail in Wharton Hookley's properly furnished background, but as a powerful little female in her own right, holding sway over a circle of admirers who listened respectfully to her shrewd worldly conversation. Overhearing her at times Wharton groaned inwardly at the world-weary comments on love and sin with which he had often delighted to shock her now being repeated, contrasting so devastatingly with her charmingly childish figure, bright innocent eyes, Latin lisp. People must surely get the wrong idea from her talk, he thought desperately, but there had been too many years of gentle scolding her for prudery, ignorance, and convent-narrowness to start reproaching her for the exact opposite. He dared not remember the evenings in the country when he had read aloud to his four daughters and Nita, carefully explaining all hidden meanings, scatological or sexual (nothing to be afraid of, let us face these matters openly), insisting on his superior masculinity, furious at himself for blushing or stammering when the five female faces remained dutifully blank and unimpressed. Now he found his wife's vocabulary astonishingly racy, and when some involuntary reproach escaped him she would mildly remind him that these were good old Anglo-Saxon words long in use, and he was perforce silenced by this parroting. Sometimes a glib quotation from some radical nincompoop, some facile praise for an anarchistic artist or philosopher exasperated him to the point of screaming protest, his sensitive nose glittered like a rock in Painted Desert and it seemed incredible for Nita to answer, troubled and wide-eyed, "But, Wharton, have you changed your opinions, then, after you worked so hard to make me see things your way?" Every scarecrow that had ever appalled him from his sister Elsie's mental pastures he had held up for Nita's fright, but it turned out his scarecrows scared nobody but himself; they leered at him on all sides, from sister, wife, and even his four little daughters.

You couldn't trust women, Wharton thought, sipping his brandy, moderately soothed to see fellow diners taking out watches and hastily paying their checks to get back to their wretched desks while he, one of the master men, could dawdle all day if he liked without losing a penny. Still, it was his second brandy, a rare indulgence for midday, and with a sigh he signed his check, placed the exact tip on it and strolled to the checkroom. The checkroom girl was helping a young man into his overcoat, the young man, being a little drunk, waved his arms clumsily and winked at Wharton. Wharton allowed himself a discreet flicker of a smile in response and when the lad gave an impatient oath Wharton inclined his head sympathetically. To tell the truth the young man had a sudden and utterly unreasonable appeal for Wharton, perhaps because his thoughts had been so overrun with women. It seemed to Wharton that there was about this young man, as there had been about himself at that age, absolutely nothing that would capture a woman's fancy. He was a swarthy, undersized, wiry little chap with wide ears, a knobby black-thatched head, close-set beady little eyes, a comedy button nose, crooked mouth, and an outthrust impudent chin— a little monkey you might say, and his arms swung about like monkey arms, too long for his body. Wharton wondered how he happened to be in such a place, for he looked as if he belonged on the other side of an all-night lunch counter, maybe in a turtle-necked black sweater with a dirty apron tied around his waist. Here was a young man who must have been born knowing everything; there was nothing you could tell this one, judging by the knowing mockery of the face. You wouldn't catch this one being harassed by the complexities of femaleness, or cornered by his own weaknesses. Here was the kind of son he should have had, Wharton thought, the ugly essence of masculinity itself, arrogant, fearless, raw. There was something familiar about him, and it was as he was smiling involuntarily at the outlandishly big coat the boy was getting into that Wharton realized the familiarity was in the coat itself.

"Why, that's my coat!" he exclaimed, startled out of his good manners.

The young man laughed, shrugged, the girl hastily pulled off the coat and handed it to Wharton, who found himself apologizing ridiculously for claiming his own property, even though there was his name woven in the lining for all to see

"But you didn't have a coat when you came in, Mr. Hookley, I'm sure," the girl murmured, confused.

"Perhaps I left it here last week," Wharton graciously allowed. "Usually I wear—"

As a matter of fact usually he wore his new topcoat. It came over him that he hadn't worn the one in his hands for at least a year. In fact he could have sworn he'd left it in the country. Mystified and embarrassed he tipped the girl and followed the young man out the hallway to the street. Not at all perturbed by the episode the young man was swinging jauntily down the street, a derby hat on the side of his head, twirling his cane like some old-time vaudevillian.

Wharton's eyes followed the cane. It was a ram's-headed cane capped by a dainty little goat's hoof.

. . . the animal lovers . . .

The enormous portrait of the four Hookley girls which hung in Wharton's library was an unfailing comfort to everyone and well worth the ten thousand dollars extorted by the artist, Laidlaw Whitfield, that charming gentleman-painter whose exhibitions were reviewed in the society columns instead of on the art page. Wharton's plan had been to have the four girls, great galumphing grim replicas of himself, curled and socked, and pearled, grouped around their mother in the Boston garden. This turned out to be such an ungentlemanly enterprise, the lovely little Nita amid the four gargoyle girls forming a satirical fantasy that would have ruined the artist's social success, that the four girls were done alone, long heavy locks and costumes given especial attention to soften the reality. Visitors, unable to compliment the children, could speak effusively of the beautiful painting, the velvet so "touchable," the lace so *real,* the sunlight on the flowers so charmingly done, Bluebell, the great Dane, so true to life. Wharton could look at this soothing idealization and flatter himself on being superior to all women for he had produced four himself, and could honestly boast, conscientious mother that he was, that he had plotted, planned and guarded every thought and move of their lives. It was he, not Nita, who directed their diet, dentistry, reading, recreations, dress, friends, schools, manners, and when they were at home he was at them indefatigably every minute, so that he seldom heard their own voices except the docile, "Yes, Father," "Thank you, Father," and "Good-morning, Father." Their aunt Elsie, who had heard them conversing beyond this point, loved to report elsewhere the delicious news that these exquisitely trained girls spoke a most regrettable, and probably incurable Brooklynese caught from their first nurse (medically irreproachable), and their riding master (a jewel, also, in his own field). Further reports from Elsie were that her brother could not distinguish between his daughters, so similar were they in appearance and so abysmally ignorant was he of any shades of difference in the female character, anyway.

"Just four junior Whartons in different sizes," she jubilated. "I think he had them by parthenogenesis."

Elsie, teeming with a marvelous new idea, had taken it into her head to drop into her brother's duplex on Gracie Square without warning, quite aware that to have pinned him down to a definite appointment would have put him on his guard. Whenever she popped in like this, Wharton was furious with himself for not forestalling this inconvenient visit for it was always inconvenient, as everything about his sister was and always would be. Nita was never any help in these difficulties, and today she herself was put out. She was expecting guests at six and Wharton was already cross because they were part of the new group he did not know. She was sure Elsie would stay and make everything worse by shouting family matters at Wharton. It was long after five and for special reasons she wanted to spend more time arranging her charming little person to perfection. The maid reported that Elsie had brought her great Dane which had started the dachshund yapping, and it so happened that the children had brought in Bluebell herself, Brucie's mother, to see the vet. Out of sheer high spirits Bluebell had immediately disgraced herself at sight of the new Ispahan in the hall and was at the moment confined upstairs to the children's bathroom, refreshing her fagged old gums with some nubbly bath towels and wet nylons.

"Elsie will have to wait till after my bath," Wharton called out testily from his bedroom. "She knows she should have telephoned me first or come to see me at my office."

"It's *your* sister, Wharton, dear," Nita called back from her mirror-walled dressing room. "The sooner you see her the sooner she'll go away."

"Why couldn't Gladys have told her I was out?" Wharton asked peevishly.

"Darling, you know Gladys is absolutely petrified of her," Nita retorted. "You *must* get down there, and do try to keep her from staying."

Elsie was not at all unconscious of the flutter her calls always occasioned. The instant her firm voice sounded at the door, "Tell Mr. Hookley I'm here, Gladys," there were scampers and scurries and whispers and tiptoeings all over the place as if it was a prohibition raid. Then the cautious stillness, indicating that everyone was in their hiding place holding their breath. Elsie knew something special was afoot by the way the Hookley's ancient retainer Gladys recoiled from the door, palsied hands uplifted as if this was the devil himself.

"And how are you these days, Gladys?" Elsie raised her voice a good octave to the eminence she deemed proper for addressing inferiors. This kind inquiry set Gladys to trembling all over again though she managed a terrified smile even as she backed away, quavering "Q-q-q-q-uite n-n-n-ic-e, madam," her faded blue eyes begging for mercy. Gladys had worked in the Hookley homes for fifty years out of sheer terror. She was afraid of all Hookleys and everything else. She believed the world was a lunatic and she was its trembling nurse. If she only could manage to coax and soothe it it might not leap at her, but on the other hand it might, just as Brucie or Bluebell might. The slightest overture found her backing warily toward any door with a fixed oh-I'm-not-afraid-a-bit smile, wide frightened eyes and little gasps of Yes, please, it is a warm day, oh *please,* yes of course it is, dearie, now, now, of course you know best, and please, oh *please* I'm very well, and there, there, everything's going to be all right, please—oh dear—*Yowie!*

Today's encounter with Elsie and Brucie, coming so soon after the *affaire* Bluebell, left the poor woman shaking like a leaf, knowing she was to blame for everything, even for Brucie's instant recognition of his mother's traces on the rug and dutiful lifting of leg to follow example. Having set the household rocking on its heels Elsie stalked straight into her brother's library, Brucie loping behind with poor Gladys scampering around for mops and Airwick.

Elsie selected a cigarette from Wharton's special hoard and seated herself before the portrait of the Hookley daughters. This never failed to amuse her, and she sat there smiling at it, till it occurred to her to torture Gladys further by shouting for her to bring a bowl of water for Brucie and a double Scotch for herself. Gladys was apparently too spent to accomplish this mission alone and it was Williams, the butler, who bore the tray, obviously resentful of being hurried from his own tea into his party coat.

"Thank you, Williams." Elsie ascended the scale to the master voice again. "Thank you very much. Leave the bottle."

She critically studied the drink Williams had poured and then added a proper amount more and was resuming her artistic pleasure in the Hookley portrait when she realized that she herself was being examined. Eight-year-old Gloria, already five feet tall, Hookley-nosed, baby fangs fearsomely clamped in steel, lanky fair locks dripping about her head like an inadequate fountain, legs bruised, bitten and vaccinated, startlingly bare from ankle socks to bloomered crotch, stood in the doorway.

"Did my mother invite you to her party?" the tot inquired without preamble, her eyes disapproving first of Brucie sitting on the love seat with Aunt Elsie, and then of Aunt Elsie sitting on the love seat with Brucie.

"Not a bit," Elsie answered genially, pulling off her gloves and adjusting her Filene's basement hat with great care at an angle leaving only one eye diabolically visible. "How are you, Gloria?"

"Very well, thank you. Did my father give you that hat?"

"No, dear. Your father did not," Elsie answered, and then, as she was really sorry for her nieces, foreseeing a grim girlhood for them either under her brother's thumb or on their own sparse merits, she said, "You look very nice today. Gloria."

"Thank you very much, Aunt Elsie," said Gloria, graciously seating herself on the ottoman opposite her aunt. "You have very nice new shoes. Did Father give them to you?"

"Indeed he did not, darling," replied Elsie, thinking the girl has no more business wearing bobby-sox than I have.

"Did my mother say you could have that highball?" Gloria went on politely, her attention focused on Brucie's pursuit of fleas. "Would you like me to bring you something to eat?"

The girl is too damn tall, Elsie thought, you feel like snapping at her as if she was a grownup. She always had to remember not to get angry, for the children always asked these same questions of everybody as a kind of courteous repartee. Where did they learn it? No matter what faults Wharton had, or Nita, either, they certainly never credited themselves publicly or privately with grandiose benevolences, and it was strange where the girls got the idea that their visitors were thanes of the family. Cooling her irritation by trying to figure out the source of this childish obsession Elsie concluded that it was born in them, as it was born in all rich people, excepting, of course, in rogue elephants like herself. All friends and relatives of other rich people are supported by them. ("I met a nice little couple at the Lambreths' the other day; they drove me home in their new Cadillac." "What? So the Lambreths are buying Cadillacs for their protégés now!") The Born Rich eye strips every other guest in a friend's house of talent, beauty, personal ability and independence and makes them at once the dependent of the other Rich—else why should they be there? What other bond is there between human beings? It entertained and soothed Elsie now to reflect on the industrious instruction Wharton had lavished on his wife and children, and how Nita had learned something unforeseen from it, and the daughters had allowed it to roll off their knobby little skulls like tropic rain, leaving the basic I.Q. undisturbed by any philosophy except I-AM-RICH, WE-ARE-RICH, YOU-ARE-NOT-RICH.

A strange moaning sound echoed suddenly through the upper hall. Aunt and niece exchanged a nod as Brucie pricked up his ears.

"Bluebell?" asked Elsie.

Gloria nodded with a beam of anticipation.

"She's locked in my bathroom, but she always smells Brucie, doesn't she? Will you let Brucie visit her again this summer, Aunt Elsie?"

"I doubt if your parents will allow it," said Elsie. "You know what always happens."

Aunt and niece were silent, smiling reminiscently, united for the moment in pleasant memories of the glorious days when Brucie visited Bluebell's kennels in the country. The great dogs had to be locked up separately but there was always the day when one or the other broke loose and freed the other and they streaked off to town, rejuvenated, like sailors on leave. They loped joyously down the highway, chasing anything that moved in the bushes, stripping clotheslines of the day's wash in back yards, scattering chickens, detouring traffic, and heading always for Mulligan's Bar at the edge of town where they had once been taken and been made much of by a highly temporary former gardener. Police, state troopers, veterinarians and sundry public officials were alerted by indignant or frightened citizens, the Hookley home was soon called and in a matter of hours the mother and son, tired but triumphant, were back in their reinforced kennels while Wharton furiously wrote checks making amends for lost laundry, broken bottles and glasses in Mulligans', lost chickens, rabbits and sundry properties.

"They have fun together, don't they, Aunt Elsie?" Gloria said dreamily. "Big dogs like to play the same as little ones, don't they, Aunt Elsie?"

"Of course, my dear," Elsie said, looking at her niece more kindly.

Wharton came into the room, cloaked in the manner he reserved for his sister, that of a preoccupied, harassed, weary man of Christian patience and forgiveness, resigned to any personal slurs or impositions, a man not too well and given to pressing a throbbing temple or overworked heart but never mind, it's really not your fault, it will be quite all right if you will not tax him too much with your idiotic demands. He kissed Elsie tenderly on the brim of her fedora, patted Brucie and Gloria twice each on the head and said solicitously, "I hope nothing's wrong, Elsie, to bring you away from your colorful little cocktail bars." Having established his impression of Elsie's slavish devotion to bars and the fact that her visit would have to be a matter of life and death to excuse it, he remained standing with an arm around Gloria's shoulders, smiling carefully at his sister.

"I came for the cane," Elsie said briskly, with the easy confidence of one who has the power of being a nuisance. "You've been so frightfully busy and couldn't get it to me."

The sound of guests arriving in the outer hall saved Wharton, and the next moment a loud wail from upstairs provided distraction. Brucie threw back his head and yowled back.

"My dear Elsie," Wharton exclaimed sharply, "you know how often I've asked you not to bring Brucie when Bluebell is here! There's always bound to be trouble!"

Elsie put a fond restraining hand on Brucie's collar.

"My dear Wharton," she replied easily. 'Bluebell is Brucie's mother after all. Can't you ever forgive or understand animals having family feelings even if human beings don't? Brucie and I will be off in a minute, as soon as you give me Uncle Carpenter's cane, there's a dear boy."

More guests were arriving and at last Nita's voice could be heard greeting them in the living room. Wharton threw out his hands in a gesture of polite exasperation.

"Really, Elsie, for someone who has never taken any proper pride in the family and has done her best—yes, I'm going to say it!—to belittle the name, this sudden sentimentality about Uncle Carpenter is too ridiculous. As I recall only too well you were too busy chasing after that phony Count of yours to even come to Uncle's deathbed and now—"

"Phony, Wharton?" Elsie interrupted ominously. "You refer to the Baron Humfert as *phony* in just what sense, may I inquire? I too can recall all too well the offensive way you used to roll out all the Humfert titles and connections to impress your friends. Surely you're not trying to imply his title is phony just because he's no longer in the Hookley family."

Hypertension, watch out for hypertension, Wharton strove to watch himself.

"You know perfectly well what I mean, Elsie, my dear," he

said with a steely smile. "He was phony in the sense that he was not a true royalist at all, insisting on giving up his title and joining the underground like any peasant. We've been over this too many times for you to pretend you didn't know he used the money we settled on him to promote all sorts of uprisings."

"I think it was the finest thing he ever did, Wharton," declared Elsie ringingly, who thought no such thing and had a private conviction that her ex-husband would have joined any church or any cause, even a good one, for a price.

Wharton controlled himself with difficulty, maintaining his patient smile which he directed now significantly at the drink in his sister's hand.

"Is that stout you're drinking, my dear?" he asked. "It's very dark for Scotch, isn't it?"

"I like it dark, old boy," Elsie shouted, "just the way your mother always liked it and all the red-blooded women in the family, right back to the original Hookley barmaid in Lancashire. I hope you've told little Gloria here all about that great-great-grandma."

"No, he didn't, Aunt Elsie," Gloria piped up, her beady little eyes leaping hopefully from father to aunt while she stroked Brucie's hide vigorously.

Wharton's emotions were now discoloring his nose just as she feared, and he raised a hand for truce, even though he would have found great relief in a real out-and-out no-holds barred fight with Elsie.

"May I ask you to lower your voice, Elsie?" He was mad enough now to be able to use his most dulcet tone, even though he knew it acted like a red flag to his sister. "We have guests here, nice people if you'll forgive my using such an old-fashioned expression, gentlemen and ladies, if you please, who wouldn't want to be subjected to the inside story of the Hookley barmaid even by her reincarnated descendant. Now, let us get to the point of this visit, Elsie, as quickly and quietly as possible."

Elsie swallowed her drink and put down the glass.

"Gloria, dear, I know you love Brucie but would you mind not pinching him? He still has his teeth, you know." She spoke very kindly and then composed herself in her chair leisurely before answering her brother. Lighting a fresh cigarette provided a further delay. "I have come to the conclusion, Wharton, that you must have lost Uncle Carpenter's cane and that indicates that perhaps a great many more of his treasures, which, as you know, are half mine, may be lost or misplaced. I'm not accusing you or Nita, of course, but you have had sole use of his house for all these years—"

"I grant you that, Elsie. I've always told you I can't understand why you've chosen to live in comparative squalor instead of in any of the family houses at your disposal," Wharton said impatiently. "If you choose to pass up your legal rights—"

"Don't be so sure of that," Elsie interrupted with a pleasant nod at little Gloria. "Your peculiar attitude in refusing to give me poor Uncle's cane, a simple little memento like that, has made me realize it's about time I should protect my other rights."

Wharton stiffened.

"And might one inquire just what it is you are proposing to do?" he asked with a glacial smile.

Elsie pulled her felt brim further over her right eye and then flung her head back sidewise, in a regal gesture revealing half an eye beamed ominously at her brother.

"I propose to look over the Narragansett property myself and select what items I wish in order to realize cash on them," she stated. "Moreover I shall then go to Boston and talk to Mother about reopening the Marlborough Street house. I see no reason why I should not spend a season or two in Boston after all my years in squalor as you call it."

Wharton whipped out his kerchief and pressed it to his lips to stifle a scream of rage.

"Elsie! You know Mother's condition!" he shouted. "You know she has a stroke every time she sees you!"

"Nothing major," corrected Elsie calmly. "May I ask you not to raise your voice unless you wish to excite Brucie? As for an only daughter wishing to visit her ailing mother, only a man without human feelings like yourself could regard it with such astonishment. How do I know if Cousin Beals is doing the right thing for her?"

"Cousin Beals is doing everything that can be done for a senile old lady in her eighties," Wharton said, breathing heavily but getting himself under control. "She won't recognize you, and if you attempt to move her from the Vendome you'll kill her."

"It's a chance you yourself have often taken, Wharton, when it suited your book," Elsie said, lowering her head to give him the benefit of the full crown of her hat.

He was outmaneuvered and he knew it. He had been braced years ago for Elsie's illogical brainstorms but today he was prepared only for the silly cane struggle. He dared make no objection to her demand for the Narragansett property, though after exclusive use of it for so long Nita had come to regard it as completely theirs and he knew she would scold him for surrendering anything in it. He was licked, but at least the battle was over temporarily, he did not have to explain the cane mystery, and perhaps she would change her mind about the monstrous Boston plan. At any rate she would go away.

"Why not call at my office and pick up the Narragansett keys?" he suggested, knowing his calm surrender took away part of her pleasure. "Naturally there is nothing I can do to keep you from upsetting Mother if that is your peculiar desire. And now forgive me if I join Nita's guests. I would ask you to meet them but you know how insupportable you always find our friends, my dear. A pity we will have so little time to see you what with this being Isabella's first season out."

"I'll run up and see Isabella now," said Elsie, but Wharton raised his hand hastily in protest.

"The poor girl has worn herself out already," he said. "She has taken to her bed and doesn't even join in our family meals."

"You drove her too hard," Elsie said firmly. "Absolutely barbaric to hound the poor child to land a husband the first year. The whole town's talking about it."

"I can trust you to keep me informed on the town talk," replied Wharton, smiling brilliantly.

Both rose, feeling a little regretful that they could not extend their always bracing quarrels, and though the room still seemed to reek of gunpowder they looked at each other with a kind of fond admiration. Gloria, who had been enjoying the battle, turned away in disappointment and petulantly gave Brucie a good pinch. With a howl Brucie bolted through the door, an echoing howl resounded from the upper floor, and the next moment Gladys could be heard screaming as she streaked, white-faced, down the stairs. The noise had electrified the quiet little group just assembled in the great living room though Nita had laughingly explained it was only the dogs.

"Bluebell and Brucie always have wild reunions," she was saying in her fetching Spanish lisp. "Sit down, everybody, they won't hurt anybody, they just want to get at each other. It is just a little incest like anybody else. Wharton will quiet them."

Fortunately Bluebell had not succeeded in breaking down the bathroom door because Brucie was trying to break it down from the other side. Elsie, with great presence of mind, took a tray of caviar, whipped sour cream and smoked salmon from Williams as he was bearing it to his mistress and took it upstairs as lure for Brucie. The strategy proved effective and the hors d'oeuvres dulled Brucie's filial passion to the point of allowing Elsie to lead him downstairs again with amiable docility. Wharton, mopping his brow wearily, paused at the door of the living room. His bout with Elsie and Brucie left him with little strength to face Nita's guests, for this was one of the newer cultural groups which always had him at a disadvantage anyway. Nita hurried out into the hall, sparkling and happy seeing that her sister-in-law was about to leave with no further disaster. She was looking even prettier than ever, hibiscus in her black hair and a huge cluster of scarlet taffeta flowers at her tiny waist and trailing down the white skirt to her hem. She embraced Elsie tenderly, reproaching her for not staying with them for dinner when there were such nice people here.

"Now, now, darling," Wharton interpolated with a warning look at his wife, "you know Elsie always finds our friends too respectable for her."

"Oh I don't know. I might have one highball," Elsie said just as he had feared, hooking Brucie's leash on to the newel post with dreadful finality.

As she strode into the living room Wharton transferred his irritation to his wife who should have known this would happen.

"I don't even know some of these people," he muttered crossly.

"Do be nice to Mrs. Grover," Nita whispered to him. "In blue over by the window."

But Wharton had stopped short as Nita went forward with Elsie. A curious puzzled expression came to his face and he did not seem to hear people greeting him, his eyes fixed on a swarthy young man standing by the mantelpiece, thumbs thrust nonchalantly in a fancy waistcoat, short legs spread apart and bowed as if astride a horse, a black lock falling over his low forehead, a crooked smile quivering on his lips.

"This is Elsie, Wharton's sister," Nita was saying, looking very tiny beside Elsie. "Elsie, this is Nigel di Angelo. He was in my art class and we're in the same dianetics group now."

"Pleasure," mumbled the young man.

Elsie blinked. Now really. No, it simply could not be.

"Nigel?" she repeated. "Did you say Nigh-jell?"

The young man returned her stare with a defiant grin.

"Nigel di Angelo," Nita said. "You've no idea how gifted he is."

Elsie nodded with a faint smile.

"I believe I'm familiar with his work," she said musingly. "I think Mrs. Jamieson in Gloucester has his very first oil painting."

The young man tugged at his lock as if it was a bell rope and evidently memory answered the summons.

"That's right," he said. "I remember. Four clams on a green plate. Let's see, this Mrs. Jamieson you mention—"

"Had a Buick," Elsie said, obliging him to meet her significant gaze.

The young man blew a smoke ring at her, unperturbed.

"I picked out an M.G. for her later," he said nonchalantly. "I like English cars."

"Of course," Elsie said. English cars! Nigel! "I wish you'd help me pick one out sometime."

It was fun to see the greedy little black eyes sparkle at that.

"Be glad to," he said. "Let me get in touch with you."

An overwhelming desire to laugh came over Elsie and to Wharton's great relief she snatched the drink he offered her and gulped it down.

"Must get Brucie home," she gasped, making for the door.

"I was sure you'd find it too dull for you," he replied. As she untied Brucie's leash from the newel post he glanced around the hall and coatroom, glad to see no sign of the young man's cane, but wondering why he had not carried it today and what this signified. Nita's new interests were increasingly curious, he thought wearily, and this odd young man's presence here was as baffling as his having the damnable cane and his own topcoat.

Elsie managed to get out on the street with Brucie tugging at his leash before the laughter came.

Niggy of all people! And calling himself Nigel, if you please. Memories of that fantastic summer on the Cape came back to Elsie, and since they were naughty memories a fond smile curled her lips. Niggy had been the Portugee of the year, and the summer ladies, always undermanned, had talked of nothing but Niggy. It was Niggy this and Niggy that. They fought over him in bars, they ruined his fishing by following him in their speedboats; they gave up husbands, jobs, reputations, for the Niggy chase. Elsie recalled her disgust at the hysteria, not having yet seen him, and picturing a slumbrous-eyed Latin of incredible beauty and delicious stupidity.

And then her prim, hymn-singing, Baptist Iola, the best cook on the eastern seaboard, had tried to kill herself for love of this hero. Outraged, as well as mightily inconvenienced, Elsie had taken it upon herself to confront the cad and bring him to account. She was astonished to find the heartbreaker one of the ugliest little monkeys she had ever laid eyes on. How did he get away with it? Evidently good girls are forewarned against wickedly handsome males but their guards are down before such disarming ugliness, so before they knew what was happening he had them all—the maids, the arty spinsters, the bored matrons. Elsie well remembered the stern scolding she had given him to leave poor Iola alone if he did not mean marriage, and to protect and console Iola she had sent her, virtue only slightly nicked, flying back to New York City to recover.

The day after she had straightened out Iola's problem, Elsie had strolled down to the docks to watch the fishing boats come in. Intellectual curiosity was what she termed it, as she stood watching the ugly little monkey scrabbling around his wretched little boat, always grinning, always legs sprawled apart astride an invisible beast—porpoise or billygoat, perhaps. He looked scared to death when he spotted Elsie standing there, tall and formidable in her oilskins.

"Want a fish?" he asked tentatively.

"Bring it to the house tonight," Elsie had commanded regally.

He was there, grinning, after dark, amused to be at the front door instead of the back, and just as he had impishly guessed, the fish was not mentioned.

He was impressed with the way this tall lady ordered him around, and he was respectfully awed by her superior gift for mischief on a grand scale. She didn't give a good damn, he marveled! He was glad to give up his fishing future to trot at her heels, cruising around at her expense, learning something all the time.

Elsie chuckled as she remembered how she had arrogantly forced the higher circles of the lower Cape to accept Niggy, and his own delight in her instructions. A real monkey he was, learning the art and music chatter as she fed it to him, learning the book talk, the patter about places. You get a higher type of girl that way, she had explained, and was rewarded by his grateful industry in bed.

He learned too much too fast, Elsie reflected. I'll never forget the day I told him he could have that secondhand motor bike for his birthday. "I want a Buick!" he kept yelling at me, absolutely furious. So I lost him and now it's an M.G. To tell the truth I did a lot better with him than I did with Jerry Dulaine. I wonder if I couldn't—

She was so absorbed in her sentimental meditations that Brucie had dragged her half a dozen blocks down the East River Drive before she remembered she hated this part of town and hailed a cruising cab.

PART THREE

. . . journey over the bridge . . .

•

He should have taken the subway, Dalzell Sloane reflected, watching the taximeter jump with what seemed to him a kind of demoniacal complacency to a new pair of ciphers led by a proud figure three. Still, he might never have found the place at this hour, for once they left the lights of Flushing the road was pitch-dark. It had started to drizzle, too, and the sharp wind coming up from the river reminded Dalzell of the winter he had spent in these very environs with a fearful bronchitis, one that lasted even after he was able to get back to Manhattan, and everyone said, "You have one of those Paris colds, it's those old buildings!" He squinted out the window, rubbed the mist off the glass as they passed a street lamp, and saw the hulk of an old mansion in a tangle of bushes and broken walls, the impressive stone steps and arched entrance still standing proudly, the side walls and chambers scattered about in odd heaps of bricks, tin cans, pipes, rubble. Nothing had been done to it in all these years, indicating a civic reverence for antiquity, Marius used to say, that Europeans don't credit us with having.

"A few yards more," Dalzell instructed the driver, who was twisting his head around to scrutinize his fare suspiciously and who now said, "Say, mister, we're getting into the wilderness here. Have a heart, I gotta get back to the other side of town. I hope you're not counting on my waiting on you if your party ain't here."

"No," said Dalzell, thinking how fantastic of him to count on the party being there. He hadn't been near the place for nearly eight years, and that time it had been Marius who had suddenly walked in the door in the middle of the winter night with a big load of Bohemian rye bread, a blackjack of salami and a bottle of genuine rotgut bourbon. It had been his own fourth week of hiding out, Dalzell recalled, and he was down to a very clever schedule of taking his one meal of a can of beans or chile with a solitary glass of hot wine at midnight so that the gnawing in the stomach was lulled to sleep until time for the next day's pot of coffee and carefully doled out pieces of bread. Marius was down and out then, too, but when two of them were in the same condition it seemed almost like success. Together they had the courage to tap Ben for a touch, and on the twenty-five dollars Ben managed to squeeze out of his wife—this one fortunately had a regular salary as a schoolteacher, owning a cottage in Maine to boot where Ben lived cozily, leaving the Queens dump to whatever hobo cared to fix it up—they roared with laughter and drank and worked and bragged and argued for a good two months, when Marius' dealer came through with the money to buy a suit, pair of shoes and a ticket to some midwestern university where he'd been offered a teaching job. Dalzell had gotten some money from Cynthia Earle—or was it from his brother-in-law?—to go to Arizona, and later, when he tried to find Marius, his only answer was a vituperative letter from Marius' mistress—the German one who produced all the children for him—saying that she was not going to have Marius ruined by his parasitical friends when his children needed care and even if she knew where he was she wouldn't tell his evil companions, particularly Dalzell Sloane or Ben Forrester who were notorious for their devilish attempts to force liquor, naked women and godlessness on a decent family man unable to make a living anyway, what with his obstinate devotion to painting.

"Old Trina," Dalzell murmured aloud, and thought she certainly must be dead, too, or she would have been stampeding around the town, unless she was still afraid of his legitimate wives popping up.

Three dollars and ninety cents, the driver said, stopping the car, and from his voice it was clear that nothing less than a dollar tip would avert the ugly business for which the neighborhood was noted. Dalzell got out in the rain, handing the driver the exact sum with the suitable tip, nothing to elicit a thank you but satisfactory enough to draw a "Some neighborhood you got here, brother, some neighborhood," and the headlights of the taxi swept over the can-strewn lot, past the fallen oak and uprooted dead bushes left from old hurricanes, and recognizing these old landmarks Dalzell would not have been surprised to see the same old goat carcass as of long years ago, but rats or buzzards must have disposed of that, certainly the local authorities could not have done so. The lights, as the taxi turned, covered the big house at the top of the slope, showed the broken windows, the chimney bricks tumbled on the porch roof, the drainpipe dangling uselessly from the eaves.

So the place was still there, Dalzell marveled, his heart beating fast as the vanishing tail lights of the taxi bumping down the road reminded him of past encounters in the night with unsavory derelicts. The wind from the water was brisk, the rain cut like hailstones and he pulled his muffler over his ears and chin, standing still for a moment until he could get his bearings, remembering the unexpected ditches and garbage pits underfoot. He sniffed the old smell of burnt or rotting wood with the whiff of river rats and the drowned, the moldy cemeteries of ancient burghers. "Paris!" Marius had cried out—was it in 1928?—like Columbus discovering America, this is the smell of Paris, and this will be our Paris!"

There were the soft, furtive sounds of footsteps somewhere

nearby, the low growl of night-prowling mongrels, whisperings, and a car without lights slithering by, but these were not the things Dalzell feared, these were not oblivion, disgrace, poverty, loneliness, these were the friendly, human sounds of footpads, burglars, gangsters, killers—these were not *Things*. *Things* were what lay in wait in his familiar places, certainly in that cozy room prepared for him in his sister's midwest home. He stumbled up the pathless bank of weeds and his feet found the remnants of the gravel path, they crunched on broken gin bottles, tripped over tangles of barbed wire and dead bushes where tree-toads yipped rhythmically as if it was their industry that produced the rain. He felt movement under his feet, toads, rats, lizards, snakes, per-haps, and they cheered him as if these materializations exorcised the intangibles. The garage doors that had dangled by a thread for years had finally fallen, he noted, and the roof, too, judging by the rain falling through. There used to be a door from the garage into what had once been used as an office, and if this was still open, a closet would lead to the middle portion of the mansion that had remained solid through decades of fires, bank-ruptcies, storms, lawsuits, and other scavengers. In the eighteen-nineties this had been Ben's grandfather's home and the seat of his small coal business; when the business went the place was left to neglect and quarrels among the heirs all over the country. As a child Ben remembered playing among the ruins, later on camping out for days there with amiable young women. The city had threatened for years to sell it for taxes but until it did this was the last retreat for the three friends. Evidently the city had still forgotten about it.

He groped his way along the muddy wall, found the step to the old office, and even the door, which pushed open. There was the fireplace wall, more broken glass underfoot, then the place for the closet door—yes, it was there, and Dalzell gave a little laugh of triumph! But it did not push open as of old, and he realized something must be shoved against it on the other side. Someone was there, then. Indeed he could smell coffee boiling. He tried to look out through the paneless french windows to see if some ray of light outside might guide him, and he saw a faint glitter as water dripped from the eaves onto some gleaming metal. He lit his cigarette lighter and peered out, saw that the narrow old porch was still there but the railing had fallen off, dragging down the dead ivy vines. This side of the building faced a dumping lot that stretched through swamps and sewers to the old wharf, and now Dalzell could see the lights on the bay winking throughout the mist, and after a full minute of incredulity he saw that the little pinpoints of glittering reflection he had observed were raindrops on the metal of an automobile parked by the porch. In the late twenties such a sight merely indicated bootleggers or highjackers making use of the place as a temporary hideout, and later it had meant some adventure-loving heiress involved in a temporary amour with Marius or Ben. Dalzell had no idea what it meant now, beyond the fact that somebody was obviously making use of the place. He heard sounds of furniture being moved on the other side of the closet, and quickly collecting his thoughts knocked vigorously on the door, rather than be caught as a snooper suddenly when it opened. The bureau or whatever it was on the other side was being pushed aside and the door opened suddenly. A man stood there and Dalzell put up his hand, shading his eyes from the glare of the flashlight on him. Behind the man a ship's lantern on a charred work bench flickered over a mottled plaster wall and the strips of oilcloth blocking the windows. The fumes of a rusty old oil heater blew out from the room and while Dalzell was blinking the other man reached out to seize his hands and pull him into the room.

"Sloane, you old son of a gun, how did you know I was here?"

"I knew in my bones, I swear! "

The next minute they were roaring with delighted laughter, slapping each other's shoulders, trying to look each other over in the dim light. Then for want of sensible words, bursting into laughter again, and shouting that it was just like it had always been, how one would arrive at the Cavendish not knowing anyone else in London and next day the other breezes in from Marseilles; and the time Marius was being thrown out of his studio on the rue Mazarine, the concierge shoving his easel out the door, when up the stairs comes Ben, pocket full of dollars, just arrived from New York, and two hours later in pops Dalzell, just landed from Rome, innocently looking for the vacancy advertised on the front door. Never needed to write each other, those three, let the years pass without a word between them, then they get a hunch and hit the same spot again—sometimes the three of them, sometimes two.

"I'm not surprised to find you here, not one bit," Dalzell said, looking around. "What does surprise me, though, is that the place hasn't fallen apart."

His eye went from the paint bucket sitting in the fireplace to catch the rain dripping down the chimney to the opened door in the corner hinting of snugger quarters further inside. At least they were still able to patch up a couple of rooms for shelter.

"Wait till you see how fine it is," Ben said, pushing the chest of drawers against the outer door once again. "Marius must have been here since I was last. An old ferry captain shacked up here, they tell me, till his wife found him and dragged him back to the village."

Ben had a bad cough and in spite of his boast that the old dump had never been cozier Dalzell noted that he was in several worn sweaters under the patched jaunty sport jacket. His beard was only a gray stubble, now, and he was bald as an owl, great frame shrunken, worn face with sunken eyes hinting at no cushioned past. He must have had it worse than I did after his spurt of luck, Dalzell thought; at least I didn't have wives, mistresses and children dragging at me along with all the other troubles. Ben was pushing him peremptorily through the corner door into a smaller room, fitted out very handsomely indeed, Dalzell saw with appropriate exclamations, for the walls were soundly weatherproofed with panels of old doors, their hinges neatly dovetailing; the floor's deficiencies were covered by layers of carpets and linoleum. A big four-poster bed, wood blocks taking the place of two missing legs, was in an alcove with a motorboat's tarpaulin draped over it, humorously ribboned as if it were the finest lace canopy. Other loose doors were latched together to make a stout screen around an oil cookstove and it was from this makeshift kitchen the smell of boiling coffee came. On a long oilcloth-covered table were two lanterns illuminating a stack of plates, jelly glasses and mugs of all sizes.

"Looks as if Marius himself might be here," Dalzell exclaimed, pulling out a packing box to sit upon.

"I've been sorting out all the junk and cleaning up," Ben said.

"Must have found traces of Marius," Dalzell said. "He was the one last here."

Ben flashed him a sharp questioning glance.

"He left a batch of work here, yes," he answered curtly.

"As soon as I heard they were having trouble locating his canvases I thought they might be here," Dalzell said. "How do they look—mildewed?"

Ben took the coffeepot off the burner and poured it into two cups.

"Most of it snug as a bug under the tarpaulin up in the dry

closet," he answered. "Mucked up here and there but easy enough to touch up. When Marius was alive and getting nowhere, being misunderstood, I thought he was a great painter. But do you know, now that he's dead and so damn well understood I don't find this stuff so wonderful. He must not have been satisfied with it himself," he added defensively, seeing Dalzell's reproachful look, "or he wouldn't have dumped it here, most of it half done. Why, remember that sketching trip we made on Staten Island around Richmond and Tottenville? He's got some half starts on those old taverns and street markets that aren't any better than mine—or yours."

"What are you going to do with them?" Dalzell asked, uncomfortable at the disparagement of their old friend.

"The fact is," Ben said deliberately, "I intend to finish them and touch up the others and tell the blasted dealers Marius left them with me in a trade."

He folded his arms and looked defiantly at Dalzell.

"Go ahead," he urged as Dalzell silently puffed a cigarette. "Tell me I'm taking too big a chance and so I'm a crook, go ahead and say it."

"I was only about to tell you I'd like to help out," Dalzell answered. "That's why I took a chance on finding you here. The two of us together could do better."

"Fine," said Ben. "Pardon my overestimating your scruples."

"A dealer who wouldn't give five bucks for my work bought three thinking they were Marius,'" Dalzell said dryly. "I could have gone on, but I decided if the only way I could get by was to pretend to be somebody else I'd better go back where I came from. Now that I've seen you I feel differently."

"It looks like this is the only way out for both of us," Ben said. "I've had nothing but bad breaks for the last couple of years and when I got the message from this guy Severgny I snatched at the chance to clear out. Left a note for Martha and one for my girl friend, then hopped in the jalopy and took off."

"I'm as good as gone myself," Dalzell said. "My trunk's in Grand Central Station. I've got about sixty bucks of my ticket money and that's all."

"You're a godsend," Ben said. "I've got about eight. We can hole in here for almost nothing. We'll work over the stuff and let it leak back little by little. I told Severgny I'm rounding up what canvases I know exist. First cash we get we can move back to Manhattan."

"Marius would think it was a big joke," Dalzell said.

"We're doing him a big favor," Ben declared. "He'd be glad artists were making a living off of him instead of dealers. All we want is enough to give ourselves a new start on our own, isn't it?"

"A fresh start, yes," murmured Dalzell.

He looked around him, filled with incredulous joy that he was here instead of on the train bound for surrender and death. His eyes took in the old rope-bound trunk at the foot of the bed with the same old *De Grasse* stickers on it, the black-painted initials M.M.M., the dangling broken lock. He got up and went to the middle partition, pushed the improvised paneling of doors gently till one of them tipped forward and showed the ladder of boards leading upstairs just as it used to be.

"This section upstairs is still fairly solid," Ben said, "if you're wondering how soon the place falls in on us."

They stood for a moment looking each other over, Ben reading the ups and downs of Dalzell's life in the familiar old topcoat, the souvenir of love in the expensive gaudy muffler, the hope and havoc in the still youthful eyes; Dalzell seeing the challenge still burning in Ben's defiant gaze in spite of the stooped shoulders.

"If we're not too old," Ben murmured, half to himself. "Good God, Sloane, we *are* old!"

Dalzell shrugged.

"We were always old part of the time, Ben," he answered. "Not Marius, of course."

"Never Marius," agreed Ben. He studied Dalzell fondly and silently for a moment, then banged on the table suddenly with his fist until the big lanterns shook. "But now we're beginning all over again, Sloane, my boy, we're young again!"

"Thanks to Marius." Dalzell lifted his glass, and then the memory of Okie's pompous words came to him and he began to laugh, sputtering out the story, all about his ticket money, Cynthia's new blond hair, the chase to ride on Marius' chariot, the five thousand dollars Okie would give for the brown-eyed boy looking at the sky—

"No!" gasped Ben. "The best thing you ever did and he thought Marius did it! That shows how easy it's going to be!"

They began to laugh again, tried to talk but couldn't stop laughing. It was wonderful to have fear and loneliness transformed at last into a great joke between friends.

How Marius would have loved the joke, Dalzell and Ben kept crying out to each other every day! Here was a merry vengeance for everything the world had made him and his two friends suffer, and they could almost hear his deep laughter in the echoes of their own. Camping out in the old Queens property, not an hour from Times Square, they were as safe from invasion as if they were cruising on some yacht in mid-ocean, while they were being sought all over New York. Someday, Dalzell was sure, when they confessed their secret, it wouldn't be funny. But for the first week of their reunion everything was funny.

"Tell me again how Okie claimed he could tell that boy's head of yours was an early Marius," Ben begged. "I can almost hear him."

"First he knew it was a Marius because Marius always got that sense of starry yearning in his children's eyes," Dalzell tried to imitate Okey's pompous lecture-hall voice, "and then there was the quality of the white paint that Marius was using at one time after he thought his old whites were fringing off yellow."

"Very good," approved Ben.

"It never struck him that we used each other's supplies, of course," Dalzell said, "and since I hadn't finished the picture I hadn't signed it. The museum scout who turned it up in that antique shop swore it was Marius and by the time Okie got through describing the special Marius touches to it I almost believed he *had* done it. I certainly would have gotten nowhere trying to prove it was mine."

"Supposing Trina shows up with whatever he left with her," speculated Ben. "She was the only dame shrewd enough to have saved anything. Remember the Sicilian model who ripped up everything in his studio and then set it on fire when she found him in bed with somebody else?"

"If Trina's anywhere in the world where she could have heard about his new reputation she would have been throwing her weight around long before this," Dalzell said. "And if Trina hadn't shoved Anna out of the picture we might look forward to Anna popping up to claim all rewards—that is if she's still alive."

"His women are all dead or they'd be brawling over his grave," Ben said.

It seemed to Dalzell that it was he and Ben who had died and gone to Heaven and not old Marius at all. That night at the Café Julien he had stepped out of his old life completely, and here in this ghost house he felt as if he was preparing for a new birth. To wake to the sound of birds, river tugs, or flapping of loose boards on the roof instead of to the creditor's knock was a kind of heaven. They had stocked up their shelf with groceries and bare necessities, and for Dalzell it was luxury to begin the day with coffee and bread that did not require his shaking out all his pockets for the pennies to buy it. Each day was opened fresh for painting instead of being snarled and gutted by arguments and futile plottings of the mind as to ways and means of getting through this day and tomorrow. For Dalzell this was a security he had not had in years, and for Ben it was the same at first. They worked over the Marius sketches and canvases diligently, planned how they were to be presented, and made notes for their own work. They took long walks along the water's edge, scarcely believing that across the river from the old abandoned ferry slip was New York itself, the city that had rejected them but would sooner or later receive them. At night they relaxed over Chianti or brandy, remembering the past, filling in the lost years. They wondered that they had done without each other so long, and even if they had only troubles to tell each other how much easier they could have borne them together!

Telling Ben about all the promised fellowships that had fallen through, the planned exhibitions that had dissolved at the last minute, the honors and commissions that had inexplicably melted before his grasp, down to the Hastings Harding misadventure, made the disappointments seem comical pranks of Fate. Dalzell dredged his memory to find more hilarious catastrophes to keep them laughing, and now it seemed to him that they were marvelous clowns who had cleverly planned their pratfalls for the grateful amusement of the world.

"Of course I had better luck than you or Marius at the outset." Ben was so cheered up by Dalzell's chronicles of frustration that he began to swell with the feeling of being a child of Fortune himself, only temporarily sidetracked. "Dough in the family, and I knew the right people. The only trouble was that whenever I was on the upgrade Martha would start being the old helpmate, shoving me down people's throats, till I'd get so embarrassed the deal would fall through."

"No!" Dalzell observed, as if he was not well aware of Martha Forrester's reputation as the aggressive agent-wife.

"Marius was the lucky bastard, though," Ben said. "I know, he had to die to make a living, but the fact was he never even tried to get anywhere. He didn't want to be anybody. All he wanted to do was paint what he liked when he liked, have the dames he liked, get as drunk as he liked. You and I tried to act decent once in a while, at least. But Marius just insulting the best people made them think he was a genuine genius. Remember when he threw Piermont Bradley out of his own house and next day Bradley buys one of his pictures?"

They roared with laughter as if their entire lives had been delightfully spiced with mischief instead of spiked with mistakes. They talked of their women, picturing themselves as pursued and bedeviled by avid females who fended off more desirable creatures. It was true that all three had left a trail of shrews, for they were the genial type that makes shrews of the gentlest women anyway in order to have their peccadillos condoned by society. Even if the ladies had been sweet and unreproachful these gentlemen preferred to sit in taverns boasting of angry viragos waiting for them with frying pans lifted, for it made their dawdling in bars and wenching more brave and manly. Dalzell, whose nature had been far from bold, was aglow with the honor of being classed with Ben and Marius.

"You were always pretty sly about your lovelife," Ben accused him now. "Smart, too, keeping from getting hooked."

"I don't call it smart always falling for somebody out of my reach," Dalzell said.

"Now there's the difference between us!" Ben exclaimed, relaxing in the luxury of candor under alcohol. "You just don't know how to go about it, that's all. I'm a perfectly frank person so let's be honest with each other—"

Dalzell had a momentary impulse to say he'd never seen bold Ben fetch down any birds that weren't already on the ground but he knew that the one thing a perfectly frank person cannot take is frankness, so he allowed Ben to continue unchallenged for a moment.

"You're just too soft, Sloane," said Ben. "When things get tough you just fold up, nary a whimper, as if you had no right to anything better. You're too damn modest, Sloane, and that's no good for an artist."

"Modest!" Dalzell shouted, suddenly outraged. "How can any man who has the gall to put a brush to pure white canvas be called modest?"

Startled by this outburst Ben retracted.

"Anyway you're not egotistical—" he started.

"I am enthusiastically egotistical," Dalzell interrupted hotly, "or else abysmally suicidal. I pride myself most on a kind of oafish stubbornness that gets me from one state to the other."

"All right, you're not modest," Ben conceded. "But you can't say you're a go-getter. Everytime a streak of luck aims at you you have a trick of deflecting it, as if you were some kind of lightning rod, so you end up with nothing but a hole in the ground. Now with me, whenever luck struck I managed to grab it by the horns and ride it till it threw me, at least. With the right breaks I could have been a first-rate businessman."

Dalzell was about to match this but decided it was neither the time nor place to boast to each other of their fine flair for business.

Ben was sick of women, so he claimed, and dismissed his wives and mistresses as such a pack of avaricious, ignorant harridans clamoring for gold, bed and babies that one might marvel how such a strong intelligent man ever fell afoul of them. But after a while a certain wistfulness crept into his voice and Dalzell suspected he was casting about for new chains as soon as he could find some.

"I married Martha because she was educated, a lady, understand, not like the arty bohemian tramps I'd been sleeping around with," Ben explained. "Nice New England family, a little money. How did I know she'd break with them on my account and turn artier than anybody? Finally I had to go on living with her because I was too broke to get away, and she could always get a teaching job. Then, out in Santa Fe, I got this girl Fitzy, a hospital nurse."

A fine, upstanding, simple country girl, Fitzy, Ben said, good drinker, good model—big hips and bosom with tiny waist on the Lachaise style. But the trouble was that after listening to him a few years she started talking art, too, just like your other women, all the stupider for finally knowing the names of all the things to be stupid about. Fitzy and Martha would have a beer and start fighting, not over Ben, but about art.

"All Martha knew about art was what she heard from me when we first married," Ben complained. "All Fitzy knew was what I'd come round to thinking later. I got it on both sides— Martha nagging at me for not being a good enough painter to earn a living, and Fitzy pitying me for being too good to make money. Then that Hoboken scene of mine that I gave Marius on a trade got printed in the papers as his and that did it."

"The girls recognized it as yours?" Dalzell asked.

"Hah!" snorted Ben. "That was the test I gave them. I was sore as the dickens at the mistake and wanted a little loyal sympathy. So, without saying anything, I showed the reproduction to Mart to see if she spotted the mistake. She just bawled me out for not being able to paint a good picture like that and make some money. I didn't say anything, just showed it to Fitzy next day and what does she do but tell me how lousy it is and why should this Marius be so famous when I could do a million times better. That finished me. When Okie started hunting me down I was ready to run out. I had a lot of Marius canvases. I threw them and my own into the old chevvy and started driving East. I'd made up a plan then what I was going to do."

"I didn't plan. It just happened in my case," Dalzell said. "When the demand began after his death I was broke and sold a couple of Marius sketches to a decorator. Then when the guy came in my studio and saw a little water color of mine he said, 'How much for that Marius?' I just swallowed hard, said 'A hundred bucks' and he took it. Next time it happened I got scared. I said to myself if the only way I can get by as an artist is by pretending to be somebody else then I might as well give up and go back where I came from, raise chickens, teach country school, be a grocery clerk. I was scared.

"I'm not a bit scared," Ben answered. "When the idea hit me I thought it came straight from old Marius himself, a kind of bequest. Whatever we get out of it you can be sure the dealers and chiselers will get a hundred times more, but at least it gets us out of the woods and ready for a new start on our own."

"I want to pay back Cynthia Earle, damn it," Dalzell confessed.

"Are you crazy?" Ben asked. "Nobody ever pays back Cynthia. Cynthia's had her money's worth, never fear."

Yes, he would pay back Cynthia, Dalzell thought, every last penny. She had never expected it and would be vexed to have no more excuse to patronize him. Once the debt had been removed between them he might be able to clean her out of his mind. For Cynthia had been his one great love. The flame had stayed alive for years, giving no warmth, merely illuminating the falseness and unworthiness of the beloved, cauterizing him against other surrenders. Knowing all about her, viewing her with cynical detachment as the enemy of everything he believed in, he had still felt slaked in her presence at the Julien the other evening. You lived and learned what a fool you'd been and wise, at last, continued to be a fool.

At twenty-six he had fallen in love at first meeting with Cynthia, braced though he was with warnings and devastating reports of her eccentricities. All the other artists knew her and none spoke well of her, but speak of her they did. She was rich and commanded you to dinner like a princess royal, but expected you to pay. She was a nymphomaniac and could easily have appeased her needs by taking you into her silken sheets, but oh no, her perverse pleasure was in climbing up your dark tenement steps and wallowing in straw ticking and dirty blankets. She could have introduced you into the soft lights of her world but it always ended with her invading yours. She promised fabulous favors but changed her mind at a minute's notice. She inveigled the best pictures out of you as gifts and in return was as likely as not to coyly send you her garter! In spite of all these legends, Dalzell had longed to meet her if only to be in on the joke. It had struck him, too, that her detractors were only too glad to hasten to her parties. Marius knew her, Ben knew her, and it seemed to Dalzell it would be an achievement just to be able to add his own personal criticisms to the common legend.

But he had capitulated at the first meeting. He was prepared for someone thoroughly pretentious, vain, and evil. Her affectations came as no surprise, but what enslaved him were certain mannerisms of which no one had told him and which seemed therefore for him alone. She was not ugly as they said, but handsome in a swarthy, gamy, medieval way. She was overtall but had a coy way of ducking her head to look up at you with a bashful little-girl smile, hands clasped behind her, all but twisting her apron strings, and she spoke in a tiny tinkling Betty Boop voice. To his surprise he found the contrast of her little-girl posturings with her full-bosomed woman's body enticing, and the sophisticated talk in the baby voice curiously piquant. He was convinced she had perfectly good brains but she seemed to make a deliberate effort to keep her conversation on an arch débutante level. Her pet artists, ungrateful by vocation, amused themselves by imitating her gestures and baby-talk. They drew private cartoons of her underlip pulled out in a bad-baby pout, wounded little raisin eyes blinking when someone had crossed her certainly full-grown will. They imitated her arch way of clapping a hand over her mouth after saying a catty or naughty phrase. She was notoriously avid for lovers, aggressive in pursuit of each new flame, primly genteel about other people's morals, but knowing all this, and seeing even more faults than had others, did not save Dalzell. He found her very vanity a virtue, and something magnificent in her never suspecting men's love for her was for anything but her own self. He had the good sense to speak of her half mockingly just as his friends did for he knew to admit anything else would be to expose himself to ridicule. He did not mind what they said about her for he exulted in a secret belief that he alone knew who and what was under this mask.

Perhaps she represented Art itself to him, and her kiss was admission ticket to the world of immortals. She represented the World, too, for he had never before met any millionaires with yachts, castles, ranches and noble kin all over the world. The stories Marius and Ben had told him of her promiscuity did not lessen his triumph when she leaped into his bed, for it seemed a proof that he was at last deemed a real artist. He saw her pretentiousness, her disloyalty and trickery, but when she finally banished him he was so stricken he could not paint for a year. Art had dismissed him. For years and years he had moments of wild thirst for her, and it was no relief to dismiss it as merely a sex need for she had been singularly unsatisfactory in that respect, eager and indefatigable though she was.

It is curious that some men lust all their lives for a woman who leaves them unsated. They are challenged by visions of unexplored delights ahead. Cynthia had obsessed him and always would, but whenever he spoke of her it was with the cool detachment of her other protégés. He had forgiven her other lovers but he had furiously resented her husbands. Why, he often asked himself? Everyone said she only married a man because she didn't want to sleep with him. There was a kind of flaunting of her basic snobbery in her marriages, for she wed only bankers or titles. All very well to amuse oneself with artists, but good heavens, one didn't marry them any more than one marries the grocery boy. Every time Cynthia was divorced Dalzell had a perfectly ridiculous feeling of victory, as if one more banker down the drain was proof of artist superiority. But he had never wished her unhappy, and when other flames of her past chuckled over her growing defeats in love, recounting gleefully some futile campaign, Dalzell felt only a twinge of sadness and reproach for the inconsiderate male who dared deny her. He couldn't be still in love, ever so slightly, with her, but it was odd how old jealousy remained long after the name and face of love have been forgotten. And here he was, bitterly jealous of dull old Okie who had never been either lover or husband and therefore had never been banished! Male vanity at its worst and most unreasonable, Dalzell told himself sternly: he wanted to be succeeded by superior men to make the object of his love more worthy and the reason for his years of desire more justifiable. He certainly didn't want to be in Okie's shoes.

He could still tingle with shame at his obtuseness to what had been transparent to everybody else at the time. Cynthia couldn't abide love in the abjectly adoring form he offered it. She must chase and snatch reluctant men from their wives or mistresses, flaunt her victories before her less powerful rivals, wear a new artist every day as Marius had once said of her. She must have been through with him, Dalzell forced himself to admit, the instant she found he had willingly given up all others for her. How blind and stupid he had been to her persistent efforts to banish him! He managed to smile a little ruefully when Ben reminded him of that moment of cruel revelation.

"Do you remember the time Cynthia summoned her whole stable to bring her that California painter, what's-his-name?" Ben asked one evening. They were drinking strong coffee laced with bourbon while they put finishing touches on two canvases Ben was going to take in to Severgny.

"The blond beast," Dalzell said, laughing as he had trained himself to do at this bitter recollection. He had had no idea at the time why she had been cross with him, picking quarrels on every occasion, accusing him of infidelities and other defections as an excuse to avoid him. Then came the day she had a pang of remorse and allowed him a quick kiss, saying, "Now stop being silly and run along. Of course I'm not angry any more, silly, I'm in a frightful rush to get out to Mother's and you keep bothering me. Now run back to the studio and stay there in case I phone you to come out to the country tomorrow."

He had stayed in the studio dutifully, happy at the reconciliation, not daring to stir outside for fear of missing the call. The next afternoon Ben and Marius had burst in, shouting with laughter. It was a wonderful joke on Cynthia, they said.

"You know that big Swede she's been chasing, the one that paints bridge builders all looking like himself," Ben said. "You know how she's been pestering all of us to bring him up every time she invites us, because he refused to come by himself. Well, she finally beat him down last fall and set him up in a fine studio in Carnegie Hall with the biggest allowance she ever gave any of us—"

"Five hundred a month he held out for," Marius chuckled.

Dalzell remembered still the sickness in his stomach and the terrible effort to laugh.

"The woman's crazy," Ben had gone on. "She got me in a corner at the Julien the day after she'd managed to make him and you could hear her all over the café bragging about Swedish technique. Her husband, the big stiff, sitting right there all the time, not even knowing what she was talking about."

"All the waiters did," Marius said.

Last fall, Dalzell had thought dumbly, this has been going on for months. So that's the quarrel she has with me.

"She always spent weekends in his studio," Ben went on, and both men shouted again with mirth at what was to come. "Then today they were having breakfast when a big blond girl walked in the room. Asked if Oley had made his proposition yet. Seems she and Oley had gotten married as soon as he started getting the allowance, but it wasn't going to be enough when they had the baby. So Cynthia would have to double it."

"Ha," Dalzell managed to say weakly. "And did she?"

"Cynthia give any money without priority rights?" exclaimed Ben. "Are you kidding? She scrambled out of the place as fast as she could, said she'd have to send the check, and then she marched in on Marius and me at the Julien, mad as hops. Outraged decency. Artist having the gall to marry somebody. Wife having the gall to have baby. Bad manners. Simply frightfully bad manners even for an artist and Swede. Well she blew off steam and we made her all the madder by laughing, then she started bawling and we put her in a cab and sent her home. Marius promised her a new doll, a young Polish sculptor."

"How about you, Dalzell?" Marius had demanded teasingly. "Or have you done your time?"

"I've done my time, thanks," Dalzell had said and he found he could laugh very convincingly. After all these years he could still feel inside his chest how much that laugh had hurt.

"That's right. We used to call him Oley, the blond beast," Ben mused now as they remembered. "He was a pretty fair painter till Cynthia got hold of him. Then he and his bride found out they could get along a lot better just selling his Swedish technique and nobody's ever heard of him since."

"Okie's her consolation prize, now," Dalzell said, casually.

In another week he and Ben were going to take an apartment in town. Gerda Cahill was going to Mexico again and would let them sublet her cold-water flat in the East Thirties. They would have money, this time, they rejoiced. Even so Dalzell dreaded New York and fervently wished he could stay hidden in the safe kindness of the rat-ridden old mansion forever.

The greatest favor Marius, the man, had ever done for Marius, the artist, was to die at exactly the right moment. Many men have triumphantly exploited a minuscule talent through life only to ruin themselves by muffing their deaths. Missing their proper exit cues they have hung around like dreary guests at a party, repeating themselves until it is made clear to all how little they ever had to say.

But Marius, bless his heart, had made death his great achievement. He had fumbled gloriously every chance in his lifetime, wantonly antagonized all who could help him, been stubbornly loyal to every outcast or dungheap that enhanced his mischievous nuisance value, stood valiantly in his own light, and then, by wonderfully timing his death, removed the enemy shadow, Marius the man, allowing Marius the artist to step into clear blaze of sun. He had been away from New York so long that journalists and art dealers had stopped smarting from his bawdy insults, husbands had lost the zeal to avenge their honor, harassed old friends once goaded into barricading their doors, beds and cellars when the big man stormed into town with all his bar friends, ladies and lads of the town, with the inevitable disasters ending in hospitals or jails, could breathe easier. Everyone was filled with the Christian pleasure of giving full praise to a man without requiring police protection from him. How considerate of him to die far away in Mexico so no one had to pass the hat for the funeral. How brilliant to choose a month barren of news fit

for publication so that editors had to pad their pages with broad-
sides against the plague of surrealism and existentialism, the sure
causes of juvenile delinquency, homosexuality and suicides! The
coincidence of a news magazine reprinting Marius' painting of a
Hoboken Square the very day Hoboken's oldest building burned
down gave feature writers and Sunday critics a nice lead into
large thoughts on our American art heritage, the neglect of our
native great men, and fulsome appreciation of the true-blue
American realism that had been wickedly pushed aside by deca-
dent foreign influences. Checking up on the artist they found
that he had just been killed in Mexico. Marius' death was a
national catastrophe, they said, and there were suggestions that
he be disinterred and given a burial in Arlington. To the very
end, they wrote, Marius was an *American* in every sense of the
word, regardless of his foreign studies and travels.

It happened that for some reason—perhaps an extraordinarily
dry decade creatively—there had sprung up from American
university campuses, European pastures for grazing scholars,
and other academic preserves a ravening horde of cultural
necrophiles. Wars, planetary bombings, invasion by Martians
and such fears of premature destruction were driving these op-
portunists into snatching chargers of long-proven might on
which to steal quick rides to glory. Intelligent enough to concede
their personal inability to get anywhere without a celebrated
mount, and too lazy to take the bellboy's job for which they were
fitted, they rushed to stake claims on the great names of the past,
boasted with a genuine sense of a deed accomplished that they
were about to write a book on Dostoyevsky, Tolstoy, El Greco,
or Bach, and dined out with dignity on nifties panned from
the richly plummed legends. Some, who had the chance, stalked
aging celebrities who might do them the favor of dropping dead
and providing juicy material for future memoirs. Sometimes a

subject who had been buying Scotch and steaks for a permanent entourage of doting biographers had the bad taste to live on and on, getting politically or socially *de trop* and allowing the biographers' rightful property, you might say, to deliberately deteriorate in value, making the once prized treasury of private journals and personal anecdote plain rubbish. Worse yet, sometimes the subject lived beyond his bad period and betrayed old followers, who had dropped him, by dying in a blaze of new glory, with new riders in at the death.

Marius, at the last, had proved his worthiness and generosity. Anyone who had once hoped to ride on his name and been brutally thrown, or else had given up, could claim whatever valuable connection he chose, for his long absence equalized all their claims. They could vie with each other without loss of face in anecdotes about long ago days when they, and they alone, had stood by the man against his enemies, heard his secrets, indeed provided him with advice and inspiration.

"You working on Marius?" they cried in astonishment to each other. "I'm working on Marius, too, but of course you knew him at a different period."

The increasing number of those who claimed to have been the dearest friends of the artist was causing a great deal of bewilderment to an honest young man named Alfred Briggs, who knew nothing of either Marius or art till his discharge from the Navy four months before when the news magazine *City Life* hired him to give a "fresh angle" to the traditional neglected-artist story. Briggs had stayed on in the Navy as a warrant officer after World War I for he was having a good time and was not at all sure of where he would fit into civilian life. The decision to be a writer had come over him while the fleet was cruising in the Caribbean, pausing in St. Thomas, Montego Bay, Port-au-Prince and other playlands where he met fellow Americans and British ladies and gentlemen lounging around swimming pools with tall frosted drinks in their hands, being fanned by tireless natives.

"Who are these people?" Briggs had asked, and on being told that these fortunate folk were all writers—novelists, playwrights, journalists—Briggs cried out, "Then that's the life for me! How do I begin?"

With the flattering letters these genial professionals obligingly wrote for someone they felt could never be a rival, Briggs had no trouble in landing the magazine job when he got out of the service. His honest statement that he had never written anything but clear, straightforward reports for superior officers charmed the *City Life* editor. Briggs had hoped for assignments in the field of sports but the editor felt that literary training and education were required for that, whereas art was a department where inexperience and ignorance would not be noticed.

Pleased as he was to have a regular job which would permit him to return soon to the Islands with some dream girl and live like a lord, and flattered as he was at the outspoken envy of freelance writers, Briggs found himself utterly bewildered by the first assignment. It had seemed like a breeze, at first. Nothing to do but call up or go see a list the editor gave him of people who would tell him about Marius, and all he needed to do was to write it down like a day's report. But no sooner had one person given him a tasty anecdote about Marius than the next person would deny it.

"I can't imagine where you heard such a ridiculous story," one man said on being asked to verify a legend. "From Dennis Orphen? Why, Marius hardly knew the man. I myself knew Marius for years, here and in Paris, and never even heard him mention Dennis Orphen. He must have gotten it from the Barrows and they weren't even there when it happened."

"Then something *did* happen?" Briggs would press patiently.

"If you mean did Marius take a love seat from a house on Gramercy Park and set it up outside the Park gates for some Bowery pals of his to have a bottle party," said the old friend who was named Ainslie Flagg, "something like that did happen in Prohibition days but it wasn't Gramercy Park, it was Gracie Square and he didn't steal it, he simply took it and why should people spread these nasty stories about him just because he drank too much?"

"This happened when he was drunk?" Briggs asked.

"Now don't go making this a big drunken story about Marius," protested Flagg angrily. "He's dead and no reason to drag his name through the dust. Of course he was drunk. When he wasn't painting he was always drunk. Anyhow the next day after this thing happened he got all dressed up and went back and made a beautiful apology, I give him credit for that."

"Then it did happen or he wouldn't have apologized?" craftily pursued Briggs.

"As I say it was a handsome apology only it seems he picked a different house by mistake this time and they thought he was crazy and had him thrown out so he landed up in jail."

"Jail?" Briggs pricked up his ears. "Marius was in jail once?"

"He was always in jail for something or other, how do you think he got those jail pictures?" the loyal friend shouted. "And let me tell you I'm absolutely disgusted with people pretending to be Marius' friends and then rushing to tell you newspapers every scandal about his private life. I refuse to be part of such a dirty deal, I don't care how big your magazine is."

Baffled, Briggs called on the next friend on his list, explained his purpose, said he had just talked to Ainslie Flagg about Marius.

"Ainslie Flagg?" the latter repeated, knitting his brows. "I don't think he was ever a close friend of Marius. Oh yes, he's the rich old crock who tried to have Marius arrested once. I've forgotten what it was about, something about stealing his sofa or some silly thing. No use trying to get any information about Marius from *him*."

Small wonder what young Briggs was beginning to think those hibiscus-wreathed fortunates lolling around tropic swimming pools had betrayed him into a most maddening profession. Marius was supposed to be worth four installments, yet how could you get anywhere forever crossing out? And what could you do when so many times he had barely mentioned the object of his call before the old friend would brush him off hastily with, "Frankly we'd done all we ever could for Marius and if his wife told you to ask us for funeral expenses we'll just have to refuse." This sort of answer stopped after the publicity started really rolling, for after that everyone was eager to talk. Briggs knew nothing of the art world so he had to copy down very carefully every phrase he heard and every explanation of Marius' technique, and when the next person contradicted this he crossed it all out with equal care.

"At this rate," he meditated gloomily, "I'll have crossed out all four installments before I've got even one written."

Then came the lucky day he visited the museum which had managed to flush four large Marius canvases out of its basement and was displaying them with proper pomp in its best room, one on each wall. It was the first time he'd ever been in a museum and he was more concerned with how to behave in a big mausoleum than he was with the pictures themselves. Huge clumps of marble in the main hall studded with a recognizable human eye or navel made him glad that at least he was not required as yet to have any dealings with this form of art. He marveled that the young visitors trudging through could take so calm a view of these amazing creations, which he feared would bring on a fit if he looked twice at them. He was relieved to reach the Marius room without mishap and to be soothed by the simple, almost photographic pictures. But again he saw how backward he was in his reactions, for here the jaded young visitors suddenly came to life, gazing in incredulous amazement at the walls, seemingly paralyzed by their emotions. He listened to their excited cries, their bewildered comments.

"Look, it's a real room!" one said. "Out the window you can see the bridge so it must be around Fifty-Ninth Street. Look, there's that corner store where my uncle works. Imagine a fellow painting a real room like that in a real place. What do you know?"

"This one called 'Burlesque,' " another young man said. "A naked girl right there. I read somewhere that they used to have these shows right on the stage with live naked girls."

"It looks real, all right," granted another. "It couldn't have been here though. Must have been Paris or Chicago or someplace like that."

Mr. Briggs got out his notebook and jotted down these comments and then sought out the young lady in charge of public relations. She seemed very cross since it was almost six, closing time, and Mr. Briggs had already asked questions of a sort to indicate he would do the cause of art no good whatever he might report.

"All right, all right," she said irritably. "This new generation was brought up on Picasso and Modigliani and they think women have three heads and two guitars. Naturally when they see Marius' paintings they are all bowled over—like people were when moving pictures started talking out loud."

"But look, Essie, this dining-room table has real spaghetti on it!" someone was exclaiming.

"Next they'll be trying to dig it out," muttered the museum girl to Briggs. "You should have been here when we showed Harnett and some early American primitives. We caught a screwball trying to get a revolver out of one painting to shoot himself right here."

"What imagination to have a real little girl with a real doll in a real rocking chair!" another voice exclaimed in awe. "You can almost see it rocking."

"They always go for that one," said the girl, as she turned to leave. "Real chair, real girl. He called it 'Little Ellenora' first, then changed the title to 'The Live Dolls,' I suppose because the doll looks as if it was being squeezed to death. The way it's pushing its arms out as if it was trying to get away."

Studying this picture Briggs felt an almost irresistible temptation to push the child's pale brown hair out of her eyes. He looked around hastily, hoping no one had guessed his naïve reaction but the visitors had marched on and there was only the girl in blue seated on a marble bench in front of the portrait. He looked at her twice, puzzled, for there was something exceedingly familiar about her. She looked away from him and rather self-consciously lifted her hand to push back a stray bang. A light burst on him.

"Why, you're the Live Doll!" he exclaimed. "I know you are."

He was pointing a forefinger at her as accusingly as if he'd caught her red-handed digging out one of Harnett's convincing props.

"Can't I be allowed to look at myself?" the girl inquired. "How did you guess?"

It must have been the gesture of pushing back the hair, Briggs reflected, then he wasn't sure. The girl was now in her twenties but she had the kind of special little-girl face that some women carry from the childhood to the grave. He realized he had been conscious of her sitting there as motionless as the picture, ever since he had come in the hall, and there was the same waiting expectancy in both. He was pleasurably amazed at his new perception. He had actually recognized someone from a painting by detecting an identical inner quality in picture and model. Briggs was thrilled, prouder of his own newborn perception than of the painter's. His eyes behind the thick, black-rimmed spectacles sparkled.

"I didn't know I was that smart," he exclaimed excitedly to her. "It's funny what goes on in the back of your head without your knowing it, I saw you sitting here when I came in, then after I look around you're in the same position and—well, all of a sudden it just hit me. Something said, that's the girl. Isn't it uncanny?"

The girl looked at him with amusement.

"It is, except that after you go to galleries a lot you usually can tell that the person sitting very still in front of a portrait is either the artist's wife, the owner, or the original," she said, and hastened to add kindly. "No, really, it was clever of you and I'm sure no one else ever could have guessed."

"Of course you're wearing the same shade of blue as the child," Briggs acknowledged, peering closer at the portrait, "and the nose is the same, a special kind of little tilt to it—well, maybe it wasn't so smart of me. Only you see I'm writing a piece about Marius and this is the first time I've gotten hopped up about him. Look. When he paints a room like that one over there you just know the kind of person who lives there. You almost know who's going to come in the door. It's real, but there's something else he gets—like past and future. A sort of magic key."

The girl smiled a little.

"Maybe that's it," she admitted. "Let's see if you can tell the past and future in my picture here. What's my key?"

Briggs looked from her to the picture and back again.

"Believing, that's what it is," he said, and scratched his head. "I mean like always believing in Santa Claus, always believing everything is on the up and up, just—well, just believing."

He was a little disconcerted at her burst of laughter.

"You're absolutely wonderful," she said. "I really believed he was going to change me into a fairy princess, just as he promised. I went on believing it ever since, without ever seeing him again. But I'm glad I got over that."

"Oh no you didn't," Briggs said positively. "You've still got it."

She looked at him, quite startled and he could see he had impressed her.

"Oh dear, I suppose it's true," she said ruefully. "So that's my jinx."

"Don't lose it," Briggs begged her. "Nobody has that look any more. It's beautiful."

He felt unreasonably pleased with himself and intolerably brilliant. He could see by her face that she thought he was brilliant, too, and he wished he could go on shining for her, but she had risen and was pulling on her gloves.

"Good luck with your piece," she said.

"Oh please!" Briggs cried out impulsively. "I mean I was hoping you wouldn't leave me. I don't know much about Marius or art and you clear things up so wonderfully. Couldn't you give me about half an hour—have a drink with me, say?"

Ellenora hesitated.

"It would help so much," he said. "You really must."

"There's a place next door," Ellenora said. She sighed, thinking that here was another example of how easy it was for anybody to bully her. Once you had your feelings hurt badly you couldn't bear to hurt even a passing stranger.

"Let's go to that place Marius used to like," Briggs urged eagerly, hurrying her through the hall. "That will give me the atmosphere don't you see? What's its name—the Café Julien?"

"The Café Julien," Ellenora murmured uneasily. "It's pretty far downtown and I have to be back uptown."

"So do I. I'll bring you back," Briggs promised. "I have to cover a shindig in honor of Marius that a Mrs. Earle is giving so I won't keep you long."

A taxi slid conveniently to the curb beside them and Briggs had firmly helped her in before she could change her mind. He was so pleased with his conquest that it was several blocks before he remembered he was supposed to pick up Janie at six to take her to the Earle party. He could telephone and explain he was detained by an unexpected assignment but he'd have to think up something good. Janie wasn't the believing type herself.

"Maybe you have some objections to the Café Julien," said Briggs tentatively. "Maybe you know some other place he hung out."

"Objections to the Julien? Oh no, of course not," Ellenora feebly assured him.

Unless you counted it as an objection that she had tried to avoid the place ever since she had fled from it that last night with Ricky. Unless it was an objection that she looked upon it as an old friend who had betrayed her. Unless you called it an objection that the mere mention of the café reminded her that here she had all but offered herself to a man who was already planning to leave her. Idiotic to go on blaming places and people for your own weaknesses, she scolded herself. Besides she was cured now. At least, almost. No one could ever know, of course, that once or twice a year in the middle of a gay party she gave in to an insane, uncontrollable impulse to telephone the Café Julien and ask for Mr. Prescott. Luckily he was never there.

"Marius always went to the Julien when he was in town," Ellenora informed the young man. "When I was a student we saved our money to go there just to spot the older artists."

"They told me to hang around there for the right Marius atmosphere," Briggs said. "I tried to get something from the waiters about the good old days. I asked them did Lillian Russell eat there? Was it true that Scott Fitzgerald and David Belasco and T. S. Eliot and Wendell Willkie used to go there? This one waiter just looks at the other one and shrugs his shoulders. 'Why not?' he says. 'Everybody's gotta eat somewhere, maybe here, I don't care.' "

"That's the way the Julien is," Ellenora laughed.

Briggs shook his head.

"I give up," he said. "I can't picture Marius there, a guy supposed to be full of life. A bleak old dump like that."

"It's the way it strikes you at first," Ellenora said defensively. "Then you find yourself coming back again and again, not quite knowing why. The tables look bare, the lights cold and bright, so the people and the talk become the only furnishings, and you come back to find just that."

"I guess you love the place," Briggs said.

Ellenora was silent, thinking that everything had begun and ended in the Julien. Each time she had started up with Rick she had entered the café an eager, confident woman, and after each breakup she had left it with her pride and love shattered. It did no good to tell herself she had expected something that had never been promised, for then she felt ashamed for assuming he was as caught as she. After each parting she had deliberately set to work to build up a completely new Ellenora. She changed her work, her friends, her neighborhood, her coiffeur, and above all tried to stamp out the damaging softness—yes, the young man was right—the "believing" in her nature. She taught herself to lunch with Maidie Rennels and not wait for mention of the beloved name, not even to ask, because she was foolishly afraid all of his friends must have guessed her infatuation—perhaps he had boasted of it himself so she must babble of serious beaux for them to report back to Rick. This did not work out with good old Maidie who said one day, "I can't understand why none of your love affairs seem to work out, unless you deliberately pick out men you know you'll have to drop. You just don't *want* them to come out right. Like Rick Prescott, always getting mixed up with girls he really doesn't care about, so he can have a free hand."

A form of fidelity for both of them, Ellenora had thought, perilously consoled, and the next instant scolded herself for lapsing into believing again. That was the way it went. As soon as she thought she was safe and strong, happily absorbed in her work either illustrating books or designing screens for a decorating firm, a crazy wire or card would come from across the world, and work, new friends, new self collapsed again. She should have had an affair with him that very first night, she argued sometimes, and then it would be all over and forgotten. It angered her that because she had denied herself to the one man she wanted she should be unable to go through an affair with any other man, as if he had demanded this vow of her. She strove so eagerly to find worthy superiority in her men friends that they could not get out of love with her and Ellenora fervently wished she could surrender to them instead of brewing her fantasy of true love out of nothing.

"Here we are!" Briggs's voice reminded her, and there they were at the Julien.

It was easier than she had imagined. She found she could walk right in the café door without a qualm. She didn't quite dare look around to see if anyone was there she knew, and she hastily ducked past Philippe's tables to the opposite corner in the back. Except for the new waiter at their table the place hadn't changed a bit, there were the same marble tables, the same pleasantly subdued excitement, but evidently she was cured, for her heart didn't turn over nor did she swoon with memories. She was glad this young man had obliged her to make the test.

"I understand pernod is the thing to drink here," he said, beaming. "I've never tried it."

It had turned out that they were almost old friends, having nearly met several times before. Ellenora's decorative screens had been given a nice plug by the household editor of *City Life* whom

Briggs sometimes met in the office elevator; Ellenora had illustrated a children's book written in a hangover whimsy mood by one of Briggs's Caribbean author chums. At the *City Life* annual ball Ellenora and escort had left early because it was too rowdy at almost the exact moment when Briggs and Janie had left because it was too stuffy. These remarkable coincidences, patched up in the taxi coming down, served as a splendid background for a warm future friendship.

Briggs was feeling enormously pleased with himself. He looked around hoping someone he knew might be witnessing his arrival in this well-known spot with a beautiful new girl. He wouldn't have cared if even Janie could see him, because she was too smart a girl not to realize that any man would stand her up for a girl like Ellenora Carsdale. At least he thought so. Janie was a good scout, with brains, but the only reason he kept on with her was a lurking fear that he might not be able to do any better. Janie knew quite well where she stood, and as a matter of fact had gotten sore about it last night at the ball. She had made some crack about feeling pretty seedy in her Budget Shop navy blue taffeta in the midst of all the diamond-studded glamour girls with bare sun-tanned midriffs, but instead of telling her she looked fine Briggs had made the mistake of saying, "What do you care how you look, you've got more brains than any of them. Let's dance."

They had started quarreling about everything else, then, as they rumbaed, and Janie had said she was sick and tired of either getting all dressed up or else all undressed and then having him tell her what a fine brain she had. He tried to say that he wouldn't be offended if she complimented him on his brains and she had countered, grimly, "You would if I did it in bed."

After that they gave up trying to have a good time and went to Costello's bar on Third Avenue where he built up a big thing about brains being the only thing in the whole world he cared about next to money and porterhouse steak. Janie was calming down after a few bourbons on the rocks and after his admitting a dozen times that he had always been a dumbbell with a psychopathic worship for a real intellect, but then he overshot himself by leaning across the table to burble, "Why Janie, honest-to-God, if I had your brains you'd never see me again."

Janie's chief from United Nations came up just as she was about to blaze away and that was all that saved him then, but Briggs knew he had a great deal of fixing to do, and tonight he had planned orchids, poetry, diamond fizzes (she had some gin and he would bring some cheap champagne) and lots of talk about her good legs and her dandy complexion and her big old blue eyes.

Yet here he was with another girl a good fifty blocks from where he was supposed to be meeting Janie, and instead of talking about brains he was getting himself all worked up about art. In a minute or two he would telephone Janie, but first he would order drinks and sit for a while just in case this dear girl he had captured might elude him. She had started to tell him how Marius came to paint her, and of course he could not interrupt, so presently he forgot about Janie.

"It was one of those crazy mix-ups Marius was always getting into," Ellenora said, "the sort of thing that drove his friends to distraction. It was that hot, hazy summer my father died and Mrs. Addington, the one that's always the Empress Theodosia on a float for the benefit of blind miners, had given Mother a cottage on her estate near Pawling."

"Two pernods," Briggs murmured to the waiter.

"I'll have a martini," Ellenora said firmly, determined to have no holdovers from the Prescott days. "It was the summer of '36, the summer that Marius' friends had sold Mrs. Addington the idea of his doing a portrait of her. She always had the artist do two portraits of her, one in formal dress for her husband and one thrashing around on a chaise lounge with nothing on for the artist. Like the Duchess of Alba. She'd never seen any of Marius' painting but she'd heard he was a big he-man and that was enough."

"Was he married then? " Briggs asked, taking out his pencil.

"Oh please don't take this down," Ellenora implored hastily, and Briggs obediently put away his pencil. "Mrs. Addington wouldn't stand for any wives. She thought they were sort of obscene and an artist should be dedicated when she herself wasn't around. Anyway it was such a terrible summer that I've never forgotten it, because everything went wrong."

"How?" Briggs's pencil made another appearance and was frowned away.

"First Mother was annoyed because she said we were just to be a cover-up for Mrs. Addington's fun," Ellenora said, "Then Marius kept being delayed and wild wires kept coming from all the taverns along Route 9. After days and days he finally rolled up the driveway, drunk, in an ambulance he'd hired. Mrs. Addington had been told what an amusing character he was so for quite a while she thought it was all great fun. Then he started pouncing on the maids when he was supposed to be pouncing on Mrs. Addington. Then he chased Mother and then he insisted on painting me instead of Mrs. Addington. He was such a great big bear Mother was scared stiff of him, but I adored him. Mrs. Addington got jealous of Mother and told us we must leave, and Marius was so outraged he disappeared. Mrs. Addington sent detectives after him—"

"Poor guy," Briggs murmured. "He was always being hunted down."

"—and she tried to make him give back the two thousand advance. But his other creditors already had it so she took the portrait of me and gave it to the village thrift shop just for spite."

"Are there two *d*'s in Addington?" Briggs asked.

"Oh you couldn't print that," Ellenora cried out.

"No, I suppose not," Briggs sighed.

"You see now she claims to have discovered him," Ellenora said.

"It's tough on a guy being dead so anybody can say what they like about him and he can't deny it," Briggs said. "Everybody seems to have been his best friend but they were perfectly content not to know where he was for the last five or ten years. Nobody would give him a show but now all the dealers are claiming him. Take that picture of you, worth thousands now, and all Marius got out of it was a few weeks' board and a new passel of enemies. What I can't understand is how a man could go through life always breaking up his luck, making the same mistakes over and over."

"It's hard to understand," Ellenora agreed, adding half under her breath, "but awfully easy to do."

"Say, this stuff is good," Briggs exclaimed, holding up his glass. "Let's come here again sometime and spend more time on it."

He was nice, Ellenora admitted. Something about his glowing black eyes behind the horn-rimmed spectacles reminded her of Ricky—but as soon as this thought occurred she was disgusted with herself for always comparing, then always discarding some promising future for a past that was little more than a dream.

"I suppose you intend to write other things besides your magazine work," she said flatteringly. "Novels? Plays?"

Briggs's writing ambitions had gone no further than the desire to put off getting fired as long as possible, but Ellenora's words excited his fancy, and before he knew it he heard himself popping away with his thoughts on literature as if he was himself one of the anointed he had admired around the tropic beaches. He did not deny that his brain was teeming with ideas for novels though he managed to hint that his impossibly high literary standards prevented him from actually putting anything on paper. Or to be honest he wasn't really so full of basic plots for novels, it was just that he knew how he was going to go about writing them once the mood did strike him.

"The trouble with most novels is that they don't tell you the things you want to know about people," he said with an involuntary glance over his shoulder to make sure that Janie's sardonic little face was not behind him. "Now the minute I meet a man the first thing I want to know is how much money he makes, what rent he pays, whether his folks have money, whether his wife has a salary or income and if there's any inheritances expected. That's what makes him the way he is. I notice how he tips and what he considers the most important item on his budget. No matter what else we talk about it's a person's financial status that forms his point of view about everything else. I propose to X-ray each character's bankbook as soon as they enter so everything falls into place. Is that so crazy?"

Ellenora resisted a desire to burst out laughing. It wasn't so crazy. She had been vaguely wondering if he knew how expensive the Café Julien was and if he had enough money with him, or if he would appeal to her when the check came, and she would have to fork over her last five dollars.

"I think a character's situation should be clear," she said.

"For instance, here's what has me baffled about Marius," Briggs plunged ahead, earnestly. "They say he was always poor, but how poor is poor? He came to the café here and drank pernod which was eighty-five cents a glass. He went back and forth to Europe and even in those days a round trip would be three hundred dollars or more, wouldn't it? Some of his paintings brought him eight or nine hundred dollars, subtracting a third for his dealer, and he never sold more than one or two a year, but yet he always had women and wives and children and nobody starved to death. He often ate here in the Julien, they say, and even if he only had a beer and one egg it would be over a dollar. But he always had eggs Benedict. How?"

"People loaned him money and he never remembered it," Ellenora answered and went on patiently. "You see you can't figure out some people by arithmetic when they never lived by it themselves."

"Look how much other people are making out of him now, for instance," Briggs went on, tossing down his pernod as if it was a slug of rye and signaling the waiter for another. "Figure out that I've already made sixteen hundred dollars out of him without doing anything, more than he usually made in a year. Figure out the space rates of all the fellows writing articles on him, figure out the price dealers are getting for his stuff, the art teachers sucking out an extra course by lectures on him. Tot up the whole lot against his own figures— Supposing I were to write a novel about him," said Briggs. "First, here's what I do."

He had produced a pencil and an envelope and was busily jotting down figures between gulps of his drink. Ellenora knew it was time for her to go, but her mind had become its usual blank as soon as statistics were mentioned and besides the waiter had brought two pernods again, regardless of her request for a martini. How clever of him, she reflected dreamily, and how pleasant it was to be here again, remembering only the gay moments and that ever present atmosphere of something delightful about to happen.

The café was crowded today, and people kept strolling around looking for tables or else pausing to speak warmly to acquaintances whose appeal was in having empty chairs at their tables. These fortunate table holders, possibly avoided as bores at any other time, could avenge themselves on old snubbers now by withholding invitations to sit; in answer to the eager "May I join you?" they could look coldly toward the door saying "I'm expecting friends" and perhaps win much better company. For his part the visitor never asked to sit unless he had first looked carefully around to see if finer friends were available. Everyone smiled a little, knowing the game so well and experiencing mischievous triumph in out-maneuvering the other.

Out of the corner of her eye Ellenora caught glimpses of Philippe toddling back and forth holding his tray aloft, steering himself by it as if it was an outboard motor that propelled his plump little body. She saw other familiar outposts pegged out across the room, the Van-Dyked old gourmet with the velvet-draped Brunhilde wife laying into an angry-looking lobster about to be drowned in Piper-Heidsieck. She saw the Wall Street Sunday painter who came to the Julien to watch the professional artists, and she saw the pompous painter and his sculptor wife who were Sunday brokers, keeping themselves artistically fit by playing the stock market. There was the savage drama critic, fearless in print but cravenly dragging his palsied old mother wherever he went as bomb shelter from exploding playwrights and actors. There was the voracious columnist who could wedge into any famous group by using his frightened little pregnant wife and golden-haired child to run resistance and was now, Ellenora saw, pushing them masterfully upon the unsuspecting university professor who leered wolfishly across the table at his latest pet pupil. Ellenora thought she detected reproachful glances at her own escort as if she had no right to be in this café without Ricky, and indeed she felt guilty herself. She noted with amusement that Briggs, who had vouchsafed such great curiosity about the Julien, was oblivious to everything but his literary mathematics. He passed his notes across for her inspection.

"Why don't you have your characters all checked by National Credit Association?" she inquired. "Make out a chart, like those maps in historical novels, with their credit ratings."

"Now you're kidding," Briggs accused, disappointed that she should be as skeptical as Janie. A furtive glance at the clock told him it was nearly seven and if he got hold of Janie by phone to head her off he might beguile his new friend into giving up her own date for him. He motioned for more drinks and excused himself to telephone. Ellenora picked up the paper, mystified by Briggs's figures, but then two and two making four had always baffled her. He was a nice young man, though, and she mustn't laugh at him.

"Eggs Benedict, $1.85," she saw had been crossed out, the idea of adding up Marius' own expenses abandoned in favor of assembling the sums other people were making out of him. As these figures were approximations and made no sense to her anyway she took his pencil and wrote down "Legitimate Expenses, Taxi $1.40, E. Carsdale Art School Tuition, $2000, Pen for keeping score $1.95—Pernods at $.85 each—" giggling.

"Here she is," she heard a voice beside her say and saw Philippe beaming at her. The next moment a mirage of Rick Prescott slipped into Briggs's seat opposite her and speechless, she picked up her glass as he picked up Briggs's. It couldn't be. But it was.

"I see you ordered for me," he said, offering her a cigarette. "Nice of you to hold a table, too."

At first her heart had done a complete flip at the incredible joy of seeing him and she looked around for Philippe to thank him for his demonstration of Julien magic but he had darted back to his own table, his stout little body quivering with suppressed chuckles. Then Rick's triumphant grin filled her with pent-up indignation that he should assume she would always be there, ready to play whatever little games he chose until he tired of it. This time she would show him that she was no more a sitting duck for him. This time there would be no pretty talk around the main issues. If she couldn't keep her nature from always believing, then perhaps she could make it find something worth believing. Don't you dare let him get you again, she commanded herself fiercely, clenching her fist tightly. Don't you dare.

"I'll never forgive you," she burst out.

The smile left Rick's face. She couldn't bear it.

"It's the third time you've forgotten my birthday," she heard herself say. "I'd hoped for a bicycle."

The smile returned.

"Did you really think I'd forgotten that?" Rick asked reproachfully. He put down his glass and came around the table to take her hand. "Just come out and see what's standing out at the hitching post right now a-stomping away."

He reached for her other hand and she let him pull her to her feet.

"With a handlebar basket for my skates?" she asked, letting him lead her unresisting out the café door.

"My skates, too," he said and held open the outer door for her. A cold blast of air came in. "Now shut your eyes and count up to a little drink around the corner."

Here we go again, she sighed inwardly, not even aware that she'd left her scarf in the café and was firmly clutching her drink, as if it was a sure protection against folly. He kept a tight grasp on her arm, hurrying her across the Square, neither of them speaking, and turning the corner to his own apartment.

"But this isn't a bar," she said.

"Of course it isn't, my poor fallen creature," he said unlocking the door. "I have brought you here to reform you if it is not too late. Now, sister, step inside the mission and tell me what brought you to this pass."

It was the little games again, Ellenora thought desperately, when there was so little time; she needed the truth not a paper hat and this time she wouldn't play.

"It was a soldier that set me off, sir," she said as he closed the door behind her. "His regiment was to sail at dawn—ah well, the old, old story."

PART FOUR

. . . we'll all go up to Cynthia's house . . .

There was no sign of Janie either at her home, Costello's bar, her girl friend's apartment, or in the U. N. lounge, Briggs's telephoning informed him. He was hardly more than an hour and a half late for their date and it made him sore that she should have gone out instead of waiting around like a lady for him to stand her up. He went back in the café and sat down, surmising from Ellenora's absence that she had gone to the powder room, since her gloves and scarf were still on the chair. He sipped his drink thoughtfully, trying to figure out what his approach should be to get her to go to the Earle party with him, and serve Miss Janie right, too.

"You're the new art man on *City Life,* aren't you?" Briggs looked up to find himself surrounded by half a dozen men, all seeming at first glance to be the same Hollywood country squire type in different sizes. The largest, a middle-aged, beefy fellow in black beret, black flannel shirt and plaid jacket, was thrusting out his hand. "Saw you in the lobby as we came in. We've met before at the magazine. I'm Hoff Bemans."

"Oh yes," Briggs said, meaning oh no for he could not recall the man at all and he saw they were ready to pounce on his table.

"I spoke to you about appearing on my Fine Arts discussion panel on TV, you remember," Mr. Bemans said, firmly pulling out a chair. "Sit down, fellows. This is Briggs. These fellows were on my show just now. Ever been on TV?"

"No," said Briggs, extending a feeble paw to the bevy of panelists looming behind him, all looking alarmingly like spacemen with their black-rimmed goggles, berets, vast woolly mufflers and briefcases bulging with interplanetary secrets. Desperately he held up Ellenora's scarf to ward them away from his table. "I'm sorry, I'm with a friend—"

"The lady left with Mr. Prescott," the waiter interrupted.

Briggs looked at him blankly.

"I think she left note," the waiter said, pointing to the notepaper, which Briggs picked up, saw his own figures and then Ellenora's postscript about taxi and pernods which he couldn't understand unless somehow she had taken offense at his commercialism.

"They went across the Square," volunteered one of the panelists.

That would be his luck, Briggs thought irritably, and it was all Janie's fault, too. Assuming an air of knowing just what had happened, he paid the check offered by the waiter. He remembered Hoff Bemans very clearly all of a sudden as a fellow reputed to be always joining you with his friends and leaving you with his check.

"I understand you're doing the piece on Marius," Mr. Bemans said. "We talked about him today on the show, and of course you know I've done a biography of him, coming out next month. I knew him in the twenties, of course, and that's one reason I wanted to talk to you. These chaps are all avant-garde critics, teachers, editors. What say to a beer, fellows?"

"I can't," Briggs shouted, for the place was getting crowded and nothing less than a shout would deflect Bemans' chosen course. "If my friend should come back—"

"They won't be back," insisted the youngest space-man, leering.

It was the sort of thing that was always happening in Briggs's life and he wished he had hung on to Janie, now, just to have on hand in such emergencies.

"Anyway I'm due at a party at Mrs. Earle's," he said more feebly.

At this Bemans let out a cry of joy.

"Cynthia? Is Cynthia Earle having a party? Why, that's great. Come on, boys, we'll all go up to Cynthia's house, one of my oldest friends. What a gal!"

"Now wait a minute," Briggs protested, for he hated people who said gal even when it stood for gallon as was too often the case. "It isn't a party, really, it's a sort of symposium of what old friends of Marius remember about him, speeches, letters—"

"Fine! We're all vitally interested in Marius," Bemans said jovially, propelling Briggs outward through the café door while the others looked wistfully back at a passing tray of highballs. "Besides I get these guys to come on my program for no dough and the least I can do is try to give them a little treat afterwards. Always plenty of liquor at Cynthia's. Haven't seen her for years. Great old girl. Understand she's going to do her life story, is that right?"

Briggs muttered that rumors had reached him that the lady had a terrific book she wanted to write and was looking for a writer, a big name, who would write it for her and leave his big name off of it. Outside the Julien he tried to shake off Bemans' grasp with every intention of plunging back into the café or someplace far from these resolute companions closing around him.

"Scotty's station wagon will take us right there," Bemans said. "Pile in, boys, I'm going to show you one of the splendors of the Prohibition Era."

"I hope there's something to eat there, I'm starved," said the young man, evidently Scotty since he was unlocking the station wagon.

"Don't worry about that, and all free, too," Bemans cried.

"Look here," Briggs said firmly, backing away from the car. "I haven't any business taking all you people. I don't even know the woman. I'm only going because the magazine sent me. How can I show up with all of you bastards?"

"I guess you don't know Cynthia," Bemans said with a patronizing grin, cuddling his pipe in mittened hands. "I guarantee you Cynthia will be okay. Maybe a little beat up by this time, and that reminds me, fellows, a word of warning. Everybody stick together when it's time to go. Lady wolf got no chance if six little pigs stick together."

Everyone guffawed, piling into the car. Six little pigs and the lady wolf, by George, that was good, and they drove away quite overcome with laughter, as if their manly honor was constantly besieged by lecherous heiresses. Anecdotes to that effect were soon forthcoming, chief raconteur being Hoff Bemans who was oldest and loudest of the group and more richly stocked. Briggs could not listen, his mind on the ticklish question of whether bringing six extra guests to a dinner excused your being two hours late.

He recalled that Hoff Bemans was an old rear avant-gardist with an inky finger in all the arts, who had set himself up as general handyman for the twenties, always ready to patch up a red carpet for Millay, Fitzgerald, Hemingway or Anderson, and a fast man with the blurb for anything from pottery exhibits to the new jazz. Years ago he had "returned to the soil" with the compliments of the Farm Home Finance Company, and was now quite the country squire, sprouting children regularly from his sturdy little peasant spouse from Minetta Lane, and singing the joys of the simple life in every bar on Third Avenue. He had a real old red barn on his place richly stocked with enough old *transitions* and his wife's old still lifes to keep their goat happy for years, a quaint old-time kitchen complete with Erector sets, broken toys, diapers, and old Chianti empties, and a fine old piny library stacked with Sears, Roebuck catalogues and bound volumes of *The Swan,* to which he contributed his quarterly tithe of three thousand words illuminating aesthetics. A good life and a good hearty man, Bemans, and it was too bad Briggs detested him so bitterly.

"Hey, where are you going?" he yelled suddenly as the car nipped past another red light up Fifth Avenue. "We've passed it."

"The Earle house is on Sixty-Fourth," Hoff said. "I know."

"But she said the old Beaux Arts studio building," Briggs said.

"What?" roared Hoff. "Turn back to Fortieth, Scotty, it's at her studio!"

The brakes were jammed so hard Hoff's pipe fell out.

"Damn, I wouldn't have come if I'd known that," he shouted angrily, replacing his pipe in his mouth. "Why couldn't she throw her party in the big house the way she used to? Confound these rich girls turning arty so nobody can have any fun any more. There ought to be a law. Studio, my foot! There won't be any place to sit down and we'll have her idea of a simple artist's supper and God knows what to drink."

Briggs felt that since none of them were invited they had small right to set up such a wail of righteous indignation, and as the car turned and sped downward again he had to listen to a chorus of complaints about the hardships wrought on friends by rich girls turning bohemian. They invited you to dinner and you went thinking for once you'd get a bang-up dinner in a fine house but what did you find? The hostess in an ominous-looking apron, the cook and butler dismissed, a great pot of the same old home spaghetti on a burner, a scraggly looking salad and a few knobs of cheese! Just what you would have had every day only you'd have had it better and more of it. It was the limit the way these rich girls tried to be simple and make everybody else suffer for it. But then most of the upper middle class was playing pioneer now, giving the money they saved by having no maid or nurse to their and their children's psychoanalysts, feeling some kind of grisly virtue in banging around Bendix and babies with their own sensitive untrained hands.

"The funny part is that it's now the artists and real poor have turned stuffy," said the driver, who Briggs fervently wished would pay more attention to the red lights than to his cosmic reflections. Back and front seats chimed in agreement to the observation and upbraided the new bohemia for wallowing in its middle-class euphoria of neo-modern furnishings, TV rooms, Sunday roasts, blended Scotch, and Howdy Doody. How different it was in the twenties, Hoff Bemans said, in the days of Marius and Dalzell Sloane and Ben Forrester! He assured his panel companions that in those days he would not have repaid their work with such miserable hospitality as he was now offering them, ah no. Rich people had fine homes in those days, places you were proud to take your friends, great parties it was a pleasure to crash.

Hoff was still puffing somberly at his pipe and shaking his head over the defections of the arty rich when they reached the Beaux Arts. They were soon rising upward in the trembling old elevator. Briggs was so unhappy wondering how to explain his associates that Bemans finally sensed it and patted him soothingly on the back.

"Nobody gets mad when unexpected men come to a party, son," he said kindly. "Especially Cynthia. It's just when you take women that it ain't etiquette."

This statement turned out to be absolutely true, for Cynthia's face on seeing her door full of strange men was a pleasure to see. She was glad to meet Mr. Briggs and as for his being late, why the spaghetti had hardly started to burn yet, though the anchovy sauce had been somewhat charred during the last round of martinis, but come in, come in, and how wonderful of him to bring so many marvelous people! It turned out that like many other well-known characters of the twenties whose friendship Hoff Bemans claimed, she did not recall ever having met him, but was happy to have him none the less. Briggs expected Hoff to be disconcerted by this, but he swaggered into the room, an arm about her shoulder confidently, reminding her of that night at Webster Hall, and those jolly treks up to the Cotton Club in Harlem, the time she came to a New Playwrights party on Cherry Lane with Otto Kahn and Horace Liveright, the time she came to a Salons of America auction ball at Schleffel Hall over on Third Avenue with Marius and got mixed up and bid against herself up to three hundred dollars for a Ben Forrester watercolor tagged at ten bucks. What good times those were and since they sounded perfectly plausible and Cynthia enjoyed hearing about them, Briggs began feeling proud of himself for having brought these fine fellows.

Cynthia was wearing her Tyrolean peasant outfit and everyone was telling her she didn't look a day over ten, a perfect child in fact. This flattery incited Cynthia to skip about and look up roguishly at the boys, all but fluttering her fan, and then look modestly downward with a clatter of eyelids, weighted as they were with layers of iridescent eye shadow and heavily beaded false eyelashes. Her golden hair was flowing freely tonight, bound Alice-in-Wonderland style with a gold ribbon. The large bare studio contained a great square couch on which several men and two women clustered; a dozen ladies in décolletage befitting a coronation party and men in dinner jackets stood in little groups holding warm martinis or New York State sherry. A large lumpy snowy-haired gentleman named Okie welcomed Briggs to the big work table on which the goblets and refreshments were laid out. Through the window could be seen the twinkling lights of Bryant Park and the red glow above Forty-Second Street.

"I understand you're doing the *City* piece on Marius," Okie said affably to Briggs, handing him a cocktail. "I'm doing a book and everybody here is interested in the man, critics, dealers, all friends of his. As a matter of fact this is sort of a belated wake for him, that's why you'll be interested, everybody telling what they remember of Marius and over there we have a tape recorder taking everything down. I think it's a great idea, a thing like this; as a matter of fact I suggested it to Cynthia. A get-together of all his oldest and dearest friends. Dalzell Sloane, the guy over there with the beard, and Ben Forrester, the big fellow with the funny-looking mustache, they just showed up."

"There are folks here that have been dead for twenty years," a wizened pixie-faced, brillo-haired little woman named Lorna Leahy said, giving Briggs a sunny smile. "I'll introduce you."

If he could hold out long enough and keep from getting tight, Briggs told himself, he should get enough material right here to finish up his piece without putting himself out in the least, so it was really a good thing that Janie and Ellenora had failed him after all.

"It's just like old times, by Jove!" Okie kept crying out, and the phrase summoned fatuous simpers to some faces; nostrils quivered sniffing out fragrant old memories, while to others the words brought an expression of helpless alarm as if some pesky visitor routed with desperate strategy had suddenly popped back in for his hat.

"Old times!" Ben Forrester muttered in Dalzell's ear. "Let's hope *they're* not here again."

Dalzell made no answer. He was the one who had dreaded most coming back into the world, yet here he was happier than he'd been in years. Maybe it was soft, as Ben would surely say, to have present pleasure obliterate years of defeat but the truth was he felt young again, he had money in his pocket, work ahead of him, and Cynthia was being nice to him. Odd, that seeing through her made him feel the more bound to her, as if her transparency was precious and must be protected. He wanted to have her go on thinking she was powerful, beautiful, and that all men were in love with her, because that was the Cynthia around which his youth had revolved; for the capricious vanity that was Cynthia's to be shattered meant the end of hope for him, too.

"What a kick Marius would get out of this!" exclaimed Okie. "I'd give a million dollars to see him walk in right now."

"The trick would be worth it," Ben said sardonically.

"Wouldn't you love to hear him when he saw the prices Severgny is charging for him?" Cynthia cried out.

"She'd ask us to throw him out for using such language," Ben whispered to Dalzell.

Dalzell felt his face reddening and he moved away from Ben imperceptibly. He didn't feel he understood the Ben he had come to know of late. The apparent ease with which dealers accepted their counterfeit Mariuses canceled Dalzell's sense of guilt but inflamed Ben's bitterness all the more. He was jealous of Marius now, as if the dead man had personally defeated him, and he would almost have been glad if some expert had spotted his own characteristic bold brush in a Marius half-finished watercolor. But none of these fine experts could even tell the break in the originals where Marius, drunk or bored with the picture, had had Trina finish the job, a vandalism obvious to any friend who knew how Marius worked or, for that matter, knew how Trina handled a broom. Dalzell feared that Ben's smoldering rage would boil over into a damaging public outburst and confession, and was glad to have Ben's attention caught by a pretty young art student sitting at his feet.

"Now that everybody's finished eating, let's get down to the business of the evening," Okie shouted, banging on the table with a tray for quiet. "What we're here for, as you know, is to put on record a permanent tribute to Marius. You all know of the books, exhibitions, articles about him and all that, but a few of us hit on the idea of making a Long Playing record of spontaneous reminiscences of Marius, tributes to him as man and as artist, the sort of thing that pops in your head just sitting around like this. We have Mrs. Earle's tape recorder and it will catch everything that's said. Later we cut it down to record size. I'm glad Hoff Bemans came in tonight, as he is familiar with radio discussions and has volunteered to act as sort of m.c. And what a thrill we'll have afterwards with the playback!"

What a perfectly marvelous way of paying tribute to Marius, people exclaimed, filling their glasses to pave the way for spontaneity. Older guests smiled as they recalled old Marius anecdotes they would narrate, and they could not help feeling relieved at the chance to shine in reflected spotlight, so to say, knowing that if the master himself had been present they would not have a chance to open their mouths.

Sitting on the floor beside Lorna Leahy in front of the table on which the recording machine rested young Briggs took out his ball-point pen and a notebook, and being moderately drunk adjusted his reading glasses for better hearing. He squinted intently at the notes he had already jotted down during the evening, and Lorna looked over his shoulder at them with considerable curiosity.

Cynthia's Studio Rent, $150 per mo.

Ford Foundation Grant to Busby—for study of Marius and his Group, $3000.

Guggenheim Fellowship to H. Bemans for Marius Biog., $2000.

Rockefeller Grant (Marsfield)—Color research from Delacroix to Marius, $4000, 2 yrs. travel.

Fulbright award (Canfield) Marius Contribution to American Thinking, $4000.

Last known Marius studio rent, $20. (Possessions seized for $80 unpaid.)

"All set, Charlie!" Okie motioned to the young man delegated to attend to the machine, and Hoff Bemans stepped over the groups clustered on the floor to take a position behind Lorna. But at this moment there was a commotion at the door. Cynthia and Severgny bustled out to the hall and came back leading the new arrival, a faded little woman in the most widowy of widow's weeds.

"Good heavens, it's Anna!" Lorna whispered. "Where did they dig her up? Look, she must have brought in some new pictures."

For Severgny was reverently placing on the table against the wall two small canvases, arranging the table lamps to illuminate the pictures while gasps of appropriate awe swept over the room. Dalzell Sloane felt Ben Forrester's hand suddenly grip his shoulder and their eyes met in something like fear.

"Just a minute while I introduce Anna Marius." Cynthia held the arrival by the arm. "Everybody knows how hard Mr. Severgny and Okie and I have been working all these months to locate traces of Marius' work and his family. We've been scouting all over the globe and now it turns out that Anna, here, Marius' first—ah—wife—was living right over on Staten Island, not even knowing Marius was dead till she read someplace about this meeting tonight. She says she never comes to Manhattan but made the trip just to bring us two of the canvases she still had and here they are and here she is."

There was a round of polite applause and a ripple of excited murmurings as the lady sat down modestly in a corner.

"Was she legally married to him?" Briggs whispered to Lorna Leahy.

"Certainly not," Lorna muttered contemptuously. "Her real

name is Anna Segal and she was always hanging around some artist or writer in Provincetown or Woodstock or Bleecker Street, wearing them down by sitting on their stairs till they'd come home and let her in, then running errands for them or begging for them. Marius was always throwing her out but she'd creep back and when he'd wake up with a hangover there she'd be with a pick-me-up and ice bag ready, showing what a good wife she'd make. She was always losing her guys by marriage or death and now I suppose all she has left is Marius' bones. She's a ghoul, that's all."

The young man Okie had invited from CBS to operate the recording machine was testing sounds around the room and in a sudden blast of monkey chatter a cracked voice shouted, *"She's a ghoul, that's all,"* and then the apparatus was subdued.

"Okay, here we go," Hoff Bemans shouted. "Everybody just act natural and forget the record."

. . . the playback . . .

"We should have had a professional regulate the whole thing," complained Cynthia much later, sitting on the floor wedged between Briggs's legs now that the young man had gotten a seat on the couch. He felt trapped and embarrassed by Cynthia's lively squirmings but she seemed quite unconscious of any undue intimacy, throwing a bare, braceleted arm over his knee or resting her sharp chin in deep thought on his thigh. "A professional could have picked up the right sounds instead of having all those whispers come bellowing out."

"It was a mistake letting Hoff Bemans try to m.c. it because he's a chronic air hog," said the young man from CBS. "He has to push in front of everybody the minute he sees a mike or a camera."

"He thinks he was chums with everybody just because he saw them eating in the same restaurant he did," Ben Forrester said. "Twenty years later he thinks he was at the same table, maybe in the same bed."

"I'll run it through again and cut out Hoff," said the young man.

Dalzell Sloane, Ben, Briggs, Okie and Severgny had stayed on for one more run-through although it was after two o'clock. Cynthia had graciously brought out her best brandy when the other guests left, for the evening had proved most unnerving for all. In the first playback private whispers and asides had come booming out drowning proper speeches and a dozen quarrels had started because someone waiting to hear his own pretty speech heard instead malicious remarks about himself made at the same time. Almost everyone had stalked out either wounded to the quick or eager to report the fiasco. Careful editing must be done by a chosen few, Cynthia had declared, and here they were, ears critically cocked, eyes on the Martel bottle. The machine whirred and voices came crackling out like popcorn.

"She's a ghoul—"

"Everybody knew Lorna meant Anna when that came out," Cynthia giggled, digging her elbow into a vulnerable angle of Briggs's lap. "But Anna just gave that patient martyr smile. Did you ever see so many yards of black on anyone in your life? That poor, rusty, humble Christian black! So like Anna! Go ahead, Charlie, skip the preliminaries."

The whirring began again.

"All the newspapers said was that it was an accident on a lonely mountain road in the Mexican interior. Nobody knows who was with him."

"You can bet it was some dame. We ought to demand an investigation and find who collected the accident insurance."

"For heaven's sake don't start anything like an investigation or we'll all be in trouble just for having known him. Don't you know they've already got him pegged as a Commy just because he was always painting ragged children and slums and beggars and women slaving away?"

"Are they crazy? Marius never sympathized with Commies or workers either. Those ragged kids were his own, the slums were where he lived, the poor women were slaving to support him. He'd a damn sight rather have painted Lord Fauntleroys and well-fed beauties but he had to use what he had."

"Nonsense, Marius just liked to paint muscles and big bottoms and hungry eyes and, boy, that's what he always had around! Don't you remember how he used to say 'Kinetics! there's your secret for you, the hell with the rest.'"

"Wonder how he managed to lose Trina and that brood. Didn't she write everybody a few years back trying to locate him?"

"Trina was a she-devil. She must have eaten her young and passed on or she'd be hounding Marius still, dead or alive. Still she was always faithful, a monstrous faithful woman, he used to say."

"That's just what drove him crazy, the sheer monotony of her faithfulness. If she'd only be faithful once in a while, he always complained, but oh no it was all the time, and it got him down."

"At least he never needed to say that about Anna—"

"Good heavens," gasped Cynthia in alarm, "I had no idea the damn machine was picking me up when I said that!"

"—One martini and she'd start tearing her clothes off. Then she joined Alcoholics Anonymous, remember, because she had waked up one morning in bed with the janitor. From all I heard she enjoyed him all the more sober."

"Wait a minute, please," begged Cynthia. "Did Anna hear that on the last playback? I think it's awful for people to listen to what other people say about them and make everybody so uncomfortable."

"She was busy telling what an inspiration she was to Marius about that time," Dalzell reassured her.

"Not that I wasn't telling the truth," Cynthia went on. "Why, I heard she stayed with A.A. right through the Twelve Steps, but one night she got tight and got into a surrealist art class by mistake next door to the Twelve Steps Club and it scared her into beginning all over in A.A. They call the art school the Thirteenth Step now, isn't that a scream?"

"I must say I thought Anna's statements were very interesting," Severgny said.

"Skip to that part, Charlie," said Cynthia, throwing her head back into Briggs's stomach so that he emitted a startled *woop*. "I missed part of that."

"'Anna,' he used to say to me, 'if it wasn't for you I'd be dead of

starvation, Anna my sweets' and I'd always say, 'Now, ducky, you know your old friends don't mean to let you down this way, and if some of those that could help haven't come through, never writing and never putting anything your way, you mustn't be too hard on them, they're just thoughtless and maybe they'd rather have their bellies full of steak and Scotch whiskey at the St. Regis and ride around in their powder-blue Cadillacs than keep a genius from starving.' And Marius would be so darling he'd say, 'Anna, old girl, I can't say I blame them at that.' Why, if Marius would be here right now he wouldn't blame any of you for letting him down, he'd act as if all of you had always been his best friends.'"

"Listen here, Anna, don't look at me because I never let Marius down and if you're referring to the time you popped in on me and said Marius had to have eight dollars for his gas bill the reason I didn't give it to you was that I knew Marius was living with Trina up in Peekskill anyway—"

"Oh, Ben, I'm not accusing anyone, and as for Marius leaving me for Trina it wasn't because he was in love with her, it was only that she had that shack on the lake and the city was so hot. You know perfectly well he came back to me when the cold weather set in—"

"Good heavens, is she crying?" burst out Severgny, for unmistakable snuffles were being broadcast.

"Of course she's crying," said Cynthia. "Don't you remember how she always cried when she was trying to wheedle something out of you, saying it was for Marius? Imagine her showing up to play the grieving widow when she didn't even know he was dead till six weeks ago!"

"Has she tried to claim insurance and how much?" Briggs piped up, but the machine drowned out any answers.

"Now don't say Marius' friends let him down, just look at all of us here honoring him tonight. The thing was Marius never appreciated what his friends did for him anymore than you did, Anna. He's the

one who never wrote. Never a word except a card about five years ago from Vancouver asking me to send money to come back east."

"Last I heard from him was from San Francisco saying the same thing. Didn't Cynthia say she got a card from Del Rio?"

"Wait a minute, what did he do with all that money if he never used it to come back?"

"Nobody ever sent him any money, Mr. Briggs, that's what l mean by letting him down—"

"People, people, we're here to tell stories about Marius not to abuse each other! This record is to be a tribute to Marius, a kind of bringing him to life, as it were—"

"If he was alive he wouldn't be invited here and Severgny and the other dealers wouldn't even handle his pictures because he owed them all, and what's more Marius wouldn't even know half of these people claiming to be his best friends."

"People, please, let's try to remember gay little things—"

You mean like the time Cynthia Earle took Marius on a cruise, and her hair was black as a witch then and she was awfully yellow and skinny. Ha ha, l'll never forget Marius said it was the longest Hallowe'en he ever had—"

"Whose voice was that?" Cynthia cried out suddenly, leaping up so that Briggs fell backward on the bed, his notebook sliding down the crack next the wall where he rolled over to retrieve it. "Let's stop this right now, Charlie, till I find out who said that."

Nobody knew whose voice it had been, and since Charlie, the expert, had gone into the bathroom the machine was left on sputtering away, ignored by Cynthia who was shouting her indignation, all the angrier for Okie's roaring to her defense. He was accusing everyone of treason to that great benefactor, Mrs. Earle, who had done everything in the world for Marius, a big peasant oaf who didn't even appreciate a fine woman's love, let alone the trouble she had trying to help him make a name. No gratitude—

"Marius had just as much gratitude toward his benefactors as they had toward *their* benefactors," Ben Forrester interrupted. "When someone gave him money left them by their ancestor Marius always said he and the ancestor were the only ones who did anything to earn it."

"When I think of all I did for that swine," Cynthia cried indignantly. "And for all his wives, too. Why I even made him bring back a Spanish shawl for one of them when we came back from Trinidad. I was always decent to them. When I'd invite him to a party I'd always say now don't forget, do bring what's-her-name. No, you can't say I wasn't a real friend to Marius, Ben Forrester."

"Like your old man was a good friend to General Motors," Ben retorted. "You got your dividends. Then when you got through with him you never looked him up even though he was right down on Houston Street. Like everybody else here tonight. If they thought he was still struggling away down there they wouldn't even bother about him."

Ben was working up to something and Dalzell gave him a warning frown, fearing an explosion of Ben's pent-up bitterness. Ben got the signal and rose. Severgny caught the look and followed Ben to the door, picking up the pictures Anna had brought on his way.

"I never claimed to know the man, Ben," he said appeasingly. "I only have the *expertise*. For instance I have a suspicion these two pictures are phonies, and from the way you two looked at them I felt you had the same hunch. What about it?"

Ben busied himself sorting out their hats and coats from the hall.

"Why should you doubt them?" he asked guardedly.

"The background," Severgny said with a quiet smile. "Marius hasn't been east in the last seven years but one picture shows a

Staten Island bus that only started running two years ago. I just happened to notice."

And the charred walls of an old brewery that had burned down only last year, Dalzell mentally added, and how could Marius have done that?

"I'd swear it was Marius' work," Dalzell said cautiously.

"Let's discuss them at the gallery when I've studied them longer." Severgny shrugged. "I think I should have a little chat with Anna. She may have talents none of us ever suspected."

Not Anna, Dalzell reflected, but who then? Who could have done that gnarled, tired truck horse like Marius? Not even Ben or himself. And if Severgny was beginning to suspect, where did that leave them?

"That's right, walk out on me!" Cynthia wailed woefully. "Walk out without so much as good-bye!"

Dalzell half-turned, but Ben significantly pushed him out the door.

"I'll call tomorrow, Cynthia dear," Severgny called out tenderly. "Get a good night's sleep. A pity the record was so unsatisfactory. Come on, gentlemen, poor Cynthia is utterly exhausted."

Dalzell hesitated, fancying he detected real woe in Cynthia's voice, but now was not the time to console her.

"Poor Cynthia, my foot! I'm not a bit exhausted," Cynthia wailed as the door closed on the three men. "I'm just the loneliest person in the whole world and everybody leaves me—"

"Cynthia dear, I'm here!" Okie cried out and in the hall the others heard her irritated retort, "Of course you're here, silly, there's never any getting rid of you."

"Cynthia, now, just a minute—"

"Oh go way, Okie, can't you ever learn when you're not wanted? For God's sake, Okie!"

With a heart-rending sob Cynthia flung herself about on her

couch, face-down in the pillows, beating her fists into them with a great jangling of bracelets. Okie had planted himself doggedly in front of her, breathing heavily, his hands clenched at his sides.

"When you wish to apologize to me Cynthia," he said in a choked proud voice, "I am willing to listen."

"Stop being such an ass!" wailed Cynthia. "You just want to stay and finish up my brandy the way you always do. Go way, I say."

She redoubled her sobs and pillow-beatings, kicking up her heels in anguish till a sandal flew off and hit Okie in the eye. It was more than even Okie could bear, especially since the young man named Charlie had come out of the bathroom and was staring at the scene with astonishment. Okie was so humiliated by this audience he could not restrain himself, and pointed a trembling finger at Cynthia's heaving back.

"Yes, you can say 'go way' but you should be glad there is one man left for you to order around because all your other men have run off years ago. I wasn't good enough for you, then, oh no. I never got invited on the big house parties and the cruises, oh no, you just had the big shots, I was always on the outside. But I could take it, just like I took it from everybody else. I knew nobody liked me, but that didn't bother me. I hung around and took all the snubs and insults, because I knew if I hung around long enough the day would come when none of you would find anybody else to take the dregs, and that's why I've got the last laugh. You've got to have me now because I'm the only one that will take the dregs, the scraps of all of you."

"Go away!"

"All the time you used to kick me around and make fun of me there were plenty others making fun of you, Cynthia, and you can snoot and snub me to your heart's content, I knew who they were really laughing at, and I could laugh too, my girl, only I'm sorry for you, because you got nobody but me and what would you do if you couldn't whistle me back? Think about that, Cynthia, and see how you like being left with nobody—nobody—"

Okie's voice broke with emotion and he gulped, looking hungrily at Cynthia's shaking shoulders but she showed no signs of listening to reason, just letting out little heartbroken gasps as she clutched the velvet spread. Taking a long tremulous breath, Okie cast a yearning look at the brandy bottle, then tossed back his white head, clapped on his Homburg and strode out of the door which the young man named Charlie held open for him as if for a great star and followed him out.

Cynthia's sob stopped the instant the door closed and she sat up, wiping her eyes. Looking around petulantly her gaze fell on the space behind the couch where young Briggs had fallen and was wedged between bed and wall, sleeping peacefully with his mouth wide open.

A triumphant smile lit up Cynthia's face.

"Left with nobody, er? Well, look who's here!" she said and leaned over to yank him back up on the couch. The motion woke Briggs who saw Cynthia's doting face above his and no one else around. Hoff Bemans' warning not to be left alone with the hostess rang an alarm in his brain, and he was out of the door like a flash, almost pushing over Dalzell Sloane who was coming back down the hall.

"Thank Mrs. Earle for the nap, will you?" Briggs shouted, just making the elevator.

Dalzell opened the studio door gently and Cynthia gave a glad cry.

"Oh Dalzell, I knew you wouldn't leave me! I'm so lonely!" she cried, holding out her arms to him. "Promise me you'll never leave me again, never, no matter what! Am I so hideous, Dalzell, am I so old?"

The mascara and purple eyeshadow were streaking down her cheeks and her nose was red. Dalzell took out his handkerchief and carefully repaired her face which she held up to him trustingly.

"You're beautiful, Cynthia," he said. "You'll always be beautiful."

. . . the bore that walks like a man . . .

In the Pink Elephant bar around the corner from Cynthia's studio Okie stood at the bar, or rather rested himself upon it, continuing the long list of grievances that the evening had unleashed. To assure himself of a sympathetic ear he had gone so far as to invite the fellow Charlie What's-his-name for a nightcap. He had a suspicion that Cynthia's ignoring of his accusations had put him in a rather weak position with his audience, and he wanted to go over the whole thing and put it into what he referred to as "proper perspective."

"A gentleman can take only so much, Charlie," he declared stirring his brandy and soda with a knobby forefinger. "Then the primitive man comes out as it did in me tonight. 'Try and whistle for me,' I said to her. They can all whistle for me—every damn one of the lot—see what good it does then! I took a lot from them."

"Sure you took a lot," agreed Charlie. "They were always trying to shake you."

"They couldn't do it, though," Okie said proudly. "I'll say that for myself, no matter how my feelings might have been hurt I stuck right along. Now I've got them all in my pocket, don't you see?"

"Sure," said Charlie. "You were right, too."

The intelligence of this comment brought an approving look from Okie, who studied his companion gravely.

"Where I made my mistake was not joining the Communist Party when I was your age," he mused.

The young man and bartender looked shocked.

"That would make me an ex-Commy, of course, right now and I could get even with the whole lot of them, Cynthia, Forrester and Sloane, all of them. I'd swear every one of them had a Party card at one time or other, and boy, it would take the rest of their lives to get out of that one. But I was too dumb to see ahead that far."

"You could be an ex-Commy without going to the trouble of being a Commy, couldn't you?" argued Charlie, rather pleased with this picture. "The real Commies wouldn't dare say you weren't one without giving themselves away. Go ahead, sic the F.B.I. on them, why don't you, and have yourself a ball watching them squirm."

"Other people do it, why shouldn't I?" said Okie reflectively.

"I think this guy really means it," Charlie observed to the bartender. "He's that mad at these characters, he'd turn 'em all in."

Okie shook his head with a sad, noble smile.

"No, my boy, anybody else would but I'm too much of a gentleman." He pounded the bar with his glass and the bartender, at a quick nod from Charlie, construed this as an order for two more drinks and poured them. "That's why I hate everybody, because they're not gentlemen. Do you realize that in all the years I've known Larry Whitfield he has never once invited me to lunch or to visit his big place there in the Berkshires? Do you believe me when I tell you that this dealer, Severgny, never once has taken me to his home or made any effort to know me? The bad manners! The rudeness! Like Ben Forrester, when he was riding high a couple of seasons there in Paris and could have taken me to some fine parties but oh no. I tell you people aren't gentlemen, that's all that hurts me!"

"Maybe they didn't want a Commy around," Charlie suggested, swigging his drink.

Okie whirled on him indignantly.

"How dare you call me a Commy?" he said.

"Wasn't you telling him you was a Commy?" asked the bartender coldly.

"No, he was telling me he was a gentleman," explained Charlie. He gave Okie a nudge. "Drink up, or the bar will close before we can order another. All that wine and sherry made me thirsty for a real drink. You should have saved your quarrel till after we'd finished the brandy."

Okie fixed bulging oyster eyes on his young friend belligerently.

"What quarrel are you referring to?" he demanded.

Charlie's jaw dropped.

"Well, when Mrs. Earle told you to go away and then you told her what you thought of her and—"

Okie put a hand on the lad's shoulder, groping past the shoulder padding to contact the shoulder proper.

"My dear fellow, can't you tell the difference between quarrels and the simple joking between friends? Cynthia and I enjoy putting on our little acts, but I'm surprised you were taken in by it. The reason I invited you here was that I thought you had a sense of humor. And now—ha ha, so you really didn't know Cynthia was kidding!"

"Were you joking about being a gentleman, too?" Charlie asked, which set the bartender off in silent chuckles of deep appreciation. Okie was looking at the bar check, holding it far away and then drawing it near his eyes.

"One-sixty!" he exclaimed incredulously. "What is this, El Morocco?"

He reached for his wallet cautiously as if it might bite off his hand and having located it in his inside coat pocket tugged away at it, evidently meeting with mighty resistance until his final capture of it almost lost him his balance. He fished some coins from his change pocket, extricated a reluctant one-dollar bill from the wallet, then restored it to its warm nest.

"I must say I don't see the point in paying out good money for drinks when we were having them free at Cynthia's," he grumbled.

Charlie looked at him in astonishment.

"But she ordered you out and you told her off, didn't you? You said what you thought of the whole lousy lot of them—"

"What?" Okie cried out, shocked. "You must have misunderstood the situation, my boy."

"What are you getting sore at me for? " Charlie said, nettled at Okie's reproving tone. "I thought you were a hundred percent right. What kind of people are they, anyway?"

Okie straightened up, frowning at him beneath proud beetling gray brows.

"They are my friends, young man, friends of a lifetime, and I should think you would regard it an honor to meet them. Instead you stand here in this common saloon making derogatory remarks about your betters, insinuating that I myself behaved badly to our hostess—"

"I said I didn't blame you!" interrupted Charlie.

Okie lifted a forefinger admonishing silence.

"I shall apologize to poor Cynthia in the morning," he stated. "If she misunderstood our little joke as you seem to have done, then of course she will be upset until I make apologies."

"You're always going around apologizing," muttered Charlie, baffled and exasperated, seeing an end to nightcaps in Okie's final gesture of buttoning up his Chesterfield.

"Because I happen to be a gentleman, my dear fellow," Okie said haughtily. "Something you young upstarts know nothing about. Have you so much as uttered one word of thanks for my invitation to a nightcap, for instance? No. There you are."

"Thanks," said Charlie sulkily.

Reluctantly he followed Okie out and stood on the corner watching him swagger proudly eastward toward Fifth Avenue, noting that the Chesterfield was too snug but still seemed the proper armor.

. . . one has one's own life to live . . .

The time had come, Elsie Hookley decided, to drop Jerry Dulaine. You took an interest in someone, knocked yourself out trying to help them get on their feet, defended them against a world of enemies, gave them the shirt off your back, and what thanks did you get? The person didn't want a shirt or to be on her feet. Your money, time and tender sympathy were all down the drain. Once you've made up your mind what a person ought to be you can't go back and be satisfied with them the way they are. Jerry had fascinated her as capable of magic transformation, but now that this had proved a false hope, Elsie felt righteously let down. She found daily justification for her decision to dismiss this friendship. There were the bills for objects Jerry had charged to her accounts all over town; there was the loan company to which Elsie had unwittingly given her name as sponsor now trying to collect from Elsie. There were the neighborhood tradesmen ringing Elsie's bell to ask for Miss Dulaine. And there was the cruel fact that the young lady herself kept away from Elsie's apartment and was never to be found by phone or knock in her own place. Once you have made up your mind to drop a person it is most inconsiderate of them not to come within dropping distance. Elsie had planned to keep a cool, polite distance, to keep her own counsel about what steps she was going to take in her own life—such as her intention of descending on her mother in Boston to wrest outright cash for splurging on the old family homestead just to show brother Wharton that from now on she was going to live on the same scale as he did.

"I'll simply make it clear to her I'm through trying to help people," Elsie told herself virtuously. "From now on I'm looking out for myself, and I shan't encourage her to tell me any of her troubles, either. When she tries to explain about all these financial mix-ups I will just shrug my shoulders."

There was no use denying that she had twinges of regret for the old happy days of friendship, and perhaps she was being unkind and unfair to her former protégée. But one had one's own life to live, after all. To avoid an open scene Elsie took pains to be out in the hours she thought Jerry would be in, and she had her lights out early at night in case Jerry might be tempted to drop in for a nightcap. But there were no encounters, and after congratulating herself on how well she was handling a rather awkward situation Elsie switched to the suspicion that it was Jerry who was avoiding her. This drove her crazy with curiosity. What was the girl up to? Maybe she was keeping her distance out of shame at the failure of their recent enterprise. Still she'd never known Miss Dulaine to be ashamed of anything.

"The least I can do is to let her know I don't hold anything against her." Elsie relented a little as she helped Brucie locate a tick on his belly. "After all, there's no reason I should go to such extremes to punish her when she couldn't help the way things turned out. Even if she did hurt my feelings—"

Elsie did not try to define exactly how Jerry had hurt her feelings but hurt they were, and it was because Jerry had absolutely refused to cry on her shoulder or accept any consolation. She, Jerry, had shrugged off her benefactor as if their positions were reversed, and Elsie, with her heart full of belligerent defenses and excuses, found her charge rejecting them. Very well, Elsie had found new interests, but she would give her eyeteeth to know what Jerry was doing without her. It seemed hardly fair that Jerry betrayed no equivalent curiosity about her neighbor's new life.

"Haven't you gone yet, Iola?" Elsie called sharply to the kitchen. "I told you to leave as soon as you got things ready and I'll do the *scampi,* when I feel like it. Now run along."

"I'm in no hurry, Miss Hookley," Iola whimpered. "I'd just as soon stay and fix 'em when you're ready."

She looked at her mistress dolefully, pale brown face smugly pious with love of duty, or was it, Elsie wondered suspiciously, malicious determination to bedevil her mistress by hanging around to see what was going on?

"Run along, I said," Elsie said firmly, and Iola with an audible sigh took off her apron and put on her coat and hat, looking reproachfully from Elsie to Brucie for being able to do without her.

"I been kinda scared lately, Miss Hookley," she said, standing in the doorway. "Couple times lately I seen somebody round this neighborhood look like that awful Portugee that used to devil me. If he starts bothering me again I just don't know what I'd do."

Elsie found another tick.

"I'd like to know how Brucie can get ticks in a city yard in winter," she said absently. "Good night, Iola. Nobody's going to bother you."

The door closed on another deep sigh. Elsie went to the kitchen and got out the ice bucket, fizz water and the bourbon. The shrimps were in the pan all ready for broiling in garlic butter, the avocados and salad greens waiting in the icebox, the chunk of provalone paired with the half-moon of Gruyère, the rice steaming gently on the stove. Elsie nodded approval and settled down in the living room with a highball.

She had just begun on her second when the door opened quietly and the young man whom Iola feared slipped into the room and grinning, without saying a word, poured himself a fine drink.

"You could at least knock, you little imp," Elsie said, not at all displeased. "I suppose you swiped my key and had a copy made."

He nodded happily.

"I like a lot of keys," he said. He looked around cautiously. "I saw Iola go. She won't come back, will she?"

Elsie laughed.

"You're still afraid of her. Iola can't hurt you."

"You never heard a dame scream like that one." Niggy shuddered. "Makes my blood run cold every time I think about it. I never knew a dame to start yelling when you made a little pass at her. She won't be back, will she?"

"Don't worry," Elsie reassured him. She looked over his suit, a gray with wider pin stripes than she had ever seen, and enough shoulder padding to float him in case of shipwreck. He flickered his sleeve self-consciously, catching her eye.

"Okay, I know. A little loud but that's my style. Nita likes it. Says it make me look like a South American millionaire," he said defensively. "Anyway I'm an intellectual now, I can dress any way I damn please. Look, can we talk or are you expecting somebody?"

Elsie motioned him to a chair.

"I expected you to phone," she said. "What are you up to in New York?"

"Old Brucie looks all right," answered Niggy as Brucie laid his head trustingly on his knees, waiting for the soothing scratch beneath the chin.

"He misses his fresh fish," Elsie said wickedly. Her guest's eyes flashed but he grinned and shrugged as she chuckled.

"Okay, you pulled me out of the fish pile but I wish I was there right now," he said. "At least I'd be making some dough."

He yanked a cigarette savagely out of a pack and lit it, his black eyes on Elsie waiting for her to say something, but Elsie kept her eyes on Brucie.

"Brains cost money," he said. "I was better off when I just had a boat."

He sounded injured and accusing, as if Elsie had made this unfair trade behind his back. Elsie laughed mockingly.

This angered the young man for he jumped up and poured himself another drink, planting himself in front of Elsie.

"All right, laugh, you know I was doing all right when you got hold of me. I made money on my boat, I played around with the waitresses at the Gull House, or the schoolteachers or the help around town, and it never cost a cent. They paid for everything. Then you fix me up with all the highbrows and rich dames and they want me on tap twenty-four hours a day and I'm lucky if I get a few meals out of it. Sure, I ride around in their cars, I drink their liquor, I sleep with their mothers or their daughters to break the monotony, but no cash, see, never a damn bit of cash."

"What's stopping you from going back to the Cape?" Elsie asked calmly, knowing he wanted something from her and enjoying the sense of power. She had every intention of giving in to his demands but she couldn't resist the desire to make him jump for his sugar.

Pouting sulkily, the lad's blue-shaven face with the snub nose and long upper lip and button eyes looked more than ever like a monkey's. Elsie found the resemblance charming and appealing. She pushed the dish of toasted almonds towards him and the nervous little monkey fingers snatched at them and stuffed them in his mouth as he talked.

"The guys there are all sore at me since I started running around with the summer people," he complained. "That's where you queered me year before last. And now that I've been around I don't want to go back to what I was. You said yourself I could paint as well as those mugs in the art classes. Sure, I can throw a couple of apples on a plate with a clam shell and a pop bottle and call it a still life but what kind of a living is that?"

"Who said it was a living?" Elsie said. "At least you met some new people through it. And now it seems you don't even paint, just go to cocktail parties and pontificate with the fine minds in my sister-in-law's intellectual group. Who pays for that, by the way?"

Niggy smirked annoyingly, and examined his fingernails.

"You've picked up a lot of camping tricks," Elsie said, deciding that she wouldn't give him a thing if he was going to act coy with her. Evidently sensing this Niggy changed his tactics.

"I worked nights in a garage up on the West Side," he said. "But damn it, Elsie, I can't go around with nice people, visit their homes and all that, maybe go on pleasure trips with them, if I have to drudge away in some dirty garage. A fellow's just got to get his hands on cash to keep up. Nita's been nice enough, letting me drive her car, letting me have some of Wharton's clothes—whatever isn't too big for me, passing out a ten-spot now and then, but I got my future to look out for."

"So?" Elsie said, determined to make it as difficult as possible.

Niggy was silent, scratching his crew cut moodily.

"Well, what's your problem?" Elsie persisted. "I take it you're sorry you gave up the fisherman's life but now you're too good for it. You like going around with rich people and highbrows only there's no money in it. You have to jump when they whistle but on the other hand you don't want them to stop whistling. Well?"

The young man took Brucie's head between his knees and gazed moodily into the dog's red-rimmed patient eyes.

"You can kid about the spot I'm in but you know you're the one that set me off," he muttered. "You're the one that told me it was easier to make upstairs than downstairs, the very words you used."

"It does sound like me," Elsie admitted, pleased. "I don't see

why you hold it against me, Niggy. You got a summer in Gloucester out of it, you learned to talk Tanglewood, you helped
make sets for summer arena theatres, you sat around the best
beaches, then you jump into philosophy and literature and end
up with my brother's wife. What more do you want?"

"Cash, like I told you," Niggy said. "So it looks like I've got to
marry Isabella."

Elsie sat up straight, staring at him.

"Isabella?" she cried. "You're not referring to my niece, by any
chance?"

Niggy nodded gloomily.

"What on earth is Nita thinking of to let you marry Isabella?"
Elsie exclaimed indignantly. "My poor brother knocks himself
out grooming the girl for a big marriage and then you step in and
ruin everything, just because you've got Nita interested in you!
What are you thinking of?"

The young man pushed Brucie aside and got to his feet. He
downed another whiskey neat and this inspired Elsie to pour
herself a revivifying swig. They banged their glasses down on
the table at the same moment and looked at each other for a
moment in silence.

"Look," Niggy said patiently. "When a fellow like myself gets
mixed up with people like you he can't call the turns any more.
He gets a lot of breaks, sure, but he has to take a lot of kicking
around too, never knowing how soon the show is over. I got good
and sick of that Gloucester setup, believe me, but I had to keep
on till I was sure of what was next. I didn't even know what I
was getting into with Nita, because we met first in the New
School. It turns out she's your brother's wife, so most of the time
she's busy doing the family social stuff and I'm hanging around
somewhere waiting for a call. Then she thinks up a deal for me
to teach Isabella art, and keeps me around, but it's a dog's life.
Isabella has a dog's life, too, let me tell you."

"I shouldn't be surprised," Elsie murmured.

"Her father has her doing this, her mother has her doing that, and she can't do anything to suit them so she just sits in the Park all day or goes to double features with me, both of us in a jam, see, only she doesn't know about mine."

"She's no beauty, of course," Elsie observed.

Niggy shrugged.

"I don't care about women's looks," he said. "They all look the same to me in the long run. Anyway Isabella's got herself set on running away with me and getting married."

Elsie was aghast.

"I always knew you were a little devil, Niggy, but I must say I never dreamed you were capable of such a dirty trick as that! Marrying that poor girl just to get a living!"

"As if it was going to be any picnic for me!" Niggy retorted angrily. "She's the one that gets the bargain. She told me she never had any fun in her life till I came along. Does that mean I have any fun? I should say not! The whole damn family bores the living daylights out of me, especially that brother of yours, and Nita being so darn cutie all the time, pretending she doesn't know what the deal is because she's such a itty-bitty. The whole bunch makes me sick but I can't go back where I used to be, so I'm stuck."

Elsie pondered for a moment and an amusing idea struck her. Wharton had never tired of reminding her how much it cost the family to pay off her Baron and how he alone had saved the family honor. Someday she might be able to reply that the sacrifice was not all his.

"How much cash do you want and what would you do with it?" she asked.

The young man brightened.

"I could get by with a few hundred," he said eagerly. "I just want to clear out of town for a few months till I get some dames out of my hair. That jam between Nita and the kid is the tough-est one but there's an old movie queen at the St. Moritz, too. I want some new territory. I'd like some fun, not this rat race."

"I went to the bank today so I've got some cash," Elsie said. "Maybe two hundred and some. And I'll give you a check."

Niggy was so excited he threw his arms around Brucie's neck and kissed him, an attention that made Brucie rise and draw back, growling ominously. Elsie went to the bedroom and got her wallet from the hatbox where she kept it. Two hundred and thirty, she counted out, and then carefully wrote out a check for three hundred. She always hated to give away cash outright, and on second thought took back three tens. Then she went back out and presented the money to her visitor. As soon as it touched his hands his cockiness returned.

"You're a good egg, Elsie," he stated. "I figured you wouldn't let me down, especially since you got me into this mess."

Little bastard, Elsie thought, highly delighted, reproaching her for giving him a leg up just as if she'd ruined his life! She de-cided she would invite him to share her *scampi* now that his business seemed settled, but she should have remembered that money in his hand always meant he would be out the door like a shot.

"You ought to be glad you have so many nice people as friends," she said primly.

"I only hope they lay off me for a while," Niggy said with his most impudent grin. "I'm fed up with nice people."

Elsie straightened up with a shocked expression.

"Ah, don't look so insulted, you know you're not nice people," Niggy exclaimed. For some reason, even though he had his money he was lingering by the door with a preoccupied air. What else did he want? Whatever it was she knew he wouldn't be long in telling her.

"I know a boat I could get for three thousand dollars," he announced. "Fellow in Boston. Wants me to come in with him taking fishing parties out, around Hyannis, summers, then take her down to the Keys winters. I'd be set for life, see."

Elsie saw. She sipped her drink reflectively, Niggy watching her out of the corner of his eye.

"Why not?" she said. "I'm going up to Boston tomorrow to settle some business with my mother. Meet me there and show me the boat. I'll be at her hotel."

Niggy jumped over a footstool to embrace her.

"Elsie, you're wonderful," he cried excitedly. "By George, if you were just a foot shorter I'd marry you tomorrow. Bye, now, till Boston."

He was gone, the door banged behind him. Elsie sat musing with a wry, doleful half smile that disturbed Brucie for he shook himself and ambled over to her, stood up and placed forepaws on her shoulders and licked her ear sympathetically.

"Dear Brucie, good old boy," Elsie said tenderly.

When she got up to put the shrimps in the broiler she saw that in his haste to leave the young man had left his cane. She looked at it incredulously and picked it up. It was Uncle's ram's-head cane, the very one she had feuded about with Wharton for so long, the one she had wanted for the express purpose of giving to Niggy.

"He got it anyway," Elsie marveled. Nita? Or Isabella? Whichever one had given it to him the idea struck Elsie as delicious and she felt more lonely than ever because there was no one with whom she dared share the joke. Presently she made up her mind and marched out to the hall and upstairs where she knocked on Jerry's door firmly. Getting no answer she knocked again and rang the buzzer. Then she tried the knob and to her surprise found the door was unlocked. She stepped inside and switched on the light.

The apartment was completely bare except for a barrel of junk in the middle of the bedroom. A pair of jet evening slippers were on top of the barrel and a crumpled magazine photograph of Collier McGrew.

. . . everybody needs a boat . . .

"I ought to get in touch with Elsie," Jerry was admitting to her old friend Tessie over a jolly lunch at Louis and Armand's. "But I can't think of any way to make her understand."

"You can't even make me understand," Tessie said, shaking her head. "You say he never makes a pass?"

"Not what I'd call one," Jerry said. "A little kiss on the forehead, a little squeeze of the hand."

"He's not married, he's not queer, and he isn't a cripple, you say," pondered Tessie. "But he has you moved into his hotel, sets up your charge accounts again, gets you set with this TV job, and lets you have me stay with you. Crazy?"

Jerry laughed.

"No other signs of it," she said. "I thought when he had me meet his aunt that maybe he meant marriage but I count that out now. Sometimes I think he's rehabilitating me."

"I wouldn't stand for anybody doing social work on me," Tessie said. "Don't he ever say anything to give you a clue?"

"He likes me to tell him things about people," Jerry said. "I don't think he knows much about people, he's got such good manners he doesn't notice anything. But he gets a kick out of hearing inside stories about them. I guess I'm his court jester."

"What do you care so long as you've got no money worries?" Tessie said unconvincingly.

"Well he's managed to get me so hopped up about him that I don't know where I am," Jerry sighed. "I don't think he'd mind if I went out with other men but he has me so baffled I just stay home and wonder if he'll show up or telephone. How did I get into a fix like this?"

"You call this a fix," muttered Tessie. "There's just no limit to the kind of fixes a man can think up. Someday I'll tell you about my marriage."

Now that they were friends again they lunched together almost every day and reminded each other of old shared experiences, more fascinating now that they had nothing to lose by telling the truth. Tessie had quit the Lido and had dieted herself back into a modeling job with Jerry as her trainer. For the time being she was following Jerry's advice in everything just as Jerry had done with her when they first met. They needed each other again and after fifteen years of experience they could admit the need. Tessie had jumped from her play-girl career straight into a kind of super-respectable suburban life. It had to be super because $15,000-a-year husbands must live religiously on $25,000 in the excessively conventional manner demanded by wives who had been models, receptionists, or hat-check girls. After a few years of this struggle Tessie had run away with a jazz drummer, worked in the chorus line of whatever nightclub he played in, working her way down to the Lido in a determined effort to go to hell, after he left her. She was glad to start over again, however, after she and Jerry had compared notes, and she was shopping around now for a glossier respectability all over again.

"I never got over the kick of calling myself Mrs.," Tessie confessed. "Bill used to tell me I Missused myself so much everybody in Mount Kisco thought we couldn't possibly be married. I passed as Missus with Hotsy, too, of course, but it wasn't the same, not being on the level. Believe me, that's what I'm after now. Big church wedding, real wedding dress, big wedding ring, calling cards with a big Mrs. Somebody Junior the Fourth."

Jerry shook her head doubtfully.

"I can see the bridal suite on the *Ile de France* and the Do Not Disturb sign on the hotel-room door," she said, "but the rest of it looks like a big bear trap to me. If you liked the life so much why did you knock yourself out to quit it?"

"I liked everything about it but Bill," Tessie said. "Him I just couldn't take. You don't know what it is to know everything a man's going to say. You get so you move heaven and earth to get the conversation around to where he won't have a chance to say it. That's marriage."

"Can we stand another brandy without falling on our facials?" Jerry asked, and answered the query by signaling the waiter for two more.

"You liked Bill well enough at first," Jerry said.

"Ever go out with a fellow who pretends he's conducting an orchestra every time any music plays?" Tessie demanded. "That was just one thing Bill did. When he was driving a car, making love, eating a steak—let him hear music and he's got to pretend he's Toscanini. It just embarrassed me to death. Maybe that's why I ran off with a drummer. At least Hotsy was a real drummer. But the real reason I left Bill was his damned boat."

It seemed that every time Bill met somebody he considered a valuable contact he got the conversation around to boats. Sailboats, motorboats, cabin cruisers, any kind of boat was his meat and he was always telling people if he had to choose between his old cruiser and Tessie he'd take the cruiser. The boredom, Tessie declared, of listening to him brag about his old *Bucephalus,* as he called her, and his troubles with the Miami Yacht Club and all the stuff about tides and bottom scraping. If she was drinking it always ended with her making a scene and there was always somebody to take sides with Bill and say, "Aha, so the little lady is jealous of *Bucephalus.* No sporting blood, eh."

"I still don't see why you worked up such a grudge against his boat," Jerry said.

"His boat!" Tessie exclaimed scornfully. "He didn't have any boat, that was the whole trouble. Same as the orchestra. It was a pretend boat. Wait till you're married to a congenital liar and see what happens. Nobody else knows he's lying, so they end up hating you for trying to keep him off his favorite subject. I just hate boats, I'd have to say, and Bill would just give that jolly laugh of his and say, 'Believe it or not, Tess won't set foot on that boat to this day.' Funny thing, that was the only thing he ever bragged about, the dope."

It was fun having Tessie to go around with and it was fun being back uptown, safe in a beautifully impersonal hotel suite with a magic pencil that could buy anything from a hat to a Carey limousine. It was a more discreet, more cushioned life than that they had ever known together before but it was otherwise the same, and what experience had taught them was that they liked it.

"You swear you won't ever tell anybody I was in the Lido line?" Tessie anxiously begged Jerry for the hundredth time. "I may tell a guy if I get matey with him but I don't want you to tell."

"I promise," Jerry said, "only you've got to promise not to tell that Collier McGrew isn't sleeping with me."

"I won't," Tessie said sympathetically. "I must say I simply don't dig it, though. He must like you, he does all this for you, he's not ashamed to take you places when he does come to town, he doesn't mind people talking—"

"Do they talk?" Jerry interrupted, startled.

"A big shot like that? Sure they do," Tessie said. "Everybody in the hotel and in the Fifth Avenue Credit Association knows who pays the bills even if he doesn't have a bed in your apartment. What's bad is that when a man doesn't put you to bed right at first he's likely to get over the urge."

"It kind of scares me," Jerry reflected. She wished she dared ask Elsie Hookley's advice but she couldn't get over the feeling that Elsie was bad luck for her. Just seeing Elsie would bring back the tense sick desperation of those days, the frantic hopes and fears, the daily failures, not to mention the danger of Elsie camping around her new home and scaring off McGrew. No, it had to be good-bye, Elsie, old dear.

"Why don't you go to an analyst about him?" Tessie suggested.

Jerry gave a short laugh.

"I'd feel like a fool showing up for psychoanalysis at this late date," she said. "I can save money by worrying. I figure it this way. He's a smart man, always too smart for the people he has to work with or for the people in his class, so he's always played a lone hand. He's like those birds, falcons, I guess, that peck out gazelle's eyes and throw the rest away. He pecks out just what he wants in people and throws the rest away. He likes my company when and where he likes it and he likes knowing he's trading that for something I want."

"Maybe he's got somebody else for the hay," Tessie said.

It was a disagreeable idea and Jerry winced.

"That would be my luck to get crazy over a man who's only crazy about my wizard brain," she said gloomily. "The gazelle's eyes falling in love with the hawk, that's about it."

They swirled their brandy glasses thoughtfully.

"How long do you give it, Jerry?" Tessie softly asked.

"I give myself forever, since I never felt like this before," Jerry said. "As for him—well, he might run for his life if I started something myself. Or maybe he expects me to. One of these days I'm afraid I'll take the chance."

"You've got that TV job, anyway," Tessie said. "What do you have to do, just line up celebrities for the show? Brother, who's that good-looking man looking at you?"

It was the producer of Jerry's show and he was only too eager to bring his good looks up for closer inspection. He had all sorts of program details to discuss with Jerry, including another drink around, and how about using this delightful young lady—

"Miss—I mean Mrs. Walton," Jerry said.

—in the fashion show. He had been admiring her carriage as she had darted in and out of the powder room and was sure she must have had show girl training. No? Well, it didn't matter. All he really wanted was her particular kind of statuesque beauty. He seemed so taken with Tessie and she with him that Jerry joined some friends at another table. In her absence the producer told Tessie he had heard Miss Dulaine was kept in great style by no less than Collier McGrew, and he wouldn't have dreamed she was the type, but maybe it was just Platonic. Tessie loyally assured him it was far from Platonic. They discovered they had both lived in Mount Kisco once, been married and divorced, and when Jerry rejoined them Tessie was telling all about the good times they used to have on her husband's cabin cruiser, the *Bucephalus*.

PART FIVE

Somebody had to take care of Marius' women before she went stark mad, Cynthia Earle declared passionately. It was true she had rashly opened the gates to trouble by sounding off in print and on the air as a Marius collector, friend and chief authority, but everybody else was doing the same. She was better placed, however, so her telephone and doorbell rang night and day with female supplicants. Gracie, Hedwig, Jeannette, Natasha, Moira, Babsie—

Marius was the father of their children, their common-law husband, their legal groom, their fiancé, anything that gave them the right to protection or support from Marius admirers. Sometimes they even brought babies, and swore they had made the trip on foot from suburban jungles or farther to share in the great man's success, and nothing less than railroad fare home would budge them from Cynthia's handsome home.

"Not a one of them attractive," Cynthia complained. "You know how Marius used to sleep with people just out of morbid curiosity. And then Anna—my God—how was I to know she was going to do a Rip Van Winkle? I admit I encouraged her at first—I was so shocked she was still around—but I never dreamed she'd come creeping up with her hat out every time I turn around! Somebody's got to do something."

This was unfair, for Anna's technique had never been open begging. She was a born poor relation and would not have been a rich relation if she could because that would mean she might have to do something for somebody else. No, in her sweet, humble way she merely rang the doorbell of the big house and collapsed on the doorstep, only sorry that it wasn't snowing and that she didn't have her newborn babe in her arms. As poor artist's neglected mate she followed these tactics shamelessly, according to Cynthia, and she had a way of getting herself up in dusty, rusty clothes, with moldy fur collars than which nothing looks poorer, and she would do this no matter how many dresses you sent her, a deliberate trick so that the mere sight of her was a reproach to you. Here I am in rags, her pious smile said, and though I am not one to blame anyone I am sure you must be ashamed of that fine coat you're wearing.

Severgny, too, was regretting that the memorial exhibition was receiving so much publicity, for he too suffered from Anna and the increasing horde of Marius' avowed connections. Lawyers must be retained to investigate claims, bouncers must be placed strategically in the gallery to dispose of weird characters eager to make scenes. A long lost brother turned up on the West Coast smelling money from Marius' name in the papers, and was only brushed off by newspaper men discovering Marius' father living alone on a New Hampshire farm.

"Neither of those boys was any doggone good," said the old man. "Both of 'em run away from home soon as they was old enough to run, wild as they come, just like the Purvises, that's their mother's folks. Willard, he's the oldest, run off with a carnival one day at milking time, the way he would, that one, and Marius was always fooling around with his paints even after he was a big boy, anything to get out of work. I knowed they'd end up in trouble, but nobody's going to take my little farm away from me now to pay for their funerals or bail or whatever it is."

Nothing would convince the old man that Marius' new fame was on the up and up.

"Those New Yorkers wouldn't stop at anything," he said dourly. "It's some trick to make me look after his family. I told that woman of his to stop pestering me years ago and this is her way of getting back at me. I won't have any part of it and you can tell that good-for-nothing Willard for me to keep his nose out of it too, if he don't want to get in the same fix as his brother."

From a San Antonio art dealer who had made the trip to Marius' last known home in Mexico had come a small package of all his landlady there could find of his belongings, at least all that she had been unable to sell or find use for. These consisted of a notebook in which recipes, restaurant addresses hither and yon, telephone numbers, notes for future sketching grounds, bus schedules, and other odds and ends were jotted down; a dozen dunning letters forwarded from as many other addresses; some snapshots of children, probably his, in varying stages of growth; a roll of used film that the landlady had been too thrifty either to throw away or have developed. The letters were from Trina and her lawyer, all written after Marius' death and obviously unaware of it. They indicated that Trina had taken the children and walked out in a huff three years before in Vancouver, returned soon afterward repentant only to find Marius gone. The letters swung from her begging to be allowed to follow him and look after him wherever he was to wild denunciations and threats. The lawyer Trina had managed to hire as tracer and his stern promises of punishments to be visited as soon as the lost one returned to his family were certainly enough to keep a man on the run. At any rate it established that Trina was still on earth somewhere far away, or had been three months ago, and was likely to loom on the scene one of these days.

Something would certainly have to be done, Dalzell Sloane had agreed, but it took a lot of arguing to get Ben to see it that way.

"We've got to do it before Severgny or Cynthia start something," Dalzell kept insisting, and finally Ben assented.

He was still grousing about giving up a date with the young art student he had collected at Cynthia's party when they took off on the ferry from the Battery.

"Whatever we find out from Anna will make things worse," he prophesied.

"Not if we find it out before the others," Dalzell said. "Whatever it is we can put the lid on it—and her—before Trina shows up and blows up the whole apple cart."

"Women are bloodhounds," Ben said moodily. "Once they get their hooks in a man they can sniff him out the rest of his life across oceans and graves. Those old hooks have just got to get back in. You don't understand that because you always managed to clear out before they got their hooks into you."

Dalzell didn't say anything. There had been hooks all right, but emotional ones only that hurt the more for not hanging on. As for women sniffing out their prey it struck him that Ben himself had been offering his own persecutors the scent whenever they withdrew the hooks. Certainly the letters coming to Ben from his Southwestern ladies couldn't have found him so easily at Gerda Cahill's apartment, where he and Dalzell were staying, without being led. Ever since their fortunes had picked up, Ben had been restless, homesick Dalzell suspected, for his old familiar ties. We get sick of our clinging vines, he thought, but the day comes when we suspect that the vines are all that hold our rotting branches together. One without vines, like himself, knew all too well one's dry rot and longed for the old parasitical leaves to mask and bind it.

"What say we stay on the ferry and go right back to Manhattan?" Ben proposed as the boat bumped into the St. George slip. "What do you expect to find out anyway?"

"We'd just be thrashing the whole thing over every day till we found out the truth—or it found us out," Dalzell said doggedly, aware that he was irritating Ben with his obstinacy, but then Ben was constantly disappointing him, too, by his belligerent self-interest. They had expected each other to be not so much the friend they remembered as the creature made up of parts they needed most and it seemed unfair that the person had developed quite differently. Their first joy in discovering bonds of mutual necessity had changed subtly to an aggrieved surprise that their aims were so different. Their disappointment in each other was the familiar discovery of age: the old friend of his youth has failed him because he fails to give him back his youth.

At the St. George station Ben followed Dalzell to the Totten-ville train which was waiting. It was midday, a time evidently not popular with Tottenville travelers for the only other passengers were a stout old German-looking couple laden with bundles, and a harassed young mother in a fishy-looking leopard coat with many glittering ornaments, twin girls in pink-flowered Easter outfits clinging to her knees and a fat little Hopalong Cassidy asleep in her arms, one boot hooked into the stirrup made by her purse handle.

"I hate this island," Ben said, looking out the window as the sleepy little villages slipped by like pictures through an ancient stereoscope, ivy-grown station shanties, old corner taverns with pointed roofs, winding roads with weather-beaten houses whose gardens were already turning green, the meadows and village four corners seeming unchanged through the centuries. "I know we used to claim this trip reminded us of the one from Paris out to St. Germain-en-Laye—but I only came here when I was dead broke or in trouble, and you know how you blame a place for that."

Dalzell was beginning to feel excited and a little afraid. He would not admit that the expedition might be a mistake for no matter what trouble came of it the risk must be taken. Now that they were nearing Prince's Bay where the old German couple were getting off, he allowed himself to think of the possible consequences to himself and Ben.

"I agree that Anna has something up her sleeve all right," Ben said. "Anybody could tell that, but is it something we want to find out? We certainly don't want anybody shaking our sleeves, either."

"I don't think Cynthia suspects Anna. She hates her too much to give her any credit for mischief," Dalzell said. "But Severgny does. We've got to check before he does."

"I'd rather have Trina to deal with than Anna," Ben said. "At least there was never any doubt about where she stood, roaring all over the place like a storm trooper. But Anna was always changing her style, laying low and biding her time, sneaking up on you, sniveling and whining till she got what she was after. You can't lick the Anna type and we're fools to even tangle with her."

The young mother and her little family and the German couple had gotten off and they were the only passengers left by the time they got to Tottenville, the end of the line.

"The end of the world!" Ben muttered, looking around the station platform, but Dalzell felt a wave of old affection for this quaint remnant of a long-ago America. The Jersey shore was hardly a ferry's length away and the old roofless ferry was waiting to cross just as it always was while to his left the cobbled street led up the hill and around and the peaceful old houses followed the curve of the bay, their wide lawns sprawling down to water's edge. If the old Queens house had given them shelter and hiding in their bad times, the Island hereabouts had offered a healing vision of long ago to wipe out today. On summer days Dalzell had wandered through these roads, reminded of the old midwest lanes of his boyhood and the little foreign villages of now. For a moment of grateful memories he forgot Anna and their mission till Ben reminded him.

"I can't figure out how Anna happened to land in this territory," Ben pondered. "Sure, she used to hear Marius and the rest of us talk about it but what tidal wave threw her up here at this late date?"

A laundry truck from the Jersey ferry came up the hill and Dalzell flagged it as it turned, saving them the hour's walk to the old brewery where they were heading. It had gone out of business years ago but the building had stayed and only burned down last year, the driver informed them. Yet one of the pictures Anna had produced of Marius' had been of an old brewery horse grazing around the charred remains of the old brewery. "Home," the picture was titled in Marius' hand. The sight of this picture, offered by Anna as an old Marius that night at Cynthia's studio, was what had shocked Dalzell into action. He and Ben had the same sudden suspicion but Ben, aware of where it might lead, had wanted to forget it.

"All right, let's say Marius couldn't paint that picture unless he'd seen the place within the last year and that means he's still alive and maybe Anna's hiding him out here," Ben had said. "It also means he doesn't want to be found out. Why should we be the ones to track him down if he wants to be dead—that is, if he really isn't dead?"

Dalzell struggled to find a logical answer. All he knew was that for a cherished old friend to wish to be dead meant an unbearable wretchedness that must be alleviated. He had been lonely himself and he couldn't let old Marius suffer the same quiet terror if he could help it.

"It isn't just that he wants to be considered dead," Ben had argued. "It's that a whole industry has been piling up on his death.

All these Marius worshippers only love a dead Marius and if it turns out he's alive they not only will lose money but will make his life worse than ever. And what about you and me? Do we confess to fixing up and painting a few bogus Mariuses, then bow out into Sing Sing? or maybe they have worse dungeons for artists than for axe killers."

"That's what we may be able to head off," Dalzell had said. "You know how Anna roused Severgny's suspicions right off claiming those new canvases were old ones from twenty years back. Then she gets Cynthia's back up. So both Severgny and Cynthia are going to check up on Anna and they're likely to find out more than they even dreamed of."

Ben reluctantly conceded the danger of this. But supposing Marius was still alive, what made Dalzell think he would not resent his old friends tracking him down?

Because, Dalzell said, of that one picture he had sent in by Anna, of the tired old brewery horse back on the ruins of his old stable.

"Marius called it 'Home,'" Dalzell said, "and I had the feeling that he meant it as a message to us."

The house was the only one for miles on the weed-grown road off the highway from the old brewery. It was that gaunt unpainted shingle house, barest symbol of home, often found on acres given over to truck farming, chickens, or temporary money-making where all funds go into the produce, not the worker. The project, long abandoned, left the husks of failure scattered over the field— unfinished sheds piled with rusted machine parts, post holes dug, broken-down chicken coops, empty paint buckets, scraps of tar paper. A few scraggly hens fluttered through the bushes and a collie was chasing a squawking rooster around the house. The mailbox at the head of the long lane was marked "Jensen," Anna's latest married name.

"Cut it out, Davey," a man's voice called out as the collie dropped his rooster chase to lunge vociferously toward the intruders.

"Marius," Dalzell breathed. "Ben, it *is* Marius."

"Either he doesn't know us or he isn't very glad to see us," Ben muttered.

"Come around the back way," Marius' voice came out.

The weary tone dampened their sudden excitement and they walked on hesitantly, wondering why they were here, frightened of what they might find. They saw him sitting in a low armchair by the kitchen stove, a blanket over his lap, a man indeed back from the grave. In the first shock of seeing him no one spoke. All that was left of the great ruddy-faced Marius was a gray skeleton with sunken blue eyes, deep lines rutting the hollow cheeks, the wide mouth drawn back in a bleak effort to smile, the hands, deeply veined, clutching the arms of his chair as if bracing against an expected attack. Dalzell's heart turned, thinking of what Marius must have been through to drain him of everything but fear.

"We got you!" Dalzell cried out, but he felt the trembling fear still in Marius' handclasp.

"You bastards!" Marius laughed weakly. "I should have known better than to trust Anna."

The kitchen was almost bare but they found a stool and chair and drew them up to the stove.

"It wasn't Anna. It was the brewery horse," Dalzell eagerly explained. "It worried us. If those last pictures were yours then we knew you had been in this section within the last year. And if somebody else had imitated you they were doing a better job than Ben and I have been doing and that worried us even more."

"What?" shouted Marius, and his laughter relieved the tension between them. "You rascals. Can't a man trust anybody even here in heaven?"

"At least you admit you're dead," Ben said. "Dalzell and I were afraid you'd try to palm yourself off as alive and bring your prices down. If you do I warn you it won't be worth our while doing any more of your work."

Marius was laughing weakly, brushing the tears from his gaunt cheeks.

"No sir, by God, I'm dead and I'm going to stay dead!" he declared and motioned Dalzell to bring out the bottle of bourbon handily sitting by the pump in the kitchen sink. "I never had it so good. But I can't trust anybody for long—Anna—even you fellows. Right now I'd like to just be an old brewery horse jogging home to graze till I hit the glue works, but it seems I'm a highwayman with a price on my head."

"How long had you been dead before you found out about it?" Ben asked.

"A good six months," Marius answered. He lit a cigarette Ben offered and looked for a moment from one to the other. "I guess I can tell you about it since you got me anyway."

"You've got us, too, don't forget," Dalzell reminded him. "We're all three in this together."

"I'd been living one jump ahead of the sheriff for years," Marius said. "Creditors, fights, dames, then borrowing this guy's car—that is, without his knowing it—Well, I had about every bone in my body broken when I wrecked it. The Indians that found me dosed me with every herb and poison known to man until all my livers and lights damn near blew up, but I was afraid to go near any villages for fear I'd get arrested for stealing the car or maybe some more of Trina's bloodhounds might catch me. The Indians looked after me but I got stir-crazy, sick of Mexico. I would have given my soul for one hour at the Café Julien. An oil truck came along bound for Acapulco and I hitched on and shipped out for New York on a freighter as dishwasher. I'd heard from Anna a while back that she'd got a farm here on insurance from some merchant marine husband and I figured she'd take me in. I'd planned before that to hide out in Rio but I thought Tottenville is further from civilization than Rio. I headed out here as soon as the ship got in and sure enough there was old Anna, sweet and silly as ever, broke and full of crazy ideas for making a fortune—dog kennels, chickens, tearooms, you know."

"Did she know you were supposed to be dead?" Dalzell asked.

"Sure, she was the one that told me. Seems she'd been trying to figure out some way of making something out of it, if Trina wasn't going to beat her to it, and she was a little put out when I showed up," he said. "I'd had pneumonia and flu and malaria and everything else with the Indians and my lungs and heart were pretty well shot, so I told her I wouldn't last long and if she'd let me stay here I'd play dead for her. No skin off her bottom. I did some pictures she could take in and sell. Lousy. I've lost the touch somehow. It made me sore she sold them so fast. But she saw being dead made me worth a hell of a lot more to her so she managed to keep quiet. But you know Anna. She'll botch it up. What I want to know is what do I do next?"

"What do you do? Why, you come right back to New York with Ben and me," Dalzell cried out impetuously. "Everybody will be so glad to have you back you'll get well in no time. You stay with us in Gerda's apartment and we'll all work together. We'll have a big celebration at the Julien."

"If I could sneak into the Julien for just one drink—" Marius said. And then he was shaking his head. He sighed, mopped his forehead with his handkerchief, then reached for his whiskey glass with trembling fingers.

"I can't risk it," he said. "I don't think I can take it any more." He grinned wryly. "Being dead has spoiled me. Gone soft."

"You're safe now, Marius, don't you see? You're a great man," Dalzell argued earnestly. "You've got the world on your side at last, and nothing to worry about. You should hear how they talk. Why, I promise you—"

He stopped at the skeptical expression on Ben's face and Marius' quizzical smile.

"You can't promise me anything and Ben knows it if you don't," Marius said quietly. "The minute I come to life I'm in trouble again."

"How about the rest of us?" Ben asked Dalzell. "People will think you and I cooked up the whole trick just to make money. They won't just accuse us of passing off bogus Marius for our own profits, they'll get us for hiding a fugitive—if Marius still is in trouble with police."

"I'm always in trouble with police." Marius shrugged. "But don't worry about signing my stuff because I'll stand up for it if the pinch comes. Just let's leave things the way they are."

"How?" Dalzell pondered.

"The most wonderful thing that ever happened to me was finding out I was dead that morning," Marius said. "No troubles, nothing to worry about but the cost of living. Damn it, why did you fellows have to spoil it? I always knew Trina and bill collectors would manage to drill a pipeline straight into my grave but I did think my old pals would respect the sleep of the dead."

"What did I tell you, Dalzell?" Ben nodded toward Dalzell, who felt helpless and defeated. Ben had been right, maybe, that they were safer to leave things as they were but when a lie was involved there was never any safety. Certainly with Anna as sole protector of the secret there was none. Through his mind there flitted all the possible reactions to the news that Marius was returned from the dead and right back in New York. There would be the initial amazement, the cries of joy, the eager questions, and then the slow mounting sense of outrage.

"If that isn't exactly like Marius!" he could hear Cynthia, Okie, Elsie Hookley, the dealers, all the old friends cry out indignantly. "That *would* be his idea of a fine practical joke, letting us go out on a limb for him, making fools of ourselves, while he has a good time laughing at us! How dare he! Here we are, knocking ourselves out to make him immortal and trying to forget what a big nuisance he always was, always broke, always in trouble, always having to be bailed out or nursed or helped! And now he pulls this! Believe me, I don't want to even see the man again."

In the silence he knew that this was in Ben's mind, too, and maybe in Marius'. Marius was looking out the window.

"I want you to go before Anna gets back from the city," he said. "She's gone down to New York for supplies for me, if I can ever get to working right again. I won't tell her you were here or that you know."

"You've seen the stuff they're writing about you, of course," Ben said. "Right up there with Titian and the old masters, my boy."

Marius threw up his hands.

"If I hadn't known it before I would have known I was dead when I read some of that bilge!" he said, and then shrugged. "What am I talking about? It was what I believed about myself. It was what made life worth living until—well, all of a sudden it—whatever it is—was gone. I was dead, all right. I couldn't figure it out. I couldn't paint. Me! Thought at first the damn harpies had killed it."

"Maybe too much liquor," Ben said.

Marius looked at him, astonished, and poured himself a new drink.

"There *can't* be too much liquor!" he said. "I decided maybe I was just under-drunk. And under-womanned. You know how a new dame can give you a fresh start. As soon as I'm well enough to light out I'll get a new one. Maybe that'll do it."

Ben and Dalzell exchanged an uneasy look.

"We've got some money for you," Dalzell said. "It's yours."

"Anna's brought me more than I ever had in my life," Marius said. "I've got it stashed away. In a couple of days I'll get the hell out of here, take the ferry to Perth Amboy and get a ship out of Hoboken for Greece, maybe Corsica. I got friends there. Always could work there, remember? If I don't get myself back there then count me out for good." He threw off the blanket and got to his feet.

"See, I can get around," he said. "Damn it, now I've got to. I'll leave Anna some stuff to sell and she'll send me some dough. I'll be staying with Sophie, if she's still there and still loves me."

Dalzell pulled his wallet out with the last sixty dollars he had gotten for a Marius sketch.

"Here's a part payment," he said. "You let us know where to send any more we get."

"*If* we get—" Ben amended under his breath. "Look, Marius, do you mean you're going to let those dealers clean up over your dead body?"

"Looks like that's the only way they can do it," Marius said. He drummed on the table restlessly. "Now will you do something for me? Beat it and forget you saw me."

"Marius, couldn't you—couldn't we—" Dalzell began but with Marius and Ben looking at him whatever he wanted to offer fled from his brain. He felt angry that the love and warmth he felt for both his friends could not even reach them or do them any good, only the sixty dollars could help. He was bitterly disappointed that Marius alive, should destroy his dream of him, and he was angry with Ben for having been right.

"Come on, Sloane," Ben said. "Marius will let us know when he needs us. Let him stay dead now."

"Thanks, Ben," Marius said. "I'll do the same for you."

They heard him calling in the dog as they walked down the lane. At the road Dalzell stood still for a moment, looking back.

A fog had rolled in from the bay and blurred out the meadow so the house seemed suspended in a ghostly haze, its two upstairs windows bleak eye sockets, its front porch railing the teeth in a death's head.

"What can we do?" Dalzell murmured.

"Nothing," Ben said gloomily. "Go back right where we were when we first heard he was dead. Forget about today. Will you have to tell Cynthia the truth?"

No, Dalzell would not tell Cynthia, he said. He did not intend to tell Cynthia the truth about anything, he thought, for the truth was what she must be protected from.

"Funny, now that we've seen him alive, I'm convinced he really is dead," Ben said, puzzled.

They were silent walking across the meadow to the Hylan Boulevard bus, depressed with the certainty that they would never see Marius again.

. . . olive branch in family tree . . .

Wharton sat stiffly upright in Elsie's cozy-looking club chair whose new slip cover cruelly disguised its broken coil springs all eager to snap at the sitter. He was going crazy. He *was* crazy! The curse of the Hookleys was upon him. He would be put away, probably in the very retreat his uncle and two cousins were patronizing—if that was the word and if they were Hookleys it was indeed the word—at this very minute. Poor Nita! How she would cry at being forced to certify him. Or *would* she cry? How did he know what might go on in that pretty but increasingly foreign little head?

He looked at Elsie, trying to keep his eyes from the corner behind her. Maybe it would be Elsie who would be the one to certify him. He was certain Elsie wouldn't like it one bit. She wouldn't like being deprived of her chief sport. It alarmed him that he could almost hear her forthright voice answering what he was thinking even while she was really saying something quite different.

"Wharton crazy? Nonsense!" It was exactly what she would say, of course. "He is obstinate, selfish, greedy, intolerably snobbish and in almost every way a monster but I will not have my brother called crazy."

"—must say I am immensely flattered at this sudden interest in my little home," Elsie was really saying.

Wharton drew a deep breath for strength and twisted around in his chair so his back would be to the corner, wincing at the punishment from the chair as he did so. No doubt Elsie had had the chair made especially for him. There! he thought in horror, I've got to stop *thinking*, that's all!

"My dear Elsie," he said tenderly, "you seem to regard a simple brotherly visit as an invasion of your privacy. I happened to be lunching at the Café Julien and thought it a good opportunity to see your flat and perhaps hear what news you brought from Boston. Do I really seem like such a *monster* to you?"

The very word popping out of his mouth upset him again and before he could stop himself he had looked at the corner by the fireplace and seen it again, or thought he was seeing it—the damnable ram's-head cane of Uncle Carpenter's. This time he stared at it steadily to make it go away, as you do when seeing double, but the cane would not go away. Impetuously he jumped up and walked over to it, touched it, more frightened than ever to find it real, the emerald eyes leering at him. If Elsie would only say something that would make it real, if it was real, or a hallucination if it was hallucination.

"I see Uncle's cane is in mint condition," he forced himself to say casually.

"Have you any objection?" Elsie snapped. "I suppose you think of me as a complete vandal, unworthy of the family precious treasures."

"No, no," Wharton protested. It was a real cane and he was not crazy but he'd opened himself up for a row and Elsie was raring to get at it so he'd have to find the explanation of how the cane got there in some more devious way.

"What about Mother?" Wharton asked firmly, sitting down in a kinder chair. "How did you find her and did she know you?"

"Of course she knew me," Elsie said coldly. "She simply refused to admit it. Mother is an imbecile, I grant you, but no more so now than she ever was, just more cunning, that's all."

"Perhaps she should be in an institution," Wharton said.

"What would you call that hotel?" Elsie answered sarcastically. "No, Wharton, Mother's act has never fooled me for one minute. She was always bored with her family and the pose of having no memory is very convenient for her, just as it was convenient for Father to pretend to be stone deaf."

This sort of talk from Elsie usually irritated Wharton to distraction but today he decided to be amused instead of getting Elsie's back up before he found out what he wished.

"Perhaps you're right," he conceded graciously. "Childhood is the happiest time, after all, so why shouldn't she want to spend her last years in a return to that happy state?"

"I never found anything happy in childhood and neither did you," Elsie stated pugnaciously. "I don't think I ever saw a smile on your face till the day you were allowed to clip your own coupons."

Wharton counted ten inwardly and went on again.

"I was surprised your visit was so short," he said. "You had told me, you recall, that you were considering opening the old house, and even making it your home again. I made no objections, you know. I didn't think it would be a wise move, for Boston is so changed—"

"Ridiculous!" Elsie said flatly.

"What I mean is that your old friends are scattered and even if you have some I don't know, still Boston does not have the—er—relaxed social life you enjoy here in New York. Besides you used to hate Boston."

That remarkably benign tone made Elsie look fixedly at her brother who was even bestowing a pat on Brucie's head, an unaccustomed compliment that made Brucie look questioningly at his mistress, then withdraw to a spot beside her where he too could watch the caller.

"I don't hate Boston," Elsie explained impatiently. "It's just little things I can't stand. The way the banks and restaurants and department stores are all like nursing homes, the very tone of voice the clerks have is that baby-talk you use on mental cases. 'Oh dear oh dear,'" she mimicked the soothing hushed voice, "'we've spilled our nice gravy on our nice little jabot,' and 'aren't we the naughty girl overdrawing our nice little checking account.'"

"So you did go to the Trust and see Mr. Wheeling!" Wharton said. She must have got Mother to sign something or give her something, he thought, and in his exasperation he forgot his plan to use the honeyed approach but plunged to the heart of the matter. "I shall have the details of that later on, of course. What I should like explained, however, is just why you should purchase a boat and why you should be brazenly running all over Boston with a man who appears from all reports to be barely half your age. Why must you drag the Hookley name again through the mud—oh you don't care, I know that—it's my wife and daughters who suffer. Actually bringing this bounder, whoever he may be, into my mother's hotel, foisting him on her as guest—"

"She cried whenever he started to go," Elsie said defensively. "Mother is lonely and she likes new people even if she just babbles."

"Elsie!" Wharton pointed his finger at her so menacingly that Brucie let out a yowl. "Carry on your routs or whatever they are in Greenwich Village where such things are common but I insist that you behave yourself in the places where my poor daughters have to bear the shame. As if poor Isabella's first year out hasn't been difficult enough as it is—"

His sister's voice tried to cut in twice before he would pause.

"Will you please listen to me now?" Elsie haughtily commanded. "It seems my good heart has run away with me again and what I did for you out of pure family pride only makes you abuse me the more."

"Now what?" Wharton exclaimed, knowing too well that no matter what deviltry he might suspect in his sister she was certain to have perpetrated something far worse.

"I merely was buying off a young man to save your daughter's good name, thank you very much," Elsie said, rising with a grand air and pulling her slightly soiled green quilted house robe about her. "You were so busy bullying Isabella about and scolding her for not doing the traditional things you never saw what was under your nose. The poor girl was being driven to running away with one of Nita's admirers."

Wharton's face paled and then the orchard shades came out on his sensitive nose, indicating the emotional confusion her words had aroused. He said nothing and Elsie's momentary glee in her advantage melted into sisterly concern.

"It's all right now, Wharton, dear," she said solicitously. "I saw what was going on and I felt it my duty to handle the situation as I saw best for the honor of the family. You say I have no proper family feeling but I'm very fond of Isabella in spite of your fears of my bad influence. I've had a little more worldly experience than you, Wharton, and I knew the man was not right for her. So—I sent him away. I shan't tell you the sum of money involved but then money doesn't mean as much to me as it does to you."

Wharton sat rigidly, staring at the cane unseeingly. Elsie, a little alarmed at this unprecedented collapse, started to speak again but he rose and lifted his hand wearily.

"Don't tell me any more now, Elsie," he begged. "I can't quite take it all in at once."

He shook out his kerchief and wiped his forehead in silence. Impressed into some sort of first aid Elsie clopped over to the bar in her wooden-soled sandals and poured out a brandy, turned to hand it to Wharton, but on second thought decided she needed one herself and poured another.

Wharton gulped the restorative. Pictures rose in his mind of the monkeylike little dark man at the restaurant wearing his old topcoat, the same little man in Nita's drawing room, the ram's-head cane, Isabella's constantly tear-stained, red-nosed lugubrious face, Nita coming in from one of her confounded culture classes with the "fellow student," the living room doors closing on the cozy laughter of the two scholars, Isabella peering in the library door and excitedly whispering, "Who's in there with Mother, Father? Can I go in?" These were the pictures but he couldn't make them fit together into any kind of meaning, and he knew he didn't want to. It was better to accept Elsie's meaning.

"I'm afraid I haven't been entirely fair to you, Elsie, my dear," he murmured. "I didn't realize that in exposing yourself to all this talk you were only saving Isabella."

"Of course you didn't realize," Elsie readily agreed. "You never do."

But Wharton did not react to the needle. It was no more sport than playing with a dead mouse, Elsie reflected, feeling unjustly deprived. There was something almost obscene, she felt, in Wharton sitting there all slumped over, letting her take cracks at him without striking back. It simply wasn't sporting. Quitting the game with the highest score just as his opponent has gotten warmed up for victory. Tears came to Elsie's eyes, and these Wharton saw. He got to his feet and patted her on the shoulder.

"I appreciate this, Elsie," he said, stiff-upper-lipping. "We'll talk it over another time."

We certainly will, Elsie thought, watching him make his way wearily out the door, we'll talk it over every time you bring up all you ever did for me, and you won't have a word to say.

But it wouldn't be the fun, she sighed, it would be just like losing a brother.

. . . the café had three exits . . .

Dalzell was having a *mazagran* in the Julien. There was small reason for him to be feeling content but he was, and he thought it was probably due to some basic masochism in his character that made surrender a relief if not a pleasure. He was down to his last twenty dollars, he had no idea where the next was coming from, but this was a state of affairs that seemed home to him. It was a pity that Ben was still angry with him, accusing him of messing up their prospects before they had gotten what they might out of them. He thought Ben was probably right: he *was* foolishly romantic and sentimental and it didn't do Marius or anybody else any good. But a person had to do the things he had to do.

"Mind if I join you, Mr. Sloane?"

It was the young fellow from *City Life* standing beside him. Dalzell motioned to the seat opposite and Briggs sat down heavily, placing a fat briefcase on the chair beside him.

"Don't let me forget that," he said. "Have you ever noticed that you can tell a person's looking for a job because they carry a fat briefcase? Like new wallets. You don't catch a fellow with lots of cash carrying a brand-new wallet."

He threw down a very new leather wallet on the table contemptuously.

"When you see a man trying to build up his morale with that sort of front you can tell his morale is pretty low," he said.

"Yours is low, I take it." Dalzell smiled.

"So-so," said Briggs gloomily. "I suppose you heard I lost my job, right after the Marius piece came out. It seems *City Life* hired me because I didn't know anything about art. Seems they like the simple average citizen approach to everything—science, medicine, books, everything. They only use the intellectual angle on sports and business. Well I started out fine from their point of view, then I had to interview so many artists and museum people that I got too smart. I was using fancy words and technical phrases. Would you believe it that six months ago I thought *gouache* was some sort of Spanish cowboy?"

"You should have kept it that way," Dalzell said sympathetically.

Briggs signaled Karl and ordered Scotch.

"It's not so bad because I had saved some money—four hundred and ten bucks," he said. "I figured that what I learned about painting would have cost me a couple of hundred in school, too, so that's something. And finding out I was really a writer would have cost me maybe a thousand bucks worth of psychoanalysis. Oh, I'm ahead."

"You don't have to take care of a family, then," Dalzell said.

Briggs shook his head.

"I'm not married yet but if things get tough I may have to," he said rather gloomily. "Oh I don't mean I'd marry a rich wife— not that I see anything wrong in your marrying Mrs. Earle as the papers say. I guess you've known her a long time and you aren't doing it for money anyway."

"No," Dalzell answered, embarrassed. "It isn't that."

"That's good, because I've noticed men who marry for money have trouble getting their hands on any cash," Briggs said. "They're always borrowing from fellows like me who have to work. They get a lot of credit on the strength of their wife's credit but that's what hangs them because they can't get their mitts on spending money."

"Thanks for the warning," Dalzell said.

"A girl with a small steady salary is the thing," Briggs said. "This girl I know, Janie. I've moved into her apartment and we can keep going on her paycheck while I work on this novel I'm planning and wait for a job. It works out fine like this. I tell her marriage would only tie her down."

Someone was waving from the doorway and Briggs nudged Dalzell. Okie came toward their table, sweeping a hand over his long white pompadour.

"May I offer good wishes, Sloane?" he said pompously. "I just left Cynthia at the Gallery cocktail party and she was kicking up her heels and acting like a child bride. What in the world made you give in to her?"

"You seem to think I was drugged," Dalzell said, nettled, even though he had known he would have to grow more armor than ever now.

"You've hardly seen her for years and you hardly know the same people any more," Okie went on pleasantly. "You've never been married and you've no idea how difficult Cynthia makes things for her husbands. I do. I've seen them all. And they were all rich and influential in their own right, too."

"Maybe that was the trouble," Briggs put in.

"If I'd known Cynthia really wanted to get married after being through the mill five times already—" Okie began and paused meditatively.

"Only four," Dalzell corrected him.

Okie looked from Dalzell to Briggs, but Briggs did not take his briefcase off the chair since he wanted Okie to go away and let him continue discussing his own affairs.

"What happened to Ben Forrester?" Okie asked abruptly.

"He went back West," Dalzell said. "He found he hated New York now and he couldn't paint here."

"Was he really good?" Briggs asked.

"Ben Forrester and Dalzell Sloane here paved the way for half the successful young painters today," Okie declared generously. "Maybe they didn't have too much success but what they tried out was the fertilizer for the talent blooming today. How do you like that for appreciation, Sloane?"

"If it's a trade-last I can't think of anything to equal being called fertilizer," Dalzell said.

Okie burst into a loud haw-haw and decided to leave on the note of good humor since neither of them had invited him to sit down. There seemed to be no other table free and he put on his hat.

"This place is getting awfully common," he said fretfully. "No wonder they talk of converting it into apartments. I prefer the Florida Bar nowadays myself."

He clapped his Homburg over his locks and sauntered proudly out.

"I think you're wrong in your figuring, Sloane," he turned to call back from the door. "I think you're Number Six."

By eight o'clock it began to be apparent to even the dullest tourist
that this was no ordinary night at the Café Julien. Guests who
had dropped in for a single apéritif, en route to an inexpensive
dinner at San Remo or Grand Ticino's in the Italian quarter,
stayed on through curiosity drinking up their dinner money very
slowly, ordering a new round just as importunate newcomers
were about to snatch their table from under them. They could
see important-looking elderly gentlemen in dinner clothes peep
in the café door, then proceed onward into the private dining
room at the rear. It must be the Silurian annual banquet, someone hinted, the Silurians being newspapermen who had been in
the trade twenty-five years.

"How could anybody afford to dine here if he's been in newspaper work that long?" argued others. It was a dinner honoring
Romany Marie, or Barney Gallant, or survivors of the Lafayette
Escadrille, others said, recalling similar occasions in the past. It
was a banquet of real estate men commemorating their grief in
selling the Julien to a mysterious concern rumored to be about to
change it into apartments. This last theory was gaining credence
when the unfamiliar sight of Monsieur Julien himself gave old-
timers the clue to what was going on. Yes, it was a dinner of the
Friends of Julien, an association of gourmets of great distinction,
and what was more sensational was the whisper that this was
their farewell dinner. Photographers from newspapers and
magazines were setting up impressive-looking apparatus in

every corner and mousy little people who inhabited the cheap little rooms upstairs and were never seen in the glamorous café
suddenly showed their frightened little faces at the door. Hoff
Bemans, leading his guest panelists into the café for a rewarding
drink at anybody else's expense, spotted Dalzell Sloane and beckoned his men to crowd around that table, so that when Briggs
returned from the men's room he could scarcely squeeze in.

"By George, I've done it again!" Hoff exclaimed proudly. "I
didn't even know the Café was going to go out of business and
here I stumbled right into the big night. So that's the old master,
Julien himself!"

Monsieur Julien was a gay bachelor of sixty who made enough
from the café bearing his name to live and usually dine at the
Plaza. He was the last of a formidable dynasty of French chefs,
inheriting the great reputation without the faintest culinary interest. But after a youthful struggle against the public insistence
that all Juliens must be cooks he had surrendered. Very well, he
would accept the unearned but profitable mantle. Cooking con-
tests, cook books, food columns, canned dainties, all must have
his name as sponsor. Wherever he went he was questioned about
this dish or that sauce. At first he had sighed candidly, "I assure
you if I had a pair of eggs and a greased griddle on the stove I
would still starve to death." Later on in his career he answered
more archly, "Ah, if I were to tell you how I make that dish then
you would be Julien and what would I be?"

His grandfather had been proprietor of the famous Julien's in
Paris and had founded the New York branch early in the century. All over the world there were people who quivered at the
name. Even those who had never tasted *escargots Julien* quickly
realized they must pretend they knew, and would sniff the air
and paw the ground like truffle hounds, sighing, "Ah, Julien's!"
Having put by a nice fortune paying French salaries and charging American prices the old gentleman was finally done in by the

shrewdness of his equally thrifty employees who sold furniture and dishes under his very nose and found many convenient ways of rewarding themselves. The Paris place vanished in World War One and the New York café had been about to give up in 1929 when a group of wealthy gentlemen from all over the eastern seaboard (and one very proud member from Seattle) decreed that the name of Julien must not perish. All those who had swooned over a Julien lobster bisque or cassoulet of duck Julien-Marie (or said they had) vowed with their hands on their checkbooks that Julien's must go on. The finest lawyers, bankers, jurists, all manner of men of affairs co-operated to insure future security. Monsieur Julien was put on salary and to keep the venture from smacking of Depression opportunism the group called itself simply the Friends of Julien, standing by the thin of the thirties to reap profits in the forties. Self-made men, lacking in clubs and college backgrounds, listed membership in the Friends of Julien beside their names in *Who's Who* for it hinted of world travel and financial standing.

Most of the Friends were by no means habitués but appeared only at the annual dinner where they toasted bygone days, the chef, the wine steward, the bartender, and above all the great Julien. Julien, who appeared in the kitchen only for photographers, always wept over these unearned tributes to his magic touch with a field salad and permitted himself to quote elegies to his skill from old rivals—Moneta, the Ambassador's Sabatini, Henri Charpentier; and he summoned sentimental memories of days when the incomparable Escoffier of London's Carlton called personally on Papa Julien to pay his respects to the only man in the world he deigned to call "Maître," or so Julien *fils* declared. The anecdotes grew more impressive each year and convinced by his own publicity Julien made himself instead of his forebears the hero.

This evening's banquet had finally gotten under way in the private room but the café guests continued to dawdle, sending emissaries back to spy on the feast and report back who was there and what was being said. The waiters' unusual speed in presenting checks as a method of clearing the café only made the guests more obstinately determined to stay on enjoying the splendid affair by proxy. Caught in the spirit of the occasion Hoff Bemans was ordering round after round of highballs, figuring that he might stick Dalzell Sloane with the check by carefully timing his own departure or if Sloane got away first there was a very young first novelist along who had been on his panel and would be too shy to protest. On the program that evening Hoff had made insulting and derogatory remarks concerning the young man's work and youthful pomposity but he vaguely felt letting him buy the drinks would atone for this. For that matter no reason why old Sloane shouldn't have it since he would be getting into Cynthia Earle's pocket any minute.

"Thought your *City Life* piece on Marius didn't quite come off," Hoff said genially to Briggs. "Some good things in it but as a whole it just didn't come off."

"Thanks," Briggs said absently. He was staring at the young novelist wondering what it felt like to have your name on a fat book, and have people talking about it as if it meant something. The novel had worried him because the author's method wasn't like his own at all. Instead of building his characters on a sensible economic structure this fellow built them on what they had to eat and drink from the breast right through Schrafft's and the Grand Central Oyster Bar; whatever they elected to eat was evidently supposed to mean something about their hidden natures. Even their retching was recorded and it didn't indicate they had had a bad oyster but meant they were having an emotional *crise*. When they weren't eating, this author's characters were all put through boarding schools and colleges, all Ivy League, no matter how poor they talked, and Briggs, having worked his way through a minor university, was irritated at having to work his way again through these fictional characters' education. What did people like about that kind of book? Maybe it was the deep sex meaning the fellow gave to those menus, for the hero was always drawing some high-bosomed girl into his arms between courses, the hot oatmeal pounding through his veins.

"I read your book," Briggs roused himself to tell the young man.

"Thanks," said the author gratefully. Briggs noted that whatever fine liquors his characters enjoyed their creator was limiting himself to simple beer, though this economy might later be regretted when he found he had to pay for his comrades' expensive tastes.

Hoff was continuing the discussion on Marius' show, pointing out errors in the critics' reviews due perhaps to their not having consulted Mr. Bemans' recent book on the subject. The *Times* critic, for example, persisted in linking Marius' work with that of Forrester and Sloane which was utterly idiotic because neither Ben nor Dalzell could paint the simplest apple to resemble Marius' touch. Hoff wished Dalzell to tell Cynthia Earle, moreover, that he felt very hurt that his contribution to the Marius Long Playing Record had been cut out and he considered that was probably the real reason the project had been such a flop. Without his key words the thing hadn't jelled, had not, as he liked to put it, "quite come off."

The café had never been noisier or more crowded. Everyone was shouting to be heard and from the private dining room there were periodic roars of applause. As the banquet progressed curious changes were taking place all over the restaurant. Certain of the banqueters were slipping out to the café between their gourmet dishes to freshen up their palates with quick shots of rye or invigorating martinis and later on grew sociable enough to draw up chairs and make acquaintance with the café customers. Some of these truants urged their new friends to return to the banquet with them, gave them their own places and went back to the café for more informal fun. Before the dinner was even half over the personnel of the Friends' table had changed in such a surprising fashion that there was a lively sprinkling of sports jackets and dark shirts and these strangers were being served roast duckling with the finest of Chambertin while out in the café their legitimate highballs and rubbery canapés were being finished by distinguished drunken Friends. It was in this interchange that Hastings Hardy wound up at Dalzell's table while Briggs, done out of his rightful place, found himself in the private dining room drinking toasts to personalities he'd never heard of. He had arrived at the moment when Monsieur Julien was making the great salad with his own hands—that is to say he took into his own sacred hands various ingredients deftly offered by assistants and poured them personally into the bowl. In the solemn hush induced by this traditional rite cooks' caps could be seen bobbing around corners as they strained to see; other diners bent their heads reverently, and down in the lower kitchen the seafood chef was sustaining himself with mighty swigs of Martel in his pride that Monsieur Julien had thought his sole good enough to claim as his own handiwork.

Toasts had been made to famous dishes, countries, high-living monarchs and again and again to Monsieur Julien until the master was shaken to tears, and many others were moved to blow their noses heartily. To restore calm the oldest living member rose to propose a health, he said, to that great chef, Henri Charpentier, inventor of the *Crêpe Suzette* which had brought happiness to so many thousands. The applause inspired Monsieur Julien to interpolate that Charpentier, excellent genius though he was, had been surpassed by Sabatini, king of them all, next of course to Escoffier.

" 'Born with the gift of laughter and a sense that the world is mad,' " shouted one of the café intruders joyously, but a neighbor yanked him down by his brown-checked coattail hissing, "You ass, not THAT Sabatini."

"Five generations of kings Sabatini served," Monsieur Julien went on unperturbed, his black eyes flashing proudly around the table, "including Umberto and the Czar of all the Russias. As for Charpentier's *Crêpe Suzette,* can it really compare in delicacy and sheer originality with the *Coeur Flottant* Sabatini created especially for that queen among women, Mary Garden?"

A Friend who had spent the last three courses in the café returned in time to catch the last words and squeezing into the group snatched up Briggs's glass and shouted a ringing toast to Mary Garden, King Umberto and the Czar himself, then sat down on the nonexistent chair dragging napery, silver, dishes and six kinds of greens to the floor with him. It was too bad that the photographer chanced to get a fine shot of this disorderly scene for it spoiled the nostalgic sentimental tone of the accompanying article on "Farewell to the Café Julien" and made many ministers give thanks that this palace of sin was finally to be routed by clean-minded citizens.

It was this picture, showing Briggs wiping salad off the fallen comrade with Monsieur Julien handing him a napkin with Gallic courtesy, that turned out to be lucky for Briggs. The very day the picture appeared he was offered the job of restaurant reporter on a tabloid. It meant postponing his literary career which grieved him but was a great relief to Janie, who loved him devotedly and without illusions.

. . . the nightcap . . .

The café crowd had thinned out a half hour before closing time
when Ellenora and Rick Prescott came in for their nightcap.
They had been coming in every night again, and tonight's news
that the rumors of the Julien's approaching end were all too true
filled them with dismay and foreboding. They had fallen in love
with what they had seemed to be in these surroundings: these
were the selves they knew: when they set foot inside these doors
each became again what the other desired. Now that they were
together so much elsewhere, their ordinary selves surrendered to
each other, they were secretly conscious of a dimension missing.
Fulfillment, so long desired, was somehow not enough. They
had to have the Julien about them, Philippe beside them, the
marble-topped table between them, their reflections in the wall
mirrors a supporting chorus.

They had spent nights and days in Ricky's apartment telling
each other everything about themselves, listening eagerly, but
failing to fit the new portrait to the image of love they had been
cherishing. Rick wanted to absolve himself of past follies and
errors by confessing everything, recklessly handing over material for an ordinary lifetime of reproaches, for part of his love for
Ellenora was his sense of guilt, a comfortable feeling of you-
dear-darling-girl-to-forgive-me-for-all the-ways-I-have-
wronged-you. She was never to be spared Ellenora thought, a little frightened at the role he had given her of forever forgiving
him and then consoling him for having hurt her, inviting more

hurt by understanding and forgiving it. She would have liked to shut her ears to his admission of other, lesser loves, but he had to know that she understood. She would have liked to know where they were heading for, now that they were lovers, but she understood her part well enough to realize she was to be near when he needed her, accept what he offered, ask no questions. It was enough that there *was* love, and the woman's duty was always to guard it, to have it ready when the man needed it.

"Calling Mr. Prescott!" The telephone operator stood in the café doorway and beckoned Rick. He blinked, puzzled. He had spent hours in this spot waiting for a call from Ellenora that never had come. Now she was here beside him and the call was just catching up.

It was Jerry Dulaine, he found when he went out to the booth. She wanted to tell him about her new job, and maybe get some advice. She was working on a television show about problems of career girls. She had moved to the Hotel Delorme on Park Avenue if he'd like to call on her.

Rick hesitated. In his confessional orgy he hadn't said anything to Ellenora about Jerry, maybe because it didn't matter or maybe because you only tell about the closed episodes. He didn't like refusing Jerry when all she asked was some friendly encouragement. He was glad things were looking up for her, he said, and he'd drop around one of these days. Maybe he would at that, he reflected, going back to the café. His eyes lit up, seeing Ellenora at their table, just as he liked to think of her, sweetly waiting for him. Where would they go to hide from their real selves when the Julien vanished?

"Wrong Prescott," he said, pulling out his chair and sitting down happily as if their feet entwined under the same café table was home enough for him.

. . . the bird's gone . . .

October was as hot as August that year and the wreckers were shirtless under the midday sun, their bare backs glistening with perspiration. Rick Prescott had been leaning against the park fence watching them for a long time, thinking ruefully that of all the happy workers in the world wreckers were undoubtedly the most enthusiastic. The whole back wall of the building was down now, and the top floors, but the handsome Victorian Gothic facade with the imposing marble steps still stood, and it was disconcerting to look through the paneless café windows straight into open garden. Now the crimson entrance canopy was a tumbled pile of rags on the sidewalk, the white letters C A F E J U L I E N almost indiscernible under rubble, and next the thick laurel vines fell in a great heap of gleaming green leaves that seemed to be still breathing and quivering with life.

"That laurel must be near a hundred years old," a workman beside Rick said. "The walls come down easy enough but those vines are strong as iron. You wouldn't think it."

"My poor birds!" quavered a woman's voice behind them.

She was a rouged and dyed old lady elaborately dressed in the fashion of pre-World War One, the low-crowned beaver hat atop her pompadour laden with birds and flowers, long peg-top brown velvet skirt almost concealing her high black kid shoes, a green changeable silk duster floating about her. She was dabbing at her mascaraed eyes with a lacy handkerchief and looked at

278 THE *wicked* PAVILION

Rick appealingly. "Their nest was right outside my window and now they're homeless. I used to feed them on the sill every morning for thirty years and more. Oh what will they do now the vine is gone?"

"Don't worry about your birds, lady," the workman said, nudging Rick. "They've gone South by now. Probably got a lot bigger nest down there in Miami."

"Do you really think so? Oh. I'm so glad." The old lady smiled tremulously. "I've cried every night worrying about them ever since they started tearing down the building. My room—right over the café window there—went yesterday. Thank you so much."

She hobbled slowly across the park and the workman winked at Rick.

"Betcha she never came out of her room till they tore the place down," he murmured. "She comes here and watches every day."

"I didn't realize people lived upstairs," Rick said.

"A lot of old-timers lived in those little rooms," the man said. "You see 'em wandering around the Park now, like her, all in kinda mummy clothes. A lot of queer old birds flushed out of their nests. They used that side entrance."

Rick took the cigarette he offered and lit it. He thought, as he walked on, that tonight at midnight he would bring Ellenora over here and they would sit on the park bench right opposite the old café with a split of champagne. The loving-cup would be the little Venetian glass slipper from Ellenora's dressing table and they would drink it the very minute of the old closing time. In the light of the street lamp at midnight they would see the old entrance steps up to the doorway and shadows would reconstruct the old café. The idea cheered him up and he quickened his steps, smiling a little to himself as he always did when he thought of something to tell Ellenora. He remembered that he hadn't told her yet he was being sent to Peru for six months but the funny thing was he didn't have to tell anything important to Ellenora because he felt she knew, without words. It was like his knowing she would always be waiting, sitting there at the café table, charming extravagant little hat—a "lady" hat as he always called Ellenora's hats—tilted at the chic angle, feathery wisp of veil or scarf making a smoke ring around her eager, radiant little face. Ellenora—keeping beautiful New York for him.

Sitting at the café table?—Rick stopped short, frightened. The nest was gone. He felt a sudden panic at the thought of his dream without the Julien frame. Where would he be sure of her waiting, loving, knowing? He couldn't, wouldn't dare leave her again with no Julien walls to hold her. He hurried frantically across the Park toward his apartment where she would be waiting—where she *had* to be waiting.

Dalzell Sloane looked again at the young man rushing past him, certain that he had seen him somewhere before. He frowned and then it came to him that the familiarity was only in the resemblance to Monty Douglass, the film actor. He walked on to the ruins of the Café Julien and sat down on a park bench opposite. It was odd that he didn't feel sad, he reflected, but then the Café had been gone from him long, long before the building came down. If it had been there in full glory at this very minute he would not have gone in, probably, for his new self might not belong there. He was not accustomed to his new self, yet, the Dalzell Sloane who was painting portraits of Hasting Hardy's entire family, at a fine fee, the Dalzell Sloane who would presently have to report at Elizabeth Arden's as he had promised to pick up Cynthia. He sighed a little, knowing just how it would be.

"Mrs. Sloane wants you to wait here until she's through," he was sure one of the beauteous young ladies would inform him. "She said for you to be sure and wait."

He would stand in a corner, fearful of smashing the jeweled perfume bottles or damaging the elegant, perfumed creatures gliding in and out, and sometimes a honey-voiced young lady would call him Mr. Earle and tell him his wife was almost through. He wondered, idly, if all of Cynthia's husbands had been called Mr. Earle after her first one since none of the other names had stuck, and whether he might not end up signing his paintings Dalzell Earle. It really didn't matter, he thought, any more than anything that happened to his new self mattered, for there was no more Dalzell Sloane than there was any more Marius or Julien. No good looking around the old neighborhood for souvenirs of the vanished past. He went to the curb and flagged a taxi.

The red-haired man sitting on the nearest bench watched him get into the cab, made a move to wave to him but thought better of it and resumed writing in the notebook spread open with his briefcase as desk.

What Dennis Orphen was writing was this:

It must be that the Julien was all that these people really liked about each other for now when they chance across each other in the street they look through each other, un-recognizing, or cross the street quickly with the vague feeling that here was someone identified with unhappy memories—as if the other was responsible for the fall of the Julien. Curious, too, that everyone connected with the café looks so small on the street. The arrogance and dignity of the old waiters is now wrapped up in a bundle under their arms when you catch a glimpse of one of them, shriveled and bent, scuttling down a subway kiosk; the men of affairs who had spent hours sipping their brandy and liqueurs, reading their papers with lordly ease, are suddenly old and harassed-looking, home and family harness collaring them for good, their café egos stowed away in vest pocket pillboxes like morphine grains.

The Café Julien was gone and a reign was over. Those who had been bound by it fell apart like straws when the baling cord is cut and remembered each other's name and face as part of a dream that would never come back.

ALSO BY DAWN POWELL

Angels on Toast

The Locusts Have No King

My Home Is Far Away

A Time to Be Born

Dawn Powell at Her Best
(*Including the novels* Turn, Magic Wheel *and*
Dance Night, *and a selection of short fiction*)

The Diaries of Dawn Powell
1931 – 1965